GOLD & SILVER

JUN'ICHIRO TANIZAKI

Translated by
SHELLEY MARSHALL

SHELLEY MARSHALL

CONTENTS

1. THE SECRET

At the time, my thinking was whimsical, and the lively atmosphere encircling me was fading into the distance. I considered quietly slipping away from the men and women engaged in various interactions. In the end, I searched high and low for a suitable hideout. I found my refuge at a Shingon Buddhist temple in Matsuba-cho in Asakusa and rented one room in the priest's living quarters.

The temple was in a noisy, little-known town at the foot of the Asakusa Twelve Stories skyscraper. The Shibori trench ran behind this aristocratic *monzeki* temple in a line from Kikuya Bridge. A long, yellowish-orange earthen wall extended on the side where slums spread over the area like overturned boxes of garbage. The atmosphere strained under a heavy silence I found calming.

From the beginning, I was drawn to the overlooked, mysterious, lonely places in the city, rather than Shibuya or Okubo in the outskirts where a hermit would live. Like the stagnant pools that appear in the rapids of fast mountain streams, I preferred a tranquil enclosure with no traffic, except in exceptional cases or for special people, sand-wiched between congested downtown streets.

At the same time, I had other concerns. I loved traveling and have walked from Kyoto, Sendai, and Hokkaido to Kyushu. I'm sure there are towns in Tokyo I've never stepped foot in despite having been born in Ningyo-cho and lived in Tokyo for twenty years. No, there are many more than I thought.

In the downtown of the big city, I know a lot or very little about places I have or haven't passed through in the countless large and small intersecting streets as in a beehive.

When I was twenty-one or -two, I went with my father to see the god of war, Hachiman-sama, in Fukugawa. I said, "Let's take the ferry and eat the famous soba at Komeichi in Fuyugi."

My father took me to a place behind the main Shinto shrine in the compound. The atmosphere was unlike the canal area in Koami-cho and Kobune-cho. The river was narrow and swelled fully at the low cliffs and listlessly pushed its way between the cramped houses crowded on the cliffs on both sides. On the round trip, two or three poles poked the river bottom to weave the small ferry boat along one side between lines of several barges and lighters longer than the width of the river.

I often visited Hachiman-sama before but never thought about what was behind the compound. I only admired the front from the shrine arch to the main shrine. Naturally, I mused over the front, a panoramic picture that stopped you in your tracks, and not the back. Now, I gazed at this river and ferry landing and saw a scene like a puzzle where the wide ground stretched into eternity. Tokyo became more remote than Kyoto or Osaka. Perhaps I saw this world many times in dreams.

I wondered what sort of town was behind Asakusa Kannon-do Temple. The situation was illustrated when I saw the bright red roof tiles of the vast hall from the alley in the compound lined with shops and hardly anything else came to mind.

Little by little, I matured into an adult. As the world broadened, I visited the homes of friends, went out on excursions to view cherry blossoms, and walked everywhere in Tokyo. I had frequent unexpected encounters in other mysterious worlds as I had experienced as a child.

That other world was the perfect place to shelter. As much as I conducted a variety of searches far and wide, I discovered places I never passed through. Although I crossed Asakusa Bridge and Izumi Bridge several times, I never crossed Saemon Bridge that stood between them.

I always turned right at a corner near the streetcar tracks to go to the Ichimura-za kabuki theater in Nicho-machi. However, I can't recall ever stepping on the land in front of this theater that extended a short two or three blocks to Ryusei-za theater. I had no idea what was the situation from the approach on the right bank of the old Eitai Bridge to the left riverbank. And I seemed to remain ignorant of many places in the neighborhoods of Hatcho-bori, Eichizenbori, Shamisenbori, and Sanyabori.

A neighborhood of a temple in Matsuba-cho was the strangest town, even for that area. At the spot that turned onto an alley with the Rokku theater district and Yoshi-wara red-light district at its tip, I was mesmerized by the creation of a lonely, old-fashioned district.

I ditched my unrivaled closest friend who said, "Tokyo is a mundane place with flashy wealth." He was not pleased with my sneaking away and hiding while he stood and quietly watched a disturbance.

My objective when I retired from the world was not to

undertake serious study. My nerves were dulled as if filed down by a blade. If I didn't encounter objects having exceptionally rich, loud colors, my interest was not sparked. I found it impossible to delight in premiere art and first-class cuisine that demand finely tuned sensitivities.

My spirit lost the ability to admire the chefs at a chic downtown teahouse, praise the skills of Nizaemon and Ganjiro, and take in all the ordinary pleasures of the city. I could no longer stand the daily repetition of an uninteresting idle life caused by inertia. I tried to throw away convention and discover a whimsical artificial mode of life.

Is there anything mysterious and strange to jiggle my nerves numbed to ordinary stimuli? Is it impossible to inhabit a wild, absurd, fantastical space set apart from reality?

My spirit got lost in a world of the ancient fables of Babylon and Assyria, visualized the detective novels of Arthur Conan Doyle and Ruiko, loved the scorched earth and the green fields in the tropics under fierce light rays, and yearned for the eccentric mischievousness of a naughty youth.

I believed by abruptly hiding from the tumultuous world and keeping my behavior a secret for no reason, I could grace my life with some kind of mysterious, romantic colors. I relished the childhood fun of having a secret. The fun of children's games like Hide-and-Seek, Treasure Hunt, and Tea Server, especially when played in the dead of night, in a gloomy shed, or in front of swinging double doors surely sprang from the mystifying feeling of hiding a secret.

I wanted to experience the childhood feelings of playing Hide-and-Seek again so I hid away in an overlooked spot downtown. The doctrine of faith of this temple, Shingon Buddhism with its deep associations with secrets, incantations, and curses, was enough to tempt my curiosity and encourage my fantasies.

The south-facing room was in the newly-built priest's living quarters. Its eight tatami mats were tanned by the sun and transmitted serene warmth to the eyes. After midday, a peaceful autumn sun faded the shoji screen on the side like a lantern. And the room brightened like a large, standing paper-covered lantern.

I arranged all the books on philosophy and art I found enjoyable on the bookshelves. I opened and scattered books filled with extraordinary explanations and illustrations of magic, hypnotism, detective novels, chemistry, and anatomy throughout the room like I was airing them out. I lay on the floor, stretched out haphazardly, and lost myself in reading the mix including works like *The Sign of Four* by Arthur Conan Doyle, *On Murder, Considered as One of the Fine Arts* by Thomas De Quincey, and fables such as *The Arabian Nights* to the French wonder, *Sexuology*.

I earnestly begged for old Buddhist paintings, beginning with a map of hell and paradise hidden by the head priest, and others like Mount Meru and Buddha entering nirvana and hung them everywhere on the four walls of the room like maps in a classroom. The purple incense smoke rose straight up from the incense burner in the alcove and embraced the bright, warm room. Sometimes, I went to a shop beside Kikuya Bridge to buy sandalwood or agarwood to burn.

On a clear day, the glittering noon sunshine hit the shoji screen full on, and the room's interior became a magnificent sight like an awakening. Brilliant, colorful old pictures of various Buddhas, monks who attained nirvana, priests, priestesses, male and female attendants, elephants, and lions swam out in the ample light from spaces on the four walls.

From the myriad of documents thrown on the tatami, assorted tools for merciless killings, anesthesia, narcotics, witches, and religions melted into the incense smoke. A small, two-tatami scarlet carpet was spread out and enveloped by the smoke. While lying on my back, I set my dull eyes like a barbarian's and drew hallucinations in my heart every day.

Around nine in the evening, when the other occupants of the temple were fast asleep, after sipping whiskey from a rectangular bottle and getting drunk, I drew back the rain door to the veranda, climbed over the cemetery fence, and went for a walk.

Every night I changed into clothes that would not attract attention and dove into the crowd in the park, walked around, and hunted for secondhand goods dealers and old bookstores.

I hung my cotton half-coat over my head, applied nail polish to my clean feet, slipped on leather-soled sandals and eyeglasses with gold frames, and stood up the collar of my cape donned to ward off the cold.

I enjoyed changing my face with a false mustache, a mole, and a birthmark. But one night at a vintage clothes store in Shamisenbori, a woman's lined kimono patterned with small and large hail on an indigo background caught my eye. I had to wear it soon.

I was captivated by it beyond simply loving its colors and stylish pattern. Not only women's clothes, but when I looked at and touched beautiful silk, for some reason, my body trembled. I often reached a climax of pleasure while gazing at the color of a lover's skin. I envied a woman's ability to indulge herself, without fear of the world, and dress up in the clothes or silk crepe I fancy.

I trembled at the pleasant thought of wrapping my body with the cold heavy cloth of the vivid, fine-patterned lined kimono in the vintage clothes store. I wanted to dress in that kimono and walk the streets as a woman…. Without a second thought, I was ready to buy the kimono and complete the outfit with a long kimono from Yuzen and a black crepe silk *haori* half-coat. The clothes seemed to be for a big woman and would fit a small man like me.

In the hushed, empty temple late at night, I quietly turned to the dressing table and put on make-up. I looked a little grotesque the instant I patted white powder onto the bridge of my yellowish nose. When I spread out the viscous white liquid evenly with my open hand, it stayed on better than I imagined. The joy of my skin was exceptional when the sweet-smelling frozen dew soaked into my pores.

As I painted on the rouge and polishing powder, my face was needlessly pure white like plaster but amusingly transformed into a woman's face with a lively complexion. More than in the work of literary or fine artists, an actress, a geisha, or any ordinary woman knows a person skilled at make-up uses her body as the test subject and learns very interesting things.

A long undershirt, a half collar, an underskirt, and the sleeves with a crisp red silk backing gave the same sensation to my body as the feeling savored from an ordinary woman's skin. I painted everything white from the nape of my neck to my wrists, covered my hair with a wig in the *ichogaeshi* style, and dared to mingle in the streets at night.

The overcast night was gloomy. For some time, I wandered the stretch of Senzoku-cho, Kiyosumi-cho, Ryusenji-cho crisscrossed by lonesome streets with many trenches. Neither the police in the police boxes nor the people on the streets noticed me. The night winds chilled my face already dried out like a stretched-out cuticle. My breath moistened and warmed the cloth of the hood covering my mouth. As I walked, the hem of my long silk crepe underskirt twisted around my leg like it was playing.

By adjusting the obi sash tightened fast from the pit of my stomach to my ribs and the waistband, blood began to flow naturally in my blood vessels like a woman's. My masculine sensibilities and posture gradually vanished.

When my hand painted with face powder jutted out from the shadow of my Yuzen sleeve, the strong lines disappeared in the darkness and nimbly floated out whiter and plumper. I was captivated by the beauty of my hands. The woman who truly possessed hands this beautiful would provoke envy. Wouldn't it be fun to commit various crimes dressed as a woman, like the young thief, Benten Kozo, in kabuki plays?

I felt sensations reminiscent of secrecy and suspicion thoroughly enjoyed by readers of detective and crime novels on my walk to Rokku through the park gradually filling with people. Like murderers, robbers, and people who commit brutal acts, I had made up my mind.

When I came out at the four corners of the opera house at the edge of the lake from Twelve Stories, light from decorative lights and arc lanterns shimmered on my face plastered with make-up. The hues and stripes of my kimono were vivid. When I reached the front of the Toki-waza theater, I slipped into the people streaming toward the huge mirror at the entrance to a photography shop at the end. The mirror reflected my figure magnificently disguised as a woman.

Beneath the white powder thickly painted on, a secret man is concealed, has a woman's eyes and mouth, moves like a woman, and smiles like a woman. Sweet scents and rustling clothes resembling murmurs arose as a group of several women passed in front and behind me. None of them doubted I was one of them. Some of the women seemed to envy the creation of my elegant face and choice of old-fashioned clothes.

The familiar disturbances at night in the park were new to my eyes that held a secret. No matter where I went or what I saw, everything was bizarre, like an object touched for the first time. While people's eyes deceived, lantern light deceived, and I hid under glamorous cosmetics and silk crepe clothes, perhaps ordinary reality should have appeared in the mysterious colors of dreams to pull back the curtain of secrecy and peer through.

I continued to disguise myself every night. Sometimes, I nonchalantly slipped in among spectators standing to watch plays at Miyatoza or an audience for a moving picture. Close to midnight, I returned to the temple, went straight to the parlor, and quickly lit the bright air lamp. My tired body still dressed lay limply on the rug. During my swift descent into sleep, I gazed with regret at the colors of the gaudy kimono and waved around the cuffs.

I stared at the reflection in the mirror of my blotchy cheeks roughened by the peeling white powder. Similar to intoxication by aged wine, this decadent pleasure aroused my soul.

With the map of paradise and hell in the background, I crawled onto the soft futon in the gaudy, long kimono like a prostitute. Until late night came, I turned the pages of strange books. In time, I became adept at applying make-up and being bold. To kindle fanciful associations, I inserted a dagger or opiates into my obi sash and went out. Without committing a crime, I wanted to fully take in only the beautiful romantic aromas accompanying a crime.

One night after only a week passed, I made the first step into a curious, outrageous, and mystical incident from an unexpectedly mysterious start.

That night, I guzzled much more than my usual

amount of whiskey and walked with confidence to the seats for distinguished guests on the second floor of the San'yukan motion picture theater. Close to ten o'clock, the crowded venue filled with air cloudy like fog blackening and billowing from the stuffiness of the squirming crowd. The air floated by and decayed the white face powder. My drunken head was pained like it shattered each time the movie's light rays, grating in the darkness and evolving at a dizzying speed, stabbed my gawking eyes.

Sometimes the electric lights that popped on at the end of the film pierced through the cigarette smoke floating above the heads of the crowd on the lower floor like clouds boiling up from the depths of a gorge.

From the shadow of the kerchief covering my entire head, I looked around at the faces of the overflow crowd in the venue. I took secret pride in the many men looking amazed at the shape of my old-fashioned hood and women stealing glances, desirous of the stylish hues of my clothes. None of the other women in the audience seemed to attract others' eyes as much as I did because of my eccentric dress and the abundance of charm in my facial features.

The chairs beside me for distinguished guests should not have been empty when I took my seat. I didn't notice when they were occupied. When the electric lights were turned on the second or third time, a man and woman were seated to my left. The woman looked to be twenty-two or -three but was probably twenty-six or -seven. Her hair was styled with three rings. She was wrapped in a sky-blue cloak. Only her vivid breathtaking beauty was showily exposed. I couldn't tell whether she was a geisha or a daughter from a fine family. From the behavior of her gentleman companion, she didn't appear to be his wife.

"… Arrested at last …" said the woman in a quiet

voice. She was reading the program about the film. While he blew tall smoke having the aroma of M.C.C. Turkish Cigarettes in my face, his big eyes gleaming more than the jewel on his finger peered at me in the darkness.

Her hoarse voice like a teacher of a shamisen was distinctive and at odds with her charming figure. I knew that voice. During a trip by boat to Shanghai two or three years ago, she was the woman named T with whom I acted on impulse and had a brief liaison on the steamboat.

At that time, I recall having difficulty telling whether she was a professional or an amateur from her bearing and clothes. Her male companion on the boat and the man she was with tonight were entirely different in presence and appearance. Perhaps countless men joined these two men as links in a chain of her past life. Anyway, she was certainly the type of woman who was always flitting like a butterfly from man to man.

When we became familiar with each other on the boat two years ago, we didn't reveal our true family names for various reasons and landed in Shanghai without knowing each other's circumstances or addresses. For good reason, I deceived the woman I longed for and stealthily covered my tracks. Since then, I only thought of this woman in dreams of the Pacific Ocean and never thought I'd see her in a place like this.

She was a little plump at that time and slimmed down to a divine weight. Her moist, round eyes with long lashes were bright like they've had been wiped clean and possessed a manly authority a man wouldn't think a man had. Only her vivid lips possibly dyed with red blood when touched and her long hairline hiding her earlobes were unchanged from the past. Her nose looked a little higher, slightly more severe than before.

Was the woman interested in me? I couldn't be sure.

When the lights came on, she was delicately flirting with her companion and showed contempt for me, the outsider and an ordinary woman, and wasn't particularly worried about me.

Now next to that woman, I despised my disguise I had been proud of. I was overwhelmed by the charm of the spirited enchantress and the freedom in her facial expressions. Her make-up applied with supreme skill made me feel like a hideous, disgraceful monster. From the perspective of femininity and her stunning appearance, I was no competition at all and withered into timidity like a star before the moon.

In the thick, foul air hanging low in the venue, a distinct outline not seen with clouds floated up. When her supple hand flitted into view from the shadows of her cloak, it swam like a fish and was enchanting. As she chatted with the man, from time to time, her eyes rose like in a dream and looked at the ceiling, frowned and looked down at the crowd, and smiled showing her row of white teeth. Each time she looked deeply interested. Her large, vibrant black pupils reflected this interest and were noticeable from a far-off corner downstairs like two jewels in the theater. The features on her face, as organs for simply watching, smiling, listening, and talking, were rich in suggestive emotions. More than a human face, hers was a sweet food that enticed men's hearts.

Not one gaze in the theater focused on me. Foolishly, I felt jealousy and rage at the beauty of that woman who stole my popularity. The charm of appearing to be a woman that I had found amusing but became self-indulgence instantly extinguished the light and ended in the regret of being ignored. Had the woman recognized me and was deliberately exacting cynical revenge?

I realized my jealousy that envied beauty was gradually

turning into love in my heart. Defeated in my challenge to her, now, I wanted victory over her as a man. Driven by my uncontrollable appetite, I thought about suddenly grabbing the woman's supple body with all my might and trembled.

> Do you know who I am? I saw you tonight after several years. I'm beginning to love you again. Do you have the heart to be with me a second time? Do you have the heart to return here tomorrow night and wait for me? I don't care to share my address with anyone. I'm simply asking you to come here tomorrow around this time and wait for me.

Concealed by the darkness, I took out a sheet of paper and a pencil from my sash, jotted down this note, tossed it in her sleeve, and closely watched her reaction.

Around eleven, she quietly watched the moving picture until the end. During the commotion of the audience rising and going outside, the woman whispered again in my ear.

"… Arrested at last. …"

With a more confident and bolder gaze than earlier, she stared at my face for a short time and eventually disappeared into the crowd with the man.

"… Arrested at last. …"

In no time, the woman found me out. This thought sent a shiver through me.

Nonetheless, would she docilely come the next night? Did I not understand my weakness and performed my mimicry without measuring the strength of my rival's many years of experience? I returned to the temple bothered by various anxieties and fears.

When I took off my overgarments as usual and was dressed only in the long *nagajuban* slip I wore under the kimono, a small square of Western-style paper drifted down from the back of my hood.

The ink traces of "Mr. S. K." transmitted light like *tamakaiki* silk cloth. I was sure the woman wrote this. During the performance, I visited the toilet once or twice. She dashed off her response and secretly slipped it into my collar.

> I meet you in an unexpected figure in an unexpected place. Although your attire is different, how could I miss the face I couldn't forget in my sleep for the past three years? From the beginning, I knew you were the hooded woman and was amused given your ever whimsical nature.
>
> I was unsure but somehow knew your meeting me was you having fun. I was too happy but couldn't tell. I will do as you say and be waiting for you tomorrow night. It would be convenient for me if you come to Kaminarimon Gate between nine and nine-thirty.
>
> The rickshaw man I'll send will look for you and bring you to my home. Like your address being a secret, I will not tell you where I'm living and have arranged for you to be blindfolded for the ride. If you don't wish to comply, I will never see you but won't be too saddened by that.

As I read this letter, before I knew it, I was a character in a detective novel. Inexplicable curiosity and terror whirled in my head. Women understand their inclinations, perhaps, I should strive to imitate them.

The next evening brought a heavy downpour. I wore a new outfit and a rubber-coated overcoat over the Oshima kimono. I went outside into a waterfall of rain pummeling my Western-style silk umbrella. A newly dug ditch overflowed into the traffic circle. I put my *tabi* socks in my breast pocket. My drenched bare feet sparkled, lit up by the lamps on the row of houses.

The downpour of rain hit and disappeared into the flood flowing from the skies. Paths down the usually lively, broad alleys were cut off. Several men with their hems tucked up dashed out like soldiers on the run from the enemy.

Except when the occasional streetcar passed through, gushing water collected on the tracks. Only light from scattered light poles and advertisements shined dimly. Everything from my overcoat and wrists to my elbows was drenched. At last, I reached Kaminarimon Gate and stood dejected in the rain pierced by light from arc lamps.

I looked around and couldn't see a soul. Hidden in a dark corner somewhere, someone might be watching me. I lingered on this thought for a time. Finally, from the darkness in the direction of Azuma Bridge, light from one red paper lantern approached. An old-fashioned rickshaw rapidly came rattling over the paving stones of the streetcar tracks and stopped in front of me.

"Sir, please get in," said the rickshaw man, wearing a deep bamboo hat and waterproof cape. His voice seemed to disappear in the echoes of the rain flowing down the shaft. The man quickly slipped behind me and wrapped a smooth silk cloth twice over my eyes. He tied the cloth so tight it pulled up the skin at my temples.

"Now, please get in."

As he spoke, his rough hand grabbed mine and hurriedly help me into the rickshaw.

I heard the rain pouring onto the musty-smelling hood. I was certain a woman was seated beside me. The scent of face powder and the warmth of body heat charged the interior

To disorient me, the rickshaw man lifted the rickshaw by the sidebars ran around and around a few times in the same place, turned right, turned left, and drifted into a labyrinth. From time to time, we came out at streetcar tracks and crossed small bridges.

The cab shook for a long time. Of course, the woman beside me was T; she sat still and was quiet. She seemed to be there to supervise, maybe, to enforce my wearing the blindfold. Even if she weren't there, I had no interest in removing the blindfold. I was thrown into a fog of mystery with everything: the woman met on the ocean, like in a dream; a cab at night during a torrential downpour; a secret in a city at night; a blindfold; and silence.

Eventually, the woman separated my lips shut tight and inserted a cigarette. She struck a match to light it for me.

After about an hour, the rickshaw stopped. Again, the rough hand guided two or three blocks down a narrow road, opened a back door with a squeak, and led me into a house.

Still blindfolded, I was left alone, sitting in a tatami room, and soon heard the opening of a sliding door. The silent woman sat and squirmed closer like a mermaid and laid face up across my lap. She wrapped her arms around my neck and loosened the knot of the silk blindfold.

It was probably an eight-tatami room. The construction and the decor were first class and made of wood. But similar to not knowing her identity, I couldn't tell whether this was a waiting room, a mistress's quarters, or a respectable, upscale house. A wooden fence surrounded the luxuriant plants beyond the veranda. From what I could see, this house was somewhere in Tokyo, but I had no idea where.

"Please come often," said the woman, as she leaned her body against a square rosewood desk in the center of the room, and her white arms crawled limply onto the desktop like two living creatures.

She looked elegant. A two-colored obi sash closed her kimono with muted stripes and a collar. Her hair was tied back in the old *ichogaeshi* style. Although she looked graceful last night, I was surprised.

"You probably think I look odd dressed like this tonight. To keep people from recognizing me, I have to change my appearance every day."

As she turned over a Western-style cup on the desk and poured wine, her manner was more dispirited than I thought. She said, "Please understand. After we went our separate ways in Shanghai, I experienced various hardships with different men but was strangely unable to forget you. Please don't throw me away this time. Not knowing my identity or my circumstances, think of me as a woman in a dream, and please be with me forever."

Each word she spoke held mournful tones like a song melody from a distant land echoed in my heart. The flashy, strong-willed, and intelligent woman from last night could show what could be called her melancholy, commendable side. She seemed to abandon everything and flung out her soul in front of me.

Attracted by a love adventure unable to distinguish between reality and fantasy with the vague *woman in a dream* and the *secret woman*, I went to the woman every night after that, stayed until around two in the morning, and returned blindfolded to Kaminarimon Gate. For one month then two, we met without knowing the other's address or name.

My desire to investigate her circumstances and house was not small. However, as time passed, a peculiar curiosity gripped me. I only wanted to know where in Tokyo the rickshaw I boarded with the woman go, or what was the destination I traveled to blindfolded from Asakusa.

The rickshaw man ran through the streets and rattled the rickshaw for thirty minutes, an hour, and sometimes an hour and a half. The woman's house where he lowered the handle sidebars may have been unexpectedly close to Kaminarimon Gate. While I was shaken in the cab every night, nothing prevented me from speculating about where I was in my heart.

One night, I could no longer stand it and pestered the woman in the cab.

"Would you let me remove this blindfold for a moment?"

"No, I cannot."

The woman was upset and tightly held down my hands then pushed my head down onto them.

"Please, don't speak so selfishly. My home is my secret. If you find out this secret, I will be thrown away by you."

"Why would I do that?"

"If that happened, I'd no longer be *the woman in a dream.* More than loving me, you are in love with a woman in a dream."

I begged in every possible way, but she wouldn't hear of it.

"If I have no choice, I will show you … but only for a moment," she said with sorrow. As she weakly removed the blindfold, she asked, "Do you know where we are?"

She looked anxious.

The ground color of the beautiful clear sky darkened strangely. A plane of stars twinkled. The Milky Way flowed like a white fog from end to end. Shops lined both sides of a narrow alley, and lantern light brightly lit the streets.

Mysteriously, despite this being a fairly lively street, I had no idea where we were. The rickshaw gradually went down an alley. One or two more blocks in front of us, I saw the signboard of a seal engraving shop with Seibido written in large letters. I glimpsed the town and house number in small characters on the side of the signboard a distance away from the rickshaw. The woman noticed.

"Oh no," she said and covered my eyes again.

Until now, I believed I'd never been to this street with the signboard for the seal engraving shop encountered in this alley with many bustling shops. I was lured again by the feelings of a puzzling world I experienced as a child.

"Could you read the signboard?"

"No, I couldn't. I absolutely do not know where we are. I only know about your life on the waves of the Pacific Ocean three years ago. I was tempted by you and thought about going with you to a fantastic country far across the sea," I answered.

In a grieving voice, she said, "Please, hold onto those feelings in your future life. Please, live in the fantastic country and think of the woman in the dream. Please, don't speak about tonight's selfishness."

Tears streamed from the woman's eyes.

For some time after, I was unable to forget the scene on the mysterious street shown to me by the woman that night. The signboard of the seal engraving shop seen at the end of the bustling, narrow alley lit brightly by lanterns left a clear impression in my mind. In the end, I struggled to find that town and eventually devised a plan.

While being pulled around and around Kaminarimon Gate as a rider every night for a long time, the number of times the rickshaws circled one place and the number of right and left turns became constant, and I somehow memorized them.

One morning, I stood blindfolded at a corner at Kaminarimon Gate and spun around a few times. When I thought, It's this direction, I ran in that direction at the same speed as the rickshaw. I had no other method but to watch the time and turn down different alleys. When I believed I reached the right place, as expected, I found a bridge and streetcar tracks. This had to be the street.

The road began at Kaminarimon Gate, went around the periphery of the park, and came out at Senzoku-cho. A narrow alley in Ryusenji-machi led to Ueno, then turned left below Kurumazaka, went seven or eight blocks down Okachi-machi street, and started to turn left. In no time, I came upon an alley.

Of course, I could see the signboard of the seal engraving shop ahead.

While keeping my eyes on the sign, I walked straight to it like I was studying the interior of a secret hidden cave. When I came out at the end of the street, I was surprised to see Shimotani Takemachi Road where I came out every night. No more than twenty feet ahead, I could see the secondhand clothes store where I sometimes bought finely patterned silk crepe.

Although the mysterious alley connected to the sides of Shamisenbori and Naka-Okachimachi, I don't remember passing here. I arrived at the front of the Seibido signboard that distressed me and lingered for a short time.

The sky of brilliant stars and the charm of the night filled with red lantern light were completely different. I was disenchanted by the sight of the row of derelict houses withered by the blazing autumn sun.

I guess the way and ran out like a dog spurred by irrepressible curiosity sniffing all the way home.

Again I crept along Asakusa-ku, turned right at Kojima-cho and right again, crossed the streetcar tracks near Suga Bridge, turned at Daichgashi to Yanagi Bridge, and came out of a wide alley in Ryogoku.

I didn't know which direction the woman chose and guessed she took a big detour. Yagenbori, Hisamatsu-cho,

Hamacho, crossed Kakihama Bridge, then had no idea where to go next.

Her house had to be on this road. I went in and out of the narrow alleys in the neighborhood for an hour.

Across from Saijo-ji Temple, the spaces between the eaves of the row of houses were tight. When I discovered an inconspicuous, tiny alley, I intuitively knew the woman's house was concealed there.

I went in. From the second-floor banister surrounded by an amazing pebble-textured fence on the second or third house on the right side, through the leaves, a woman who looked like she was dead glared down at me.

Unexpectedly, I looked up with a smirk at the second floor, an unsmiling woman gazed at me and feigned innocence. Although she was disguised, it was her. She looked different from my impression of her at night. She allowed just one request from a man and loosened the blindfold. Her expression reflected her remorse and frustration over the exposure of her secret. Quietly, she hid in the shadow of the shoji screen.

The woman was the widow of the neighborhood's rich man called Yoshino, the same name on the signboard of the seal engraving shop. The puzzle was solved. After that, I threw her away.

A few days later, I settled with the temple and moved to Tabata. My spirit gradually became dissatisfied with the lukewarm pleasure of secrets and gravitated to searching out more colorful, bloodstained pleasures.

2. THE YANAGIYU
INCIDENT

One summer night around nine-thirty, a young man visited the law office of Dr. S located in the Yamashita district of Ueno.

A bit of luck placed me at the large desk sitting across from the elderly doctor in his room upstairs and listening to the latest criminal case, a possible seed for a novel I may write. If this novel comes to be, the reader may make the deductions. The doctor has been a fan of my novels for a long time, always delighted in my visits, and offered me new material. I learned more from this elderly lawyer than randomly reading detective novels.

The doctor was a famous criminal lawyer who was a scholar of literature, psychiatry, and psychology, as well as practiced law for many years. Needless to say, I listened with great interest to the assorted secrets of criminals.

It was after nine on that summer evening when the young man knocked on the door. Only the doctor and I were in the room. A smile bursting with charm rose on the doctor's always-kindly face with white sideburns while a fan blew on the back of his baggy linen suit.

I propped an elbow beside the window looking out at

the light of the evergreen flower beds in the mountains in far-off Ueno and enjoyed my ice cream as we discussed details unknown to the general public about a murder in Ryusenji-cho reported in the newspapers' crime stories.

We might have been engrossed in our conversation and failed to hear his footsteps. His sudden, nonstop knocking on the wooden door startled us a bit. The doctor glanced at the door and simply said, "Come in," and returned to our conversation.

I was sure the doctor expected an office boy with some business-related material. By this time of the evening, most of the people working in this office had gone home. Other than the porter who lived in a room downstairs, no one should be coming to the second floor uninvited.

When I thought the door knob turned, a thud echoed like a shoe dragging a heavy object. An unknown young man staggered into the room.

"Oh, what is this? A serious criminal."

My intuition told me this immediately. Of course, the doctor realized that before me. The young man's expression was more ghastly than anything I'd ever seen in a play or a moving picture.

Any amateur would agree with certainty the abnormal criminal before them from the watchful blackness about to fly out of his eyes. The doctor and I unexpectedly paled. The doctor, who was well versed in this sort of situation, nearly leaped from his chair, gently gestured to me to hold back, and calmly stared at the young man, while staying vigilant.

The young man took a few steps toward the desk between us, stopped, said nothing, and only returned the stare.

"Who are you? What is your business here?" the doctor asked in a genial tone. The young man looked like he wanted to answer, but his heavy panting kept him from talking.

Judging from his heaving chest, purple lips, and disheveled hair, he might have been running for dear life and escaped here from the street.

He closed his eyes and touched one hand to his pounding heart. As his huffing and puffing subsided, he appeared to struggle with all his might for two or three minutes to quiet his excited nerves.

The young man was twenty-seven or -eight, aged by his grimy appearance but not older than thirty. He was wearing a long, old, threadbare, salt-and-pepper suit but no hat. His hair looked like a frayed straw sandal and trembled above his pale forehead. He wore a Bohemian necktie with soiled colors.

I first guessed from the paint stains dotting the shoulders of his jacket that the man worked as a painter, a craftsman but soon discovered elements of refinement in his features. I didn't overlook his appearance. The long hair and Bohemian necktie made him look less like a craftsman and more like a fine artist.

The man gradually quelled his heart palpitations, and blood slowly returned to his purple lips. He opened his eyes. They gave the impression of still watching that familiar dream. He didn't look at the doctor's face but stared for a long time at the desktop while his head nodded slightly.

On the desk were the cup of partially eaten ice cream in my hand and a telephone. He kept staring at the cup of ice cream with amazed eyes. He may have been out of breath and thirsty. The thought, He probably wants the ice cream, popped into my head. The next moment exposed how wrong my guess was. More than amazement, he stared at the ice cream with deep suspicion.

As he looked, an indescribable terror spread over his face. His scared eyes looked like they saw the true form of a ghost and stared at the mushy lump in the ice cream cup with suspicion. Then he took another step forward. After he scrutinized the ice cream in the cup, he released a faint sigh like he was relieved for the first time.

The doctor had been quietly observing his puzzling behavior, at least to me, and asked again in a gentle voice like he had been waiting for this moment.

"Who are you? What business has brought you here?"

This time, the doctor spoke like a concerned uncle to the young man. The doctor and I realized The young man probably wasn't a craftsman. The young man gulped air and blinked his big eyes several times. Like danger was after him, his attentive eyes scanned the door he entered. He was frightened like the prey in a hunt and couldn't stand still.

"I'm terribly sorry for showing up without an appointment," said the young man and lowered his head in a half-hearted bow. "Excuse me, but are you Dr. S? My name is K. I'm a painter and live in Kurumazaka-cho. I went to a bathhouse not far from here and decided to stop here on my way home."

Of course, the man carried a towel and a soap box in his right hand. He looked like he wore Western-style clothes to the bathhouse. He only had his one good suit and was not carrying a lightweight *yukata* kimono to change into. Moisture soaked the ends of his long hair, but his hands and face were not flushed like someone fresh from a bath.

"… I had to see you, Sensei, and ran here as fast as I could. I've come to ask for your intervention. Unfortunately, I've shown no one else. I panicked and rushed here without warning. Forgive the intrusion."

Little by little, the man calmed his words, but the disturbed expression floating in his eyes never vanished. His alarm grew and his nerves were triggered as he tried to calm down. His right hand shoved the soap box into his pocket. As both hands wrung out his damp towel, he ended his rapid-fire introduction in a hoarse voice we strained to hear.

"So you have urgent business with me. Please have a seat, and we'll calmly discuss it," said the doctor, offering him a chair. He glanced at me and said, "I have complete trust in this man. There's no need to worry about him. Please, speak freely on any matter."

"Yes. Thank you. There's an incident I wish to tell the renowned sensei. But before I do, I have a request.

"Tonight, I possibly committed the serious crime of murder. I say possibly because I don't know if anyone was even killed. Moments ago, a crowd was pointing at me and shouting, 'Murderer! Murderer!' I ignored them and fled here. For all I know, my pursuers are coming for me now.

"Thinking about it, this may all be a dream that leaves no traces and be nothing more than my hallucinations. If a murder actually happened tonight, inconsistencies are everywhere. And before this, I often experienced hallucinations.

"I have no idea how much of tonight's incident is true. If there was a murder, the murderer may be me. And from the beginning, a murder may have not occurred at all. The sounds of the crowd shouting, 'Murderer! Murderer!' and their pursuit of me may be nothing more than my delusions.

"I'm not saying this to avoid my crime. Sensei, I will confess everything about tonight's incident to you and ask you to judge whether I'm a detestable murderer.

"If tonight's murder is real and I am the murderer, I'd

like the doctor to prove I don't have the heart of a killer, and my crime was my curse of hallucinations. If my pursuers catch me here on the second floor, I ask you not to hand me over to the police until I finish my story.

"If a sickly man like me is threatened by some unforeseeable calamity and commits a crime, I trust no one but you, Sensei, to explain my mental state and speak in my defense. Even if tonight's incident amounts to nothing, I had been thinking about visiting you for a long time. Are you able to grant my request?

"I may talk for a long time, so could you give me refuge in this room until I'm done? If my crime is exposed after I finish, I promise to act like a man."

The young man spoke without taking a breath then timidly looked up at the searching but gentle eyes of the seasoned doctor. At that moment, the doctor's face overflowed with dignity and authority befitting a scholar with an unusually austere, sharp mind. He carefully gauged the young man's circumstance and did not appear to question whether or not he was a detestable murderer but only saw him as an honest young man.

The doctor was charitable and said, "Very well. I guarantee your safety until you have told your whole story. You seem upset. Calm yourself and speak so I will understand."

"Oh, thank you. Thank you," said the young man, his voice quivering. Finally, he sat in the offered chair. As the three of us sat around the desk, the story unfolded.

"Before I describe tonight's event, would it be better to cut out the beginning of this story? Where and when this incident began becomes complicated the more I think about it. I feel like I must go back to a nearly infinite past problem. In order to thoroughly explain the nature of tonight's incident, everything about my life until today may have to be revealed. It may be inadequate if I don't tell every detail of my history or my parents' traits.

"I don't have the latitude to explain this sloppily, I will simply mention my history of insanity. I suffered a severe mental breakdown around the age of seventeen or eighteen. Although I work as an oil painter, my technique is so awkward I'm ashamed to say what I do. I'll simply say my life is one of extreme poverty.

"Please understand that in advance. If you listen carefully to the situation I'll describe, at least, the sensei will understand the mysterious world I witnessed and the anguish I experienced.

"As I said earlier, I live in Kurumazaka-cho inside the compound of Jonen-ji Temple of the Jodo Sect behind the railroad tracks. I rent a room in a row house and have lived there with a woman since the end of last year.

"Yes, the woman. You could say we were intimate. She was like a wife, but our relationship was very different from that of a normal husband and wife, so I'll call her *the woman*. No, I'll call her Ruriko. She'll come up frequently as I tell this story. To put it bluntly, thanks to Ruriko, and for her, thanks to me, we fell into today's poverty. I have no regrets, but she had many grievances.

"When she was a geisha in Nihonbashi, if she hadn't run off with a yakuza like me, she would have attracted a fine man and probably live a comfortable life. Over the past year, this idea lodged in her breast. Although I'm madly in love with her, even now, a passionate woman and lustful at her core, her love for me vanished long ago.

"Occasionally, she deliberately picked a fight, stormed out of the house, visited a male friend she did not have relations with, and didn't return home until late at night. Even without that behavior, my nerves as a deeply jealous man were inflamed. In those days, I was mostly insane. I was quite aware and terrified of the feelings that drove me crazy.

"In an instant, blood rushed to my head, perhaps I grabbed the hair at the nape of her neck and started dragging her around like her body was a piece on a game board. I hit and slapped her, and like in a dream, didn't know how many times I could have killed her. However, Ruriko was not a weak woman who shrunk from this treatment.

"Later, I placed my hands together before her, rubbed my forehead on the tatami, and begged for her forgiveness. But my behavior only intensified her arrogance and selfishness. Of course, I'm not without blame for her actions.

"On top of the nervous breakdown, I've suffered from a severe case of diabetes.

"My spirit adored her flesh, but I couldn't satisfy her physical desires. I'm certain this was the powerful reason for the trouble brewing between us. An amorous woman with her health may be suffering unbearably. In a short time, this woman who took pride in her health slowly slipped into severe hysteria, flew into random fits of rage, and grew impatient.

"Riruko's flush face that glowed with life seemed to gradually pale and become gaunt. This was tragic to me, and at the same time, I was delighted. My feelings became that decadent and sick.

"The force of Ruriko's hysteria doubled and negatively affected my nervous breakdown. Sensei, perhaps you know about the close relationship between diabetes and nervous breakdowns. Although diabetes in fat people is not terrifying, you know that diabetes in a thin person like me is malignant.

"Diabetes in my case aggravated my mental breakdown or was it the other way around? I don't know which came first. These two illnesses are related and stay in step with each other. My mind and body decay with each passing day.

"I obsessed over Ruriko, drew various delusions, and was battered by hallucinations. Whether asleep or awake, I constantly saw strange dreams. The most painful one was the fear I could kill her.

"I'm not a man who has entirely wiped out my desires for art. Although I'm addicted to the love of Ruriko, having been born into this world, my constant wish is my desire to leave behind at least one fine work of art when I die.

"No matter how depraved and decadent my life becomes, I'm a man who believes an artistic life is immortal. If I became depressed and killed that woman, the footsteps I left in this world will be buried forever. Nothing terrifies me more than this.

"The fault may lie in thoughts like, Will I kill today? or Will I kill tomorrow? I'm also threatened by gruesome visions. When I woke up in the dead of night, Ruriko had straddled my body as if riding a horse and was holding a trembling razor to my throat. Blood dripped from between my eyebrows. A mysterious anesthetic coated the collar of my nightclothes. I felt like I saw this event and often felt on the verge of passing out.

"That may be why Ruriko never once resisted me with force. Although an evil woman with a twisted nature, she was exhausted like a corpse when I punished her. A cynical smile rose on her lips as I kicked, slapped, and tossed her around as much as I liked.

"However, her attitude heightened the craziness in my spirit and turned me into a brute. The more she endured, was unmoved, and looked unafraid during a beating made my fears drive me harder.

"If she showed unusual gentleness, I became more cautious. I didn't thoughtlessly drink a cup of sake or hot water she offered. If she was going to kill me, I thought the safest path would be to kill her first. Would I be killed or would she be killed? Either way, I felt a bloody crime would arise between us and become an undeniable fact.

"I planned to show nude paintings with her as the model at a fall exhibition but have made no progress in my work in this condition. From around the end of last month, all we've done is fight every day. I've had no time to pick up a brush. The desperation coming from dissatisfaction with work changed in my sick head. And my life has become increasingly hopeless. In just the past half of a month, my daily routine was to repeatedly punish, love, worship, and plead to Ruriko.

"Within a day, my feelings toward her change often like a cat's eyes. I thought about hitting her with all my might, then in the next instant, tears flowed in sorrow over my violence toward her. When she didn't comply, I started beating and kicking her again.

"The mayhem was always followed by her hiding away. Who knows what she did for half or the whole day until dawn when she always reappeared?

"She left me alone in the house, crying, angry, and drained. Holding my head and feeling like I was going to blackout, I lay down and drowsily watched time pass.

"This turmoil boiled up four or five days ago. In the biggest fight ever, I raved by giving into the despair of going insane. The fight began in the evening and continued until around nine. During the day, she looked more dead than alive.

"She mussed her hair and was looking with contempt at the objects knocked down on the wooden veranda when she dashed to the street and walked around. When I wondered why she ran out of the house? I thought Ruriko was about to run out. I'd hate to see that and intended to thwart her.

"I still don't clearly remember how I walked out or where I went. When I slipped into the darkness of the Ueno forest and went down to the edge of the lake behind the zoo, I came to my senses and sighed with relief.

"Perhaps the cold air skimming my fevered head refreshed me. Oblivious, I wandered in a lonely direction with few passersby. From there I walked past the front of the Noryo Exhibition Hall. As I crossed Kangetsukyo to Ueno, I was mostly in my right mind and vaguely understood my situation.

"Was I too violent? All my joints ache as if I fell from a high place. I'm conscious but I feel like I'm watching a movie half of the time and live in a fog. Few human feelings remain in my head as if blown away by a storm.

"The female figure I fought a little earlier and treated cruelly drifted in and out of my consciousness like far-off sounds. I stared at her features but felt no particular longing or loneliness. I passed through droves of lively people and went out to streets lit by flickering firelight.

"When I wondered where I was, I noticed the railway of the main street lined by nightclubs. While jostled this and that way by the crowd out enjoying the cool air, my walk was aimless. Perhaps it was a festival night for Marishiten, the goddess of war, or a Saturday night? The swarm of spectators from an exhibition was probably strolling around.

"Although this part of town was always lively, I thought differently about the human refuse out that night. The liveliness of that night's scene dazzled my eyes. This liveliness was fairly dizzying but did not rattle my brain. I felt more lighthearted and cheerful than ever, like listening to the music of a symphony.

"My nature is to have a dislike for a town of human refuse, but those feelings awoke only on that night to numb my nerves. The assorted passersby lurching to my left and right, the sounds, and the lights did not stop one vivid image in my head.

"I went through a haze resembling pictures in a magic lantern. I'm sure its calm enveloped me. I felt alone in a high place and had a bird's eye view of the throng of people in this world. I passed in front while crying like I did when my mother scolded me as a child.

"The street looked hazy through my tears and could see a faraway scene. I saw that exact scene that night.

"Around thirty minutes later, I turned around on the main street to go home to Kurumazaka. Of course, I don't have a clear recollection of how I got home.

"I might have decided to walk toward Asakusa Park. I turned right at the streetcar stop in Kurumazaka and followed the railway tracks for five or six blocks. As you probably know, Sensei, on the left is a public bathhouse called Yanagiyu. When I stood before the bathhouse, I thought I'd go in for a bath. I decided not to go but have the habit of going for a bath when my head is muddled.

"I sensed melancholy in my spirit and the uncleanliness of my flesh as one. When my spirit sinks, I feel like filth clogs my entire body and makes me stink. So when my spirit sinks to the lowest depths, I enter the bath several times and wash and wash. I feel the filth and the stench won't easily come off.

"During the year, I only enter the bath at these times. Although I sound like a fastidious person, the truth is I often feel so listless and have no energy to take a bath.

"As a result, I'm used to long spells of spiritual melancholy. I'm nostalgic for feelings of enjoying my filthy flesh and immense sloth. If I entered the bath when I stood before Yanagiyu that night, I believed my monotony for the past half a month would brighten slightly for a time.

"I have no schedule for going places, be it the public bath or the barbershop. I always walk the street. When struck by the feeling, my habit was to jump in as soon as I found one. That night, fortunately, I had ten *sen* in change on me and considered going into Yanagiyu.

"When inside, I realized I had never been to this bathhouse. No, let me be honest, until I passed there that night, I wasn't aware of the bathhouse. I had an inkling I had been there but completely forgot about it.

"I must highlight one thing, I flew out of my house at nine and at least three hours had passed. It was a summer night, but the bathhouse was so crowded it was intimidating.

"Thick steam floated over the surfaces. I couldn't tell the width of the bathing room. The drainboards and the buckets were slimy and slippery. The bathhouse wasn't very clean, but this late at night the griminess left behind by many people was no surprise.

"The crowd of customers made carrying the small bucket a challenge. When I came to the crowded bathing pool, I aimed for the gaps between the shoulders of the naked bathers, packed in like potatoes being washed.

"Five or six bathers waiting to cut in were lined up near me and grabbed the edge of the bathing pool. I was unnerved for a short time then sloshed the rental towel in the warm water and wet my back.

"Finally, I discovered a small space in the center and forced my way in. The water was thick like warm spit, dirty, and its stench hit my nose.

"The faces and skin of the guests in front and behind

me were hazy, exactly as I've seen in Carriere's paintings. I felt countless apparitions drifting there.

"As I said, I squeezed into the center of the pool. I could barely see anything through the billowing clouds of steam. When I looked at the ceiling, in front of me, and to my left and right, I saw steam. The five or six people closest to me looked like ghosts.

"If the babbling voices coming from the crowded pools in the women's bath and the men's bath, the racket echoing off the high-domed ceiling enveloped by steam, and the sensation of lukewarm water enveloping my limbs were absent, the feeling would have been the same as entering the fog in a valley between steep mountains.

"In fact, I was lured in by pleasurable and mysterious feelings identical to human refuse loitering on the main street or a strange lonely dream.

"The problem with this bathhouse was I felt stronger as I soaked in the bathing pool. The edges and the bottom of the bathing pool and the hot water filling the pool were all slippery and felt like I was being sucked into a mouth.

"I felt uncomfortable but not that awful. I must confess one aspect of my abnormal propensities. For some reason, I particularly enjoy being touched by slippery materials.

"For example, I've loved *konnyaku* gelatin since a boy but not because I liked the taste. I didn't put konnyaku in my mouth but simply fondled it in my hands or watched it jiggle. I found that to be one pleasure. Others were jelly noodles, syrup, toothpaste in a tube, snakes, mercury, and the fatty flesh of a woman. It could be food or anything. I could never do without all those things that evoke pleasure.

"My love of paintings, that is, my fondness for that sort of object, has gradually escalated. I think you'd understand if you saw my still life paintings, only the drawings of a body dirtied by ditch mud or a body slippery like syrup are drawn masterfully. Thus, a friend dubbed me a Gooeyist.

"My sense of touch for slippery objects is particularly refined. Through sight alone, I can immediately judge the sliminess of things like a taro plant, snot, or a rotten banana.

"Thus, that night, I remember a rush of pleasure when my feet touched the bottom of the slimy tub filled with slightly grimy water. My body slowly became strangely slippery. The skin of the people soaking near me seemed to glisten with slime like warm water. For some reason, I wanted to touch them. Just as I had that thought, seaweed seemed to stick to the backs of my legs. I thought I stepped on a denser, slimy object wiggling like an eel. I felt as though I thrust my leg down into an ancient pond and stepped on a frog's corpse.

"My toes searched the slime. Sea algae stuck to both of my legs and coiled around them. Then a thick, fluid-like lump grazed the top of my foot.

"At first, I thought a substance like an ointment for a skin ailment together with a bandage were submerged and dissolved at the bottom of the bathing pool. After fumbling around for a while, I realized the object wasn't small.

"I walked a few steps on the fluid. When I raised my foot, clinging to it was a substance with a degree of sliminess that thickened and became heavy like gum as I walked. Mucous covered the surface of the gummy substance and became slippery when I stepped with force. But no matter how I stepped, the substance billowed up. Dents appeared all around then started to puff up in a zigzag for about six feet and drifted along the bottom of the foggy hot water.

"The situation was bizarre. I considered pulling up the object with my hand. A sudden ghastly thought crossed my mind. But before I realized it, my hand was pulled in. A thought flashed into my mind, the seaweed-like substance wrapping around my shins was a woman's hair.… A woman's hair? Oh, that's it. I'm entangled in a woman's long hair.

"The heavy, gummy, entangled object is definitely human flesh. A woman's corpse is drifting along the bottom of the pool.

"No, it can't be something so stupid. Aren't there many other people in this pool right now? Doesn't everyone but me look composed? As I was about to change my mind, a slimy object wound around my shins, and the squirmy object beneath my feet swelled up.

"Despite my unusually keen sense of touch, even on the back of my legs, my judgment of a body was a mistake. I had no reason to suspect it was the corpse of anybody, let alone a woman. As a precaution, I retraced my steps from the head to the toes and found I was not mistaken.

"Beside a cylindrical shape like a head was a long narrow neck indentation. Next to that was the high tip of the breast rising like a mound to become a nipple, the belly, and two legs. There was no mistake. It was a human form. Naturally, I wondered, Am I dreaming?

"If not a dream, this mysterious thing should not be. Where was I? Maybe I was covered by a futon and asleep. I glanced around as I thought this.

"I saw dense steam and listened to the din of voices. The blurry contours of two or three guests floated like apparitions around me.

"My sole thought was this faint, misty world of steam was all a dream. This is a dream. It's just a dream. I'm sure I'm dreaming. The truth is half of me believed and half did not. Some sly trick forced me to dream. If a dream, please, don't wake me up.

"In my heart, I wished, Please, show me a dream-like, mysterious scene and a funnier and extraordinary dream. Although it's human to pray to wake up if in a dream, I was the opposite. I'm a person who values and trusts dreams that much.

"At the extreme, a man lives a life based on dreams more than reality. I realized this was a dream and did not quickly lose the sense of reality. Seeing a dream is the enjoyment of some truth like eating delicious food and wearing fine clothes. I crave interesting dreams.

"My foot played with the corpse. Unfortunately, the fun didn't last long. I asked why, but I discovered a terrifying truth in this dream!

"The sensitive sense of touch on the bottom of my foot, how do I say this? It may be a cursed, fatal sense of touch! Not only did I sense a woman's corpse, I knew who she was! Was the hair, slippery like kelp, wrapping my shins, perhaps, a large amount of hair floating limply as if blown by the wind, not her hair? I seemed to fall in love with her, at first, because of her hair.

"How could I forget that? Is that all? Isn't her flesh weak like cotton and smooth like a snake, like the feel of always glowing skin as if painted with kudzu gruel? As if I were looking at them, my toes vividly felt the shapes of the nose, the forehead, the distinctive eyes, and the position of the lips. No matter what anyone says or tries to trick me, I'm certain this is Ruriko. She is dying here.

"I had solved the mystery of this bathing pool. So I wasn't seeing a dream.

"I met Ruriko's ghost. Usually, a ghost menaces the visual sense of human beings. In my case, my sense of touch was menaced. There was no doubt I was touching her ghost.

"When I first flew out of the house, I looked at her with

eyes more dead than alive. I'm sure I accidentally killed her then. She was exhausted, slumped over on the veranda, and not trying to get up. She was dead.

"Now, her ghost appeared in this bathhouse. If not her ghost, why was no one in this crowd aware of her?

"At last, I've killed! The crime I had to commit one time happened tonight! As this thought bubbled up, I shuddered and, possibly, jumped out of the pool without washing and escaped to the street.

"Outside, the refreshed guests were still walking around the area, as lively as earlier. One animated group was followed by the next. To prove nothing else in the world had changed but me, Ruriko's collapsed form on the veranda and the feel of the wet corpse sunk to the bottom of the pool were bound together and etched into my mind.

"Over the two or three hours since then, until the streets in the dead of night quietly slept, I wandered the streets engulfed by a miserable feeling. I'll give a broad explanation without going into detail.

"I would go home to confirm the truth of this damned incident. If I confirm I committed the crime of murder, I'm determined to turn myself in tomorrow. I couldn't help believing that nothing in the world changed but me, and only Ruriko is not alive in this world. Naturally, these became my beliefs. The possibilities of Ruriko being alive and the corpse at the bottom of the bathing pool not being her ghost became more unnatural.

"However, when I returned home late that night, mysteriously, Ruriko was alive. Although her habit was to run out of the house in the wake of an argument, I brutally beat her that night, and she may not have had the strength to move her body. She was laying on her face on the veranda as before, while throwing out the unconscious body, I disheveled her hair into tufts, but she was gloriously alive. In fact, I wondered, Was that a ghost? Night ended and morning came. Ruriko waited for me.

"Of course, I did not tell her or anyone else about the bathhouse incident. But if a vengeful spirit is in this world, I thought, the ghost last night was vengeful. I saw the strange hallucination until now. It was too strange for last night's corpse to be a simple hallucination. Has anyone other than me seen that mysterious apparition?

"From then until tonight, I went to Yanagiyu at the same time for four nights in a row.

"What happened? Every night, the body was in the middle of the bathing pool and always floated by licking the backs of my legs. A noisy crowd was always there, packed in the dense flow of steam.

"That alone would be fine, but I lost patience. Until now, I touched the corpse with my toes. Tonight, I thought about plunging both my hands under the sides of the corpse to raise it from the bottom of the pool. When I did, my imagination was not mistaken. It was her vengeful ghost.

"While glimmering in the slippery scale deposits, the vacant eyes and mouth were open; the wet hair floated like arame seaweed. The face in death floating on the surface of the water certainly reminded me of Ruriko. Unnerved, I pushed the corpse to the pool's bottom again. I feverishly got out of the water, quickly changed into my clothes, and fled out to the street.

"In that instant, I thought the others in the bathhouse became rowdy. The many placid guests who submerged the body jumped to their feet and began shouting, 'Murderer! Murderer!'

"I heard a voice say, 'That's him. The guy in the Western clothes!'

"I was shocked, ran at full speed, turned down alley after alley, and ended up here.

"That's my story. I swear I've told no lies. At first, I thought that corpse was a dream, then suspected it may be a ghost, and finally believed it was a vengeful spirit.

"When I saw the crowd get unruly tonight, I thought, could this be her corpse and not a vengeful spirit or a ghost? Was everyone calling me a murderer? If so, how did I kill her? Did I commit this serious crime without knowing it like a sleepwalker?

"Somehow, her corpse was submerged at the bottom of the bathing pool. If the corpse had been in there, why hadn't anyone else noticed it until tonight? Were the events until tonight nothing but my hallucination? Have I gone crazy?

"Sensei, please explain these strange facts. Even if I were a murderer, please prove the truthfulness of my testimony in a court of law.

"The moment I fled the bathhouse tonight, you popped into my head. The sensei would understand my predicament. That's why I came to ask you."

This concluded the young man's confession. Dr. S heard it all and then responded he couldn't come to the truth without going to Yanagiyu with the young man. He was saved the trouble. Several police officers tracked the young man's path to the office and hauled him away.

Later the police told the doctor what happened. The young man suddenly grabbed a man's vitals in the pool at Yanagiyu and caused his death. The murdered man died without a sound and sunk to the bottom of the bathing pool.

No one noticed right away because the pool was overcrowded and the steam dense. When the young man raised the corpse, a bather spotted him and the wild chase began.

Of course, the young man's lover, Ruriko, had not been killed. She was called to court as a witness. I heard Dr. S say he would be the defense attorney in this case. Her testimony in court provided sufficient proof the young man was out of his mind. She launched into the following description of the young man's usual behavior.

"I hated him not because he didn't work or because I found another man. The truth is his madness worsened year by year until he only made unreasonably strange demands of me.

"I became worried when he started talking about nonexistent things as facts. He abused and punished me. Those punishments were extraordinarily subtle. For example, he'd put pressure on me, soaked a rubber sponge with soap, and rubbed it on my eyes and nose, hit places all over my body with a glue plant, and shoved tools for oil painting up my nostrils. He tormented me with that stupid behavior.

"He turned me into a grown-up doll and I cheerfully went along, but if I disagreed a little, he was quick to anger and become violent. It became horrible to be with him."

She did not seem to be the lewd, passionate woman the young man thought she was. Dr. S viewed her as an amiable, laid-back, honest woman. In a short time, the young man was committed to a mental hospital instead of being sent to jail.

3. THE PASSING OF A YOUNG MAN

The boy's name was Tajima Yoshio. He didn't know what sort of people his parents were or had any idea what they look like. His parents were dead by the time he was four years old. For as long as he could remember, he was raised in the home of his older brother Mikizo. He was five years old, and Mikizo was twenty-four.

His other siblings were Rokujiro, his twenty-year-old brother, and Ryuko, his sixteen-year-old sister who was eleven years older than the youngest, Yoshio. His oldest brother was his parent. Yoshio grew up knowing the truth that before he was born, one or two other babies died soon after birth.

Although he was one of four siblings, Yoshio was lonely as the much younger brother who lived a life apart from the others. He often heard relatives say, "Poor Yoshio-san is the most pitiful thing," because he doesn't know the faces of his mother and father.

Even if he knew his parents, his current feelings towards his siblings would not change much. While his brothers and sister talked with each other like friends, only he was a child and not a peer.

This wasn't done out of cruelty, and his sister, Ryuko, cared for him as if he were her child. He was dissatisfied with being "treated like a child" and wished to be "like a brother." Yoshio was around seven when these feelings occasionally arose.

Naturally, his eldest brother being the firstborn was the most domineering of his siblings and the brother most feared by Yoshio. Unlike his other siblings, his oldest brother couldn't bring himself to discipline Yoshio. Therefore, both Rokujiro and Ryuko had the same authority as the eldest, Mikizo, to scold Yoshio.

His older brothers and sister only seemed to clash in matters concerning Yoshio. Mikizo would summon his three siblings by name, "Rokujiro," "Ryuko," and "Yoshio." The younger three would properly address him with "Niisan," for older brother. Rokujiro and Ryuko would affectionately call each other "Roku-chan" and "Ryu-chan." Only Yoshio was formal when calling his second oldest brother and older sister, "Rokuji-niisan" and "Neesan," for older sister.

In the summer of Yoshio's seventh year, Mikizo graduated from college and became a medical doctor. Until then, every morning he put on his uniform with gold buttons and his college cap and went out. In no time, he was wearing Western-style clothes like a gentleman to work at the university hospital for the day that began around eight in the morning and ended at five in the afternoon. During that time, an uncle and aunt visited their home.

"Mikizo has become a fine doctor, but this is not too happy an occasion. Your mother and father are probably also joyous in the shadows of their graves."

Yoshio faintly remembered their joy in their nephew's success. He more vividly remembered Mikizo's coming marriage in March of the following year. The ceremony was held at Daijingu Shrine in Hibiya. In the evening, the announcement banquet was at Seiyoken, the exclusive French restaurant in Ueno.

Yoshio got into a car with his Aunt Hirosawa, who lived in Ushigome, Rokuji-niisan, and Ryuko and traveled from Hibiya to Ueno. In the car, his aunt said, "The bride is a truly, lovely girl…. Roku-chan, you're next."

"What? Before me comes Ryuko-chan."

Ryuko blushed bright red.

"Stop it, Roku-chan."

From that day, Yoshio had a new older sister. He simply called his new sister, "Neesan." Aunt Hirosawa cautioned Yoshio to call his only sister until now "Ryuko-neesan."

Yoshio found it funny to say the pair "Niisan" and "Neesan" and the pair "Rokuji-niisan" and "Ryuko-neesan."

Yoshio asked, "Is it okay to have so many niisans and neesans?" and laughed, his aunt laughed with him.

Yoshio felt strange about the new older sister and unhappy. His new sister was twenty, two years older than Ryuko-neesan. Her name was Kitako.

The day after the wedding, "Kitako … Kitako," Mikizo called to her, dropping the honorific *-san*. Would she get used to hearing that? For a time, Yoshio felt sorry for his new sister.

On the night he attended the banquet at Seiyoken, Yoshio thought both his sisters, the new one and the old one, were nice women with comparable good looks. However, that night, both wore flashy, glittery kimonos for special occasions. Their thick layers of face powder were perfectly painted on. They looked so much alike, he couldn't tell which one was prettier.

After two or three months, he judged the new sister to be prettier than the first one. The new sister had a superior face and body to Ryuko's and the same kindness and love for Yoshio. Because his brothers and sister went to the hospital or school during the day, naturally, Yoshio quickly became attached to his new sister.

He had been a sickly child from birth. As he grew, he came down with a fever or stomach or bowel problems once or twice a month. At those times, his new sister worried about him and went to fetch the doctor. Yoshio was not alone in his favorable opinion of her. His other siblings and relatives also thought well of her.

She got along with Ryuko, like blood sisters. Ryuko often let her new sister care for Yoshio who was frequently ill and slept a lot. At those times, the compassionate Ryuko said, "Yoshi-chan, you must try to not be such a burden on Neesan."

An incident to be critical of her arose. Even now, half of it remained in Yoshio's memory like a dream. In January of the year after her marriage, his sister had a baby. Yoshio remembered seeing the baby's face one time.

The baby's first cries were strong. Yoshio remembered hearing the baby from the parlor on the second floor. But later, there was no baby. Yoshio was told his memory of a birth was faulty. However, two or three years later, Ryuko told Yoshio that his memory of the birth was not a mistake but the truth. The baby was born but died a few days later. Yoshio haltingly pulled the memory from his head.

Events seen and heard during his childhood were a mystery. He distinctly remembered some parts, but many events were hazy and disjointed. Yoshio didn't know the baby died, but later, his sister gave birth two more times. He remembered these babies, like the first, died soon after birth.

Each time his sister's belly got big, everyone in the house would say this time it would be all right. They couldn't help being happy, but none of the births went well. If a baby were born, Yoshio would become a big brother and enthusiastically prayed for a baby. The family was fairly large. Even with no babies, the house was lively.

His four older siblings gathered together and were joined by their friends, male and female. They came to play *karuta* and other card games, play musical instruments, and raise a racket until late into the night.

Yoshio went to bed first around eight o'clock, but the noise kept him awake. Being a child, he was sensitive and a light sleeper. He'd watch them play cards but didn't understand the game and was bored. Nevertheless, Yoshio enjoyed their lighthearted banter during their musical gatherings and was always lurking at the margins.

When everyone was tired of singing and Yoshio looked vacant and bored, Ryuko often said, "Yo-chan, it's your turn. Which song do you want to sing?"

"Please sing for us. We have food. If you sing, you can eat, too, Yo-chan."

His other sister would join in the persuasion. Yoshio was not unhappy about entering the party of adults, but he was shy and not used to singing in front of his siblings' friends. Then Ryuko teased him.

"Yo-chan is a shy thing. But if you don't sing, I can't give you a sweet."

Kitako loved the shamisen. Ryuko always chanted a long epic *nagauta* song to her playing. His brothers were excellent card players but not skilled in musical performances. They only sang in English, performed a scene from the kabuki drama, *Kanjincho*; acted theatrically; or shouted nonsensical banter.

His oldest brother always looked serious to Yoshio, but he was funniest when playing the woman in a *gidayu* ballad.

Some of the guests who came from strange places played the violin or mandolin.

Everyone called a woman student, a cousin of his sister-in-law, "Mizue-san, Mizue-san." When she came to the gatherings, only Yoshio did not call her "Mizue-san" but "Azabu-neesan," the big sister from Azabu. She sang Western songs in a beautiful soprano voice.

She was a stylish woman and rarely performed Japanese works but was an accomplished violinist. When Mizue's turn came, everyone listened carefully. The end of the piece was met with thunderous applause. Words related to solo music for sopranos or baritones sometimes flowed from Mizue's mouth. Yoshio seemed to suddenly recall hearing her.

Mizue tended to converse fluently using English words he didn't understand. Ryuko was a mischievous woman but was no match for Mizue. Although she joked with the men, Mizue couldn't be out-talked. The other women were bad at cards, but Mizue was a strong player and always praised as the best.

AFTER MIKIZO WORKED at the university hospital for two years, he quit and hung out a placard announcing Tajima Hospital on a backstreet in Ginza. However, the family was large and couldn't move there because the hospital was too small. So as before, Mikizo commuted every morning from the family home in Yayoi-cho. The atmosphere in the house remained carefree and lively. When he opened his hospital, he telephoned his family on nights he would be late, but that rarely happened.

When Yoshio was ten years old, his sister gave birth to a second baby. As explained earlier, that baby died soon after birth. For a month after the birth, his sister was fatigued and lay listless on her bed when awake and asleep. From the beginning of the evening on the day of the usual musical gathering, Ryuko comforted her at her bedside. When Yoshio returned home from school, Ryuko sent him to Ginza to buy a record for the gramophone at Jujiya.

He knew the way to Jujiya but was a timid child and thought going so far on an errand by himself was a terrible idea. Ryuko and the maids were busy with dinner preparations and couldn't leave their work. But why did he have to go?

After he got off the streetcar in Kyobashi and shopped at Jujiya, the sky was faintly light. Yoshio hugged the package but took care not to break the record. He would appear to anyone as a child out on an errand in this far-off place. He went to his brother's hospital, which was nearby. It looked like his brother had already gone home. No one was in the reception area or the dispensary.

He had only been there a few times and was unfamiliar with the building, so he climbed the stairs and opened the door to a second-floor room. He thought his brother had gone home but found him with a woman, Mizue. Yoshio felt he saw something he shouldn't have seen but sensed leaving immediately would be bad. He stood there for a few moments.

Mizue and his brother saw Yoshio and looked away. Although their complexions seemed to change a little, they didn't act particularly upset but froze for an instant and remained quiet like they stopped breathing. Mizue was lying on the floor, and his brother was sitting at her head and lowering his face to hers.

"No, not there…. More this way, my chest hurts here," Mizue said curtly, spread her collar and tapped on her chest.

"Here? Does it hurt here?" asked his brother. He retrieved a salve from the dispensary and rubbed it where she was tapping.

Mizue stood and asked, "Yo-chan, are you by yourself?" She looked at Yoshio, smiled, and adjusted the collar of her kimono.

"Yes, I came to Ginza on an errand to buy a gramophone record," answered Yoshio, looking at Mizue but never at his brother. He half felt as though nothing mattered now.

"Oh, you were on an errand? That's admirable. Now, I will go with your brother to the musical gathering at your home. Yo-chan, you go ahead and tell your sister. We'll follow right behind you, so please get dinner ready."

Mizue then told some sort of joke to Yoshio. Although the evening musical gathering was dismal with his sister-in-law sitting on a futon like a semi-invalid woman, the others did not despair and the gloom was forgotten. Mikizo was in a good mood. As always, Mizue, who came with him, had lively conversations with everyone.

The cheerful atmosphere filling the Tajima home reached its height at that time. Everyone was happy, and the timid Yoshio no longer felt lonely.

After Kitako went to bed, the musical gathering and the card club lasted a little longer. Everyone was light-hearted, shouting over inconsequential matters and rolling with laughter. The regulars who gathered, beginning with Mizue, all felt good.

In the fall of Yoshio's eleventh year, Rokujiro became an engineer and went to work for a shipbuilding company in Kobe. The house felt lonelier. The tomboy Ryuko was not defeated by Mizue in rowdiness and, at the end of the year, she married into the Miyamoto family of Shibuya.

After that, melancholy touched the house, and the gatherings ended.

After Kitako's second failed pregnancy, she became anemic, experienced occasional dizziness, was aloof, and often slept. She welcomed guests but of the regular attendees to the musical gatherings only Mizue visited, as always, to chat and reminisce about old times.

After her recovery, she invited Mizue to join her and her husband on an outing. They also included Yoshio on an excursion to Hibiya Park. But it was not as much fun as before. One reason was Mikizo was strangely solemn and had become a moody and gloomy man.

By nature, he was always a bit of a moper with a quiet nature lacking in charm. Until now, ostentatious people seemed to be attracted to the environment of his home. However, after Rokujiro and Ryuko left, he returned to his original personality. And being relatively unsociable but generous and big-hearted, he may have secret feelings about his wife's illness, her inability to have children, and other issues.

When alone with Mizue, he was a different man and talked with a smile. One day, Yoshio was on his way to Koishikawa Botanical Garden. From the shadows of trees across the street, he spotted them walking hand in hand. In March of the year after Ryuko's marriage, Kitako suffered her third miscarriage and spent her waking hours in bed. Of course, Mizue and sometimes Ryuko, wearing her hair in the *maruge* style of a married woman, visited from Shibuya.

"Mizue-san, I must apologize to you. You visit every day," Ryuko said from her heart and explained how her health problems kept her from visiting as often as Mizue.

"No, I'm a lady of leisure and can visit every day. I'll be

your sister's companion in your place. I'm here and everything is fine," Mizue always said to Ryuko.

Her usual bright laughter echoed until late in the night as she entertained Kitako with amusing stories. Although she was not that ill, most days, Mikizo closed the hospital early to attend to his wife with kind words and compassion. Feeling guilty about her husband's indulgence, she said, "Mizue-san and Ryu-chan visit me so I'm not the least bit bored. You don't have to go to so much trouble. Were you busy today?"

Her husband's tender care was natural given her pleasant nature. Yoshio felt he didn't receive half that concern from his brother when he was ill but put it down to his sister's happy disposition.

More than envy, Yoshio was happy but felt dark concern over his brother's and Mizue's doting on his sister. Why did he find it unbearable to look at her thin pale face?

Her fatigue after giving birth was not a serious illness. However, everyone worried and nursed her. Everyone said she was lonely but affectionate. That may have been a bad omen. She later recovered from her illness, but her anemia slowly worsened. At the end of May, three months after the miscarriage, she suddenly died.

A few days before she died, she showed no particular change in her condition. She was dizzy or fainting and so giddy she couldn't sleep. One evening, Mikizo administered the usual injection to her. Beginning the following morning, she rapidly deteriorated. She suffered multiple bouts of diarrhea, like she contracted cholera, and continuously vomited a white milky substance. On the third evening, her condition became critical.

When she was close to her final breath, Rokujiro, who received a telegram and came from Kobe, and Ryuko, who nursed her the previous night, Aunt Hirosawa from

Ushigome, her Ogiwara relatives from Azabu, Mizue, Mikizo, and Yoshio surrounded her bed and called to her.

"Neesan."

"Kitako."

In the end, everyone sobbed until their noses stuffed up.

The women cried like children until their voices rose in a plea to bring back Kitako one more time. First, Mikizo, then one by one Rokujiro, Ryuko, and Yoshio followed by everyone else moistened Kitako's lips with the deathbed water to say goodbye. As they performed this ceremony, the soul departed from Kitako's bright eyes, slowly disappearing to some faraway place.

Even Yoshio understood his sister was dead. Her eyes were closed, and both hands were placed on her chest. For a short time, everyone sat heartbroken and silent beside her corpse. A dreadful situation seemed to occur. The departed soul may not have gone to some far-off place but roamed the room.

"The telegram surprised me. Why was it so quick?" Rokujiro whispered to Mikizo, sitting beside him.

"… It was acute intestinal catarrh. A stronger person could have been saved, but she was debilitated …"

The look on his eldest brother when he answered worried Yoshio. He peeked at his brother. Mikizo's face was paler than the dead Kitako's. When his gaze met Yoshio's, he seemed shocked and hung his head down. Yoshio paled, too.

Following the all-night wake, the funeral, and the first memorial service after seven days, faces from the old musical gatherings assembled and were fairly lively. After the ceremonies ended, Rokujiro went back to Kobe. From time to time, Ryuko and Aunt Hirosawa came to burn incense at the Buddhist altar and console Mikizo and

Yoshio. Eventually, the occasional visitors disappeared. The cheerful laughter of the most frequent visitor, Mizue, was healing during the lonely time, but for some reason, her visits stopped.

Every day, Mikizo rose early and visited the graveyard in Somei then made the long journey back to his hospital in Ginza. When Kitako was alive, he always returned home at sunset. These days, however, he didn't return home until late on many nights. Some days, Yoshio did not see his brother's face at all.

Yoshio was an ordinary sixth grader who always came home from school around two in the afternoon. He never got used to only the cook, a young woman named Waka, and the elderly maid, Moto, being there when he got home. He was always outside playing when the evening lights came on.

Although he could forget his loneliness to some degree during the day, he didn't understand whether his dreary feelings at night were the unreliable feelings of true loneliness.

After eating dinner, Yoshio was bored and went to the servants' room. He flopped down beside them busy at their needlework.

"Young master, it's already eight. Please go to bed. If your brother comes home late and you're still up, you'll be in trouble," said Moto and then went to a small, four-and-a-half tatami study a short distance away, laid out a futon, and hung up a mosquito net.

After Ryuko married, Yoshio had the habit of visiting her home alone and sleeping there. He hated doing this since Kitako's death and, as much as possible, went to his brother's room or the servants' room on the second floor to sleep. He was dismayed when he confessed his fear of sleeping alone to Mikizo, although he harbored negative feelings toward him and had to be patient with Mikizo.

Since the night of Kitako's death, Yoshio struggled not to come face-to-face with his brother and look into his eyes. Nevertheless, he worried about what his brother thought of him.

The large difference in age with his brother kept Yoshio from opening up to him. Their dispositions were also at odds. Yoshio believed his brother thought ill of him since that night. This belief was lodged deep in Yoshio's heart, and he couldn't warm up to Mikizo.

Yoshio felt better when he drove out the thought, If my brother truly thinks ill of me, why? More than being afraid of his brother, Yoshio felt he was a terrible child.

He decided not to look at his brother with suspicion but couldn't escape that thought. Every night, particularly on nights his brother came home late, he stayed wide awake and brooded over this sole thought.

After Kitako died, Yoshio left the electric lights on, but the room where Yoshio's mosquito net hung was dim like hazy smoke. If he stared for a long time at one spot, he could see unseen things. If his sister became a spirit, Yoshio was sure, more than anyone else, she would come to him. He found that likely, and his nervousness intensified and he couldn't sleep. Time after time, he woke with a start on the futon.

On many nights, the clock struck nine, ten, and eleven, and his brother still had not returned home. Long after twelve rang, Mikizo returned home drunk.

One time when Yoshio woke up during the night, the electric light was turned off, and the room was dark. Questions popped into his head. What time is it? … Is Mikizo home? … To make sure he was in the four-and-a-half-mat room, he stretched out his hand, felt the hem of the mosquito net, and searched for the shoji door at his pillow. Everything seemed fine but his bedding was ripped from his head. He usually waited for two or three minutes and turned on the electric light. No matter how late it got, he did not easily fall asleep.

The longer the darkness lasted, the more Yoshio tried to sleep, but the more wide awake he felt. He blamed faulty electricity. Yoshio had a hunch something he could see and hear was quietly sneaking up on him.

The mystery was why this didn't frighten him this time. He thought Kitako would never scare him. She had no reason to scare me or be envious of me wherever she went. Did she want to ask me something? If not, maybe she wanted to tell me something. She would be kind and only speak to me with compassion like when she was alive. These thoughts brought back memories.

"Neesan ..." he quietly called out.

He felt he immediately heard a small and sad voice answer from the darkness.

"Yo-chan ..."

The room adjacent to the four-and-a-half tatami room where Yoshio slept was Kitako's sitting room when she was healthy. Her vanity and wardrobe remained there, unchanged from the past.

Suddenly, Yoshio felt an inexplicable excitement completely unlike himself as the constant scaredy-cat. The thought he heard his sister's voice filled his heart, but he had no intention of controlling it. He slipped out of the futon and groped in the darkness for the adjoining room.

These days, few went in and out of this room during the day. The damp tatami smelled musty. Each sticky step disgusted Yoshio who felt like he was wandering around a dream. His dark-adapted eyes saw what looked like a bag motionless in the corner where the wardrobe stood.

From somewhere in the dense darkness surrounding his eyes, a bright foam lazily floated out fluttering toward him then vanished in an instant. He already had that feeling two or three times but nothing more. He began to walk again on the sticky tatami staying close to the wall beside the wardrobe, advancing like a spider. Yoshio was surprised when his hand touched something.

It was Kitako's shamisen hanging on the wall. Like he was tempted by the devil and strong curiosity to taste a terrifying experience, he plucked a string. The hair on his body stood up. After the reverberating tone died away in the depths of the darkness, he thought Kitako's voice would echo, but he heard nothing.

He plucked a string again, held his breath, and listened. A dim brightness appeared in a part of the darkness. He could make out the latch of the shoji door he couldn't see until now. Barely audible creaking sounds of footsteps snuck this way down the hall outside.

Like a ghost was about to slip in, his brother dressed in his nightclothes and carrying a portable candlestick holder quietly slid open the shoji door. While the tip of the candle glowed red between his eyebrows, he stood quietly at the threshold.

His face floated into the darkness like the Buddha inside the miniature shrine lit by the votive light on the side opposite the flickering candlelight. The shadow of his high nose fell black on one cheek. With his shoulders stiffened and shrunken, his gaze froze on Yoshio.

Yoshio cowered in the corner of the wardrobe and the wall. Both fists were clenched tight like a newborn's under his chin. Incomparable trembling consumed his entire body. The sight of his sister's phantom could not have been more frightening than the terrible look on his brother's face.

He had not seen this look on his brother's face since the night Kitako died. His brother's eyes gazed back with animalistic horror. In his brother's eyes, Yoshio thought they were filled with horror touched with madness equal to his own.

"Yoshio, … what are you doing over there?"

His voice was not austere enough to be more terrifying than his eyes. He looked at Yoshio and the shamisen beside him. More than a reprimand, his tone was charged with extraordinary gentleness used to make a plea.

"Huh? What are you doing? Did you do something just now?"

Yoshio said nothing more than "No" and stared without looking away deep into his brother's eyes. This was not defiance. Fear fixed his gaze on his brother.

"You're not doing anything? Really, you didn't do anything?"

As his brother spoke, he looked at Yoshio with a doubtful but threatening expression. Then he looked fearfully at the shamisen and thought a little about what to say and whether to say it.

"Did you just play the shamisen? Well? You did," he said and changed the hand holding the candle to better see Yoshio.

The shadows of objects strung with strings in the room vibrated with this instrument. The shadow of his sharp nose—shaped slightly differently than before—lay black on his brother's cheek. His face was flatter and brighter. However, his complexion shining red until now, and the brightness in his eyes strangely clouded and dim vividly revealed his brother's drunkenness to Yoshio.

"No …"

Yoshio braced his entire body and he stubbornly repeated the same phrase. He was afraid his brother, drunk

this time for a different reason, would act in an unimagin-
ably ghastly way.

"But you came into this room in the middle of the
night to do something. It looks like you've been rummaging
around in here for a while. Were you dreaming and half
asleep?"

Yoshio faintly said, "Yes," and nodded. His wavering
drew a doubtful stare from his brother, who seemed not to
believe him and was suppressing his irritation.

"All right. Go to bed and don't play around in here."

He appeared to be a little embarrassed and avoided
Yoshio's eyes following him into the hall on his way back to
the second floor.

The night was over, and the next day came. Yoshio
wondered if he would be scolded again, but his brother
didn't mention that night for several days. However, the
shamisen that previously hung uncovered was soon covered
by a yellow bag.

His brother said nothing, but his gut feeling was Yoshio
was a strange child. A casual observer could see deep suspicions about that night still nagged him. Yoshio found no
way to get friendlier with his brother.

"THAT'S HOW IT IS. It's not easy to find a house I like. If we
talk about this, the discussion will never end. I wonder if
we can move."

Yoshio caught snippets of this conversation four or five
days after that nighttime incident. On the thirty-fifth day
after Kitako's death, his Aunt Hirosawa and Ryuko visited
the home in Yayoi-cho to discuss some matter with Mikizo.

"Well, you may be interested in this. Young people
these days don't think about these things, but it's said the

deceased can't leave the house for forty-seven days. I'm old-fashioned and think you should wait a little longer."

"Auntie, you are truly old fashioned," said Ryuko from the side, supporting her brother.

"… This place was too cramped before, but now with just you and Yo-chan living here, it's empty and gloomy. You'll never forget about Kitako if you stay here and should move to some cheerful place."

His aunt didn't strongly oppose this idea and finally agreed.

Soon under orders from the busy Mikizo, the household moved to Hara-machi in Koishikawa. Their new home was a newly built, rented house constructed on a hill and faced south. This house had fewer rooms than the home in Yayoi-cho but they were bright and cheerful.

Yoshio felt like he was being chased by Kitako's ghost but now felt like he'd been rescued and could sleep peacefully at night. When they moved, Mikizo did not put her shamisen, koto, and vanity in any of the rooms in the new house.

Everyone but Mikizo and Yoshio noticed after the move, the home slowly became a melancholy and cold place.

Naturally, Mikizo, who was so much older, didn't bother about his youngest brother, an ordinary student. It was that way when Kitako was alive. Yoshio believed this was unnatural and biased. This bias became rooted in no time, and he worried deep in his heart about things he saw his brother do.

One day, Yoshio came home from school to find a long absent visitor, Mizue.

"Oh, it's been so long since I've seen you. I've been busy and a little lazy but thought I should visit once," she said in her casual voice always echoing with spirit, hugged

Yoshio like she used to, pressed her cheek against his, and stroked his head.

She said quietly, "Yo-chan, how are you? Did you miss me? Were you lonely? I think you were lonely every day."

Tears poured from Yoshio. He didn't answer but was enchanted by stray hairs of Mizue's bangs hanging down lightly over her eyes as she peeked down at him. He only raised his eyes to look at her face framed by a pillow of black hair like he wanted to wash away his overwhelming sadness.

"Oh, I've been awful. Yo-chan had forgotten, but I brought back those memories. I'm so sorry. Please, forgive me."

Her beautiful eyes shined pink like a cherry and glistened with tears. Her honesty was powerfully drawn into Yoshio's heart like he could not doubt her.

"How is Mikizo these days? When does he get home from work?"

"Hmm, what time? ... I go to bed early and don't really know."

"What? He comes home that late?"

Mizue's eyes widened in surprise. She worried and again asked, "Really? So how is he doing?"

"Mikizo hardly talked anyway and never talks to me," said Yoshiro, looking troubled and frowning.

A smiling Mizue stared at him. Her eyes narrowed in amusement, and she teased him.

"Yo-chan, does Mikizo scare you? Well? Is that it?"

She grabbed both his hands like she used to and massaged them in her supple palms.

"He's not scary, but ... sometimes he comes home drunk."

"What? Drunk? What an awful big brother! But the loneliness has been hard on him since Kitako died.

Drinking sake helps him forget his troubles. It's nothing more than that. You may not understand but ..."

Mizue's eyelids graced with long lashes seemed to blink too rapidly over her dark eyes that bulged like convex mirrors. Tears slowly appeared again and shined like a mucous membrane. Yoshio looked up doubtfully at her as she stroked his forehead.

She explained in a compassionate tone, "Your brother loved Kitako so much and will never forget her. He's drained of energy. It's not right to think poorly of Mikizo. Do you understand? ... It's natural for anyone to lose spirit when that sort of thing happens. Nobody was as fine a woman as Kitako...."

She immediately saw and wiped away his tears.

"Ah, I'm sorry for bringing that up again. Please, forgive me. Let's stop this. What can we sing? From now on, I'll visit often to play with Yo-chan. You won't be lonely and everything will be fine. I'll come often."

She lit an incense offering at the altar. After she chatted with Yoshio for an hour in his room, she left but often visited him after that. Mizue usually came by two or three in the afternoon and took Yoshio to see a moving picture. They strolled down Hongo-dori Avenue. She bought him a boys' magazine and then went home without seeing Mikizo.

"Yo-chan, could you ask Mikizo about the music gathering? I have a wonderful song to teach you. Will you sing it with me?"

In no time, Mizue returned to her former vivacious self and sang with spirit. While gazing at her bright plump cheeks, Yoshio found comfort in her kind actions and words but felt getting closer to her was somehow betraying Kitako. He believed if he became friendly with Mizue, Mikizo would be kind to him.

Rokujiro in Kobe frequently sent postcards to Yoshio. He wrote notes like this.

This is a picture of Minatogawa-jinja Shrine where the samurai Kusumoki Masashige is enshrined. I went on an excursion there a few days ago. Has anybody in Tokyo changed? Is the house in Hara-machi nice? I'll be visiting in December and will bring you a gift. We'll have fun. Study hard. Mikizo is probably lonely without Kitako, so please try to comfort him.

Yoshio always had difficulty writing back.

Rokuji-niisan, Thank you for the postcard. The new house is nice. Please come in December. It will be fun. We'll bring in the New Year together. Mikizo does seem lonely. I want to help him, but being a kid, I don't know how.

Why did Yoshio never write about Mizue's visits, not even once?

It was January of the coming year when Yoshio saw the smiling face of Mikizo he hadn't seen in a long time. Rokuji, visiting from Kobe, Ryuko, and Mizue had gathered at their home. Everyone recited poems from *Hyakunin-Isshu*. Mikizo showed as little as possible of his smiling face to Yoshio, who thought he only had lighthearted conversations with everyone else.

When Ryuko and Mizue teased Yoshio like he was a plaything, their boisterous laughter rumbled through the group, Mikizo couldn't help laughing, too. Rather than being deliberate, it felt like pity. Yoshio couldn't be as spirited when his brother was present as when he wasn't.

A puzzled Ryuko said, "Yo-chan, is something wrong? You weren't like this before and weren't acting so mature."

Yoshio's innocence gradually disappeared and transformed him into a reserved, distrustful child.

One or two months after the new year when Rokujiro returned to Kobe, Yoshio entered middle school in April. One Sunday, Ryuko came to visit him.

"You're a child and shouldn't be so nervous. You should visit me for a nice change."

She invited him to the Miyamoto home in Shibuya as if she would drag the reluctant Yoshio there.

He remembered a healthy Kitako bringing him along on visits a few times long ago. Ryuko's husband and mother-in-law were delighted to entertain him.

"Oh, it's Yo-chan, Yo-chan."

Also, there were Ryuko's younger sister- and brothers-in-law. Yoshio was three years younger than her sister-in-law and one year younger than a brother-in-law. There were also a brother and a sister younger than Yoshio. In the parlor of the large home much bigger than the Hara-machi home, Yoshio spent a lively day with the children.

A hammock hung on the sunny veranda. They took turns lying in it and swinging it from the sides, played with the parrots and canaries Ryuko's bird-loving husband kept as pets, played a toy organ, and went out to the garden to watch the geese in the lake from under the wisteria trellis. That enjoyable day felt like a dream Yoshio rarely savored.

The day slowly came to an end. He suddenly remembered he alone had to leave these lively relatives and return to the lonely house in Hara-machi and was overcome with sadness. If possible, he'd love to be a child in this family.

Here he would be happy and could call children "Neesan" and "Niisan" who were close to his age.

Ryuko asked, "Yo-chan. Will you come again? It's getting dark. Should I get someone to go with you?"

Yoshiro looked up at her and said, "No ... I can go home alone."

Yoshio felt miserable. If the fun day had to end in this despair, he was convinced not coming in the first place was better. Nevertheless, he was invited to come on future Sundays and went. On days he didn't go, Mizue came to visit. For some time, he was distracted by their kindness.

One Sunday soon after he started the middle school attached to Ochanomizu University, Yoshio wore his school uniform to Shibuya to show everyone. Unfortunately, that day, the children had gone cherry-blossom viewing with their older brother. Only the mother and Ryuko were home.

He was squatting on the veranda outside of her room, lazily looking at the blooming golden bell flowers.

"Yo-chan, today was truly miserable. I'll make you a great meal, then we'll spend a pleasant time together," said Ryuko, as she approached and leaned against a pillar and stared at the yellow flowers.

A short time later, she said, "Yo-chan ..." She broke into a smile like something funny happened, and looked like she was trying to find something in his eyes.

"Hey, Yo-chan, are you lonely in Hara-machi these days?"

"Yes."

Yoshio had no idea why she asked that question out of the blue. When he looked at her smiling face, Ryuko approached as her smile widened and her eyes crinkled.

"You seem to enjoy being here. Would you like to become a child in our home?"

He was sure she was joking but that had been his dream. Yoshio said nothing but grinned while letting go with nearly evil laughter like the plot was guessed. For some reason, he was unable to show the happiness on his face if this came to be.

"You're kidding, right? ..."

Ryuko knew Yoshio's spirit was strongly moved by this passing fancy and denied her slight panic at the wretched thing she did.

"But Yo-chan, more than becoming a part of this family, something that will make you much happier will happen soon."

This time her playful words contained an element of seriousness.

"Something will make me happy? What do you mean?"

"Well, soon a new older sister is coming to your house. You may not have heard yet, but Mikizo has found a new bride."

"A bride?"

Ryuko didn't notice the slight trembling in his voice. Her bright, delighted eyes opened wide with a child's innocence over this happy event.

"Ah, his bride's name is one you know well. And she's someone you like a lot. Can you guess who?"

"I know her ..."

In contrast to Ryuko's lightheartedness, Yoshio was pained by having no insight into the secret fear welling deep in his heart. For a short time, he was confused about whether to speak or not speak the name of the person he already knew. If he said the name and was right, he'd be questioned about how he knew—although that should not matter.

Yoshio could not answer calmly at this moment. Ryuko might become suspicious. He worried she'd have doubts if he pretended not to know about this happy affair. This situation rapidly reached a deadlock, and he said nothing. If this moment had gone on for much longer, Yoshio might have ended up trembling. Fortunately, Ryuko said the right words.

"If I say she's someone you know really well, you probably have a good idea. Mikizo is going to marry Mizue-san."

"Mizue-san is the neesan from Azabu?"

Yoshio stared far off and spoke like he was talking to himself like this meant nothing.

"Yes. Azabu-neesan will officially become your sister. That's wonderful, isn't it? Mizue-san is better than some stranger. Both Mikizo and you will probably be very happy. Your home will surely become a lively place. Since Mikizo's mood may change, the loneliness will go away."

Ryuko expected him to jump for joy after being told this news, and Yoshio had to show enthusiasm. He had to look happy to have Mizue as his sister and cheerfully said, "Is that true, Ryuko?"

His thumping heart raced. Eventually, he realized its beating was not caused by happiness.

In the instant he was delighted by Mizue's coming, he was attacked by fear of the unseen figure of his dead sister making a sad and grievous appeal in her feeble voice pass by him. He could not hide his ashen complexion and the fine hairs standing on end.

"Yo-chan, what's wrong?"

"It's nothing ..." he said but didn't fool her.

"... I'm so happy Azabu-neesan's coming here, but I thought about Kitako-san and felt sad all of a sudden ..."

"You're not a bad boy. You're like a woman worrying about that sort of thing, not like a boy at all!"

Ryuko was taken aback. She looked askance without

blinking at Yoshio and wondered why this child had such a twisted nature. Yoshio stubbornly kept his mouth shut and cast down his eyes filling with tears while the tips of his fingers, thin like a sick person, nervously fiddled with the buttons on the coat of his new uniform like he was bored.

Mikizo was going to marry Mizue. All the adults including Ryuko were simply happy for them. Did being a child make Yoshio doubt this marriage? He no longer deeply brooded over this matter. Kitako's sudden mysterious death sketched, at least in Yoshio's mind, the faint notion of Mizue not becoming Mikizo's second wife, but this idea fell into a vague shadow-like mist in his heart.

Sometimes Yoshio believed only he harbored doubts and was bothered by something about Mikizo and Mizue. He thought he was disturbed by a groundless delusion caused by his youth. Although these thoughts began to disappear, his speculation gradually became true.

Despite Ryuko worrying about him, his suspicions steadily deepened and never yielded. He was wary of his brother, the way Kitako died, Azabu-neesan who had been so caring to him, and his own heart. He couldn't tell anyone this. Everyone already thought he was a child who wasn't very childlike and no longer found him cute.

If everyone and not only Mikizo came to dislike him, Yoshio would truly be all alone. If that happened, would the deceased Kitako secretly protect him?

As Yoshio rehashed these worries in his heart, tears rose in his eyes. He had forgotten about Ryuko beside him and sat dejected while gazing at the golden bell flowers.

May brought the first anniversary of Kitako's death. Rokujiro came from Kobe to attend the memorial. Five or six days after the memorial service, Mikizo married Mizue at Daijingu Shrine in Hibiya.

Until now, Yoshio called Mizue "Azabu-neesan" and

worried it would be hard to switch in an instant to Neesan. But starting the day after the wedding, Rokujiro and Ryuko affectionately called Mizue "Neesan, Neesan." It turned out not to be horrible, so he would call her Neesan, too. Although Mizue was twenty-one, three years younger than Ryuko, their relationship didn't undergo any drastic change because they were already friends.

Like she was well prepared, Mizue rarely showed her tomboyish nature and became a modest, serene, and graceful sister. Yoshio realized this the night everyone saw Niisan and Neesan off at the Chuo train depot for their honeymoon trip to Hakone.

His new older sister poked her head out the train window and looked at Yoshio standing on the platform. She cheerfully said, "Yo-chan, we'll be back soon. Don't get sad waiting for us. We'll bring back a nice souvenir for you. All right? It's late. Go home and straight to bed."

She wore her hair in the usual puffy *sokuhatsu* hairstyle tied back into a bun. That night, however, she looked like another person and much older. Maybe the reason was the *marumage* topknot of a married woman replaced the bun she always wore in the back. Her words certainly reflected the dignity of an older sister.

Rokuji, whose train back to Kobe was next, went up to her window and tipped his hat.

"Well, take care … I'll see you soon."

"Roku-chan, take care of yourself, too. When are you coming to Tokyo again?"

"Let's see. Probably at the end of the year. Hakone is so ordinary. Why don't you come with me to Kobe?"

"That sounds like fun. Even if you didn't go to Kobe, a trip from Kyoto to Nara would be nice," said Ryuko from the side.

"… But can I go with you?" he said.

Rokujiro was a little drunk when we left the house and seemed to whisper, "I don't know," into Neesan's ear.

Neesan blushed a little and seemed flustered but had an air of innocence and a touch of bashfulness. Yoshio felt odd after seeing this part of her that was animated like a man.

After the Hakone-bound train left, Rokujiro and Ryuko talked while strolling the platform for thirty minutes as they waited for the Kobe train to depart.

"Our brother must be overjoyed at finding a new love and is probably full of life."

"It's true. He always thinks only about the past. I feel sorry for this neesan ..." said Ryuko then was quiet for a while. She appeared to slowly recall something.

"But Mizue-san seems happy. Mikizo isn't the type to cherish his wife."

"So she probably fell in love with him," said Rokujiro, looking up and laughing out loud.

YOSHIO's newest older sister sent him postcards from Hakone. After they returned, he couldn't believe how kind she was, even kinder than Kitako. When he lived alone with Mikizo, no one cared this much for him. She helped with spending money, clothes, food, and any little problem that arose. When Yoshio sweetly pestered her, she always gave in.

After they married, Mikizo never came home late at night. He usually returned around four or five in the after-noon when Mizue was spending time with Yoshio.

"Mizue-san, ..."

He dropped the honorific with his first wife and called

her "Kitako" but always added "-san" when he addressed Mizue.

"Yes," she said, then turned to Yoshio.

"Yo-chan, I'll see you later," she said lovingly, left in high spirits, and went to the parlor on the second floor with Mikizo. They chatted affectionately for a long time.

Whenever Mikizo had free time, he stayed with Mizue like a shadow. They didn't want to be apart. In his child's heart, Yoshio saw a compatible couple. He heard the maids say Mikizo and Kitako seemed to get along well but not this much.

Yoshio read too much into this situation, for instance, how much of a nuisance was this deeply suspicious younger brother in the heart of his brother who adored his wife this much? Yoshio secretly apologized to his brother about his wife who pampered his younger brother although Mikizo wasn't particularly bothered by that.

Around that time, Mikizo seemed to gradually hope to be friendlier with Yoshio and wanted to convey that to him. When Mikizo and Mizue went out for their evening walk, she said, "Yo-chan, why don't you come with us?"

"If you come, we'll go to Asakusa to see a moving picture show," said his brother, unable to hide his formality but smiling broadly.

Outside, Mizue slipped between the two brothers, so they couldn't speak directly to each other, only through her, and slowly grew friendlier.

"Yo-chan, is there a book you want? If there is, your brother will buy it for you?"

"What sort of book do you want? Anyone is fine because I'll buy it."

Mikizo could speak in relatively kind words without sounding too unnatural.

While mysteriously losing nerve out of frustration,

Yoshio seemed happy as he could be and thought disappointing his brother would be awful. He looked up at his brother's face and looked into his eyes for a long time. He felt he saw a glint of light that betrayed the compassion deep in his eyes. His brother noticed and was momentarily startled. Both of them panicked and looked down.

Mikizo was always worried. He wanted to avoid showing what was in his eyes and intended to be calm despite Yoshio's watchful gaze. Not used to being bold, but if their eyes met, he immediately looked away. Although he managed a pleasant smile, it seemed to be dressed in feigned innocence.

Yoshio didn't know whether his brother told Mizue to say that, but Mikizo thought a lot about Yoshio. He worried about his school grades and health, his likes and dislikes, and would ask his wife about what concerned him. Mizue told him this in a tone that said he should be grateful for these favors.

"Yo-chan, The truth is as a man of few words, your brother doesn't talk to you much. That's why he's so distant like you're a stranger, but you shouldn't take that to heart. He'd do anything for you. Your brother always says so."

Yoshio had the habit of saying nothing and raising his eyes to study her face. Only a brilliant pretty smile lit her face, and she lacked the ability to uncover his secrets.

Outwardly, Mikizo was friendlier than before. At some point, he became confused like the two had gotten closer and could coexist but had come to a roadblock. He suffered over the feeling that nothing had changed from their previous relationship. This feeling pursued him everywhere. A faraway hazy object slowly took a definite shape and was reflected in his heart.

As the days passed and his childish innocence slowly

vanished, Yoshio crept toward the real world and away from whimsical notions.

When the shadow of some object walked down a dark street at night, the ghostly thing approaching was not a ghost. While thinking, It's a person. It's human, he saw the far-off shadow of a creepy being that reached his side, lured in by the feeling that it could not be seen. The shadow was enticed by the feeling it was as invisible as possible while it pursued Yoshio.

Yoshio felt this lure was nothing more than his brother forcing himself to be kind. His brother had run out of kindness. The brother who was indifferent to his young brother, recently, began to have feelings of love and showed kindness in various ways. Alarm at Yoshio's growing up seemed to engulf him in fear. Was it a feeling of weakness that lacked hostility?

"You're already a middle school student and will soon reach the age of reason. At that time, you may gain a better understanding of what Mizue and I have done. But until now, I've thought of you as a child, instead of dismissing you, I think a great deal about you but would like to not think or talk about every little matter."

Listening to his brother's heartfelt words, Yoshio thought about what he witnessed in the room on the second floor of the Ginza hospital between his current sister-in-law and his brother at the end of his tenth year when Kitako was healthy. He recalled their surprised looks and the positions of their bodies. Mizue's collar was open and his brother seemed to be examining her, but they weren't in the examination room. Now, he wondered what was going on but was not suspicious. Although Mikizo and Mizue never brought it up, from that day on, Mikizo worried about Yoshio.

On the night Kitako died, Mikizo made a queer face

and was a little remote. This is how it appeared to Yoshio. However, Yoshio welled up with feelings that something was wrong about Mikizo and Mizue alone together at that time and seeing the two alone at the Koishikawa Botanical Garden a year later when Kitako was sick in bed. Many others thought Mikizo's worrying caused his horrible melancholy. The belief his brother turned sinister during those days overwhelmed Yoshio.

Mikizo blanched when Yoshio asked Rokujiro about his suspicions shortly after Kitako's death. He examined her and treated her illness. He gave her an injection the day before she died. Fragments of incidents like this over three or four years floated into his mind. As Yoshio asked more detailed questions, Mikizo felt vague doubts taking root in Yoshio's mind and gathering into a frightening form. Could Mikizo no longer stay silent?

Mikizo felt proof of his past crime remained in Yoshio's mind and grew distressed as Yoshio matured. Mikizo and Mizue skillfully tricked Kitako and showed love for her that dazzled the eyes of all his siblings, except for Yoshio. Mikizo surely realized the insight gradually gained by Yoshio through these events. If Mikizo's crime was nothing more than this, Yoshio believed his brother would not be as distant as before.

On the night soon after Kitako's death when the electric lights were off for the night, Yoshio's eyes opened with a start in the pitch black. Confused, he groped his way around her room strangely giddy from her loving heart.

He remembered his brother standing behind him in no time with a candle in hand after he plucked the string of the shamisen in the darkness. The look on his face was probably caused by drunkenness. His eyes didn't move like he was staring at the shadow of some dark object. His complexion revealed fear like he saw a ghost.

Even now, Yoshio still recalled various events from those days. Mikizo may not be able to bear the terror at that time when he thought he heard the sound of the shamisen alone in his late wife's room and may have even seen a specter that shouldn't be seen. Not just the sounds of the shamisen, did Mikizo see ghosts that shouldn't be seen when he heard a strange voice? Back then Mikizo came home drunk every night. The shamisen disappeared to some unknown place during the move from the house in Yayoi-cho. Tormented by his conscience, Mikizo agonized over forgetting.

Yoshio constantly brooded over this situation. He was young and a sickly child. After entering middle school, he often caught colds and slept a lot. From the winter when he was thirteen to the spring when he was fourteen, he suffered from bronchial catarrh influenza and stayed in bed for one or two weeks. At times like that, thoughts like these were natural.

On nights when his body temperature neared 104°F, Yoshio's babbling while delirious worried Mizue, who nursed and listened to him. He'd wake with a start from a peaceful sleep, mouth open like he was about to scream. His eyes opened wide and darted around nervously. His shivering body sweated a cold sweat.

When she asked, "Yo-chan ... are you all right? Did you have a bad dream?"

He only said, "Yes, I had a bad dream." He suspected telling her was not a good idea.

"It was nothing," he said and hid his ashen face from her under the ice pack.

Actually, he often had nightmares. The Mikizo who emerged in those dreams was, for the most part, no different from the real one, gloomy to a distressing degree. Yoshio was alone with his brother. They walked briskly down some unknown lonely, dark road. As they walked down the middle of the road, Mikizo suddenly said, "Yoshio ..." His tone reflected the crushing gloom in his chest.

"Yoshio, I know you are suspicious of me. You no longer have to hide it because I'm well aware of it ..."

Then he fell into a long silence but kept up the brisk pace.

"... I also know why you suspect me. On the night Kitako died, I saw your face pale. Since then, you've suspected me. Am I right?"

Yoshio peeked at his brother's expression. The tall Mikizo smirked while looking down at Yoshio.

"You seemed to think I killed Kitako because the blood drained from my face at that time. But I didn't pale because I killed her. I paled because I feared you suspected me of killing her. Of course, only you were suspicious. I thought Kitako's death was fortuitous. Thus, your suspicion was understandable, but I felt awful thinking you suspected me. That's the reason why I paled."

He spoke like he was muttering to himself.

"Mikizo, please be patient with me. It was awful to suspect you. I don't think I will dig any deeper into that because Kitako is dead although she was not murdered. I'm not happy about making you a murderer. Please don't worry anymore about this."

"That's not good enough. Although you tell me not to worry, you still suspect me in your heart. You must believe me because I had no reason to kill Kitako. Didn't she die of intestinal catarrh?"

In a dream, Mikizo explained this to Yoshio. In his heart, Yoshio knew he was still a child and didn't understand the things adults did because he wasn't an adult. His suspicion of his brother was not over, but he reassured Mikizo.

He was still a child but intended not to be deceived by what adults do, so he'd continue to closely question his brother. The more he asked, the dread when the shamisen string was plucked slowly appeared on Mikizo's face. He tottered and looked like he was about to faint.

"Yoshio, please stop talking about this. You're young so be patient. I was wrong to kill Kitako."

He seemed to plead over and over in an earnest tone. Even after he woke up, Yoshio heard these words in his ears.

The scariest part for Yoshio was the dead Kitako appearing only in dreams like this every day and asking for an explanation of how she was killed. After he woke up, he gradually investigated the facts in a way that exactly matched the conversation in the dream.

That wasn't all. Around this time, Yoshio fell ill and only slept. He saw the awful dream day and night and thought Kitako triggered this. He believed he'd be tormented until Mikizo's crime was exposed to the world.

"Yo-chan, Mikizo really did kill me. Only you know this, but why are you so quiet? You were so cute when I was alive but too reserved for a child...."

Kitako always whimpered from her grave. She forced Yoshio to see the horrible dream until he became her ally.

"Although Mizue is nursing you, as long as you're not listening to me, you will not get well. She seems to care, but she's hiding her claws to make you her ally and is a woman with the heart of a demon."

He could hear her words curse the kindly Mizue. Was Mizue really that treacherous? Maybe, Mikizo was not the only one who knew about the mysterious death of Kitako. Had he discussed it with Mizue? Mikizo seemed to take all the blame for his crime, but Yoshio saw little guilt in Mizue. Perhaps she married him not knowing about the murder?

But if Mizue truly had a demon's heart, she looked innocent, a sheep in wolf's clothing, who had no problem marrying Mikizo while aware of his crime. While thinking this, Yoshio gazed hard at his sister-in-law sitting at his bedside and knew she and his brother deceived Kitako.

Mizue showed deep affection and always treated him as *our boy*. The nape of her neck, slender, graceful, and white as snow, and facial features were much more beautiful than Kitako's. However, she displayed moments of evil several times more dreadful than Mikizo.

"Neesan, you've been very nice to me but I've been sort of suspicious of you lately. Did you know that? Are you staying by my side because my brother asked you to find out what I'm thinking?"

But if he dared to ask her, would he see a scary demonic look on her attractive face? This thought not only sickened Yoshio but sparked the curiosity in his imagination he felt when reading fairy tales.

His high fever continued for days and he slept a lot and often felt he was being carried away to some far-off place. He wondered if he would die, but around the beginning of March, he went back to school. He had been absent for so long he didn't expect good grades but managed to pass. Amazingly, he attended school for a short time.

In May, in the evening of a day just one week after the third memorial of Kitako's death, Yoshio suddenly came down with a fever and vomited a river of blood. Fortunately, in four or five days, his fever went down seven degrees, and he recovered little by little. His brother said he should not go to school and rest.

Yoshio remembered the curse of Kitako. His mind

teemed with other terrifying imaginings. He frequently fell ill. His brother examined him and gave him medicine, just as he treated Kitako. Yoshio didn't know how long he had these thoughts in his heart and inferred while feeling somewhat threatened that his suspicions arose more from the reality of his sensitive nerves than from Kitako's curse.

Kitako had been steadily plagued by this condition for six months to a year. From time to time, Mikizo gave her injections he said would cure her anemia. Then one day, her condition abruptly changed and she died.

Yoshio had not yet received injections like Kitako, but Mikizo may have put something in the medication. If he asked his brother to let another physician examine him, it would appear to Mikizo that Yoshio discovered his crime. He feared Mikizo would avoid him. If this happened and he died, that would be his fate, and he gave up. Yoshio thought he'd like to tell Mikizo that if his time came to die, he would quietly go without saying a word out of concern for his older brother.

One day, Yoshio had this dream.

Behind the old house in Yayoi-cho was a high cliff. He could climb down and slowly descend to the steep rocky narrow path with poor footing and end up in an isolated, broad field in a hollow. Unbelievably, pampas and other grasses grew rampant in this town in Tokyo. The grasses bent and rustled in the wind.

One rainy night during a gentle drizzle in the middle of June, for some reason Yoshio snuck out and went to the Koishikawa house. He went out alone, without an umbrella. He walked unhurriedly as if enticed by an unseen ghost. He still had not fully recovered but went out dressed in his nightclothes and wondered whether going outside would make him sicker.

As the back of his hand wiped away a queer slimy

sweat sticking to his face untouched by the fine rain, he pressed on with no desire to go back. He seemed to know why as he walked.

Kitako's spirit was lost and stuck behind the house in Yayoi-cho. If he went there, he was sure he'd see her. She wanted to tell him something and called him to that field.

He came to the gate of the house where strangers live now. From outside the fence, he could see the eaves of the room facing the beech tree in the garden.

"Oh, even now, that's my room over there. In that room, I talked a lot with my sister who died so young and listened to the music gatherings," said Yoshio to himself in his heart.

He went around the outside of the building to the back door and came out at the edge of the cliff. He slowly went down the hilly path with the overgrown pampas grass entangling the hem of his kimono, swaying like people laughing, and followed the path, like he was coming from deep in some faraway mountain, to land at this spot that was special to him. He waited for ten to twenty minutes to see Kitako. He stood there assured he had a firm promise. Then he heard Mikizo call from behind.

"Yoshio."

He must have trailed me, thought Yoshio and turned nonchalantly to look at his brother. Mikizo seemed timid and stayed a few steps behind.

"Yoshio, you are ill. What are you doing out here at this hour?"

He smiled like he was trying to convince Yoshio to stop his suspicious gaze.

"If you do this, you'll get sicker, which would be awful. Come now, let's go home. It's getting late. You are worrying me and must come now."

"I'll go, but you go first, ahead of me."

At this moment, the ghost of the late Kitako moved toward Yoshio's voice. As he spoke, he had an inkling Mikizo couldn't hide his listening and looked like the hairs on his body stood on end. Mikizo stared like a beast challenged to a fight upon hearing those words. He was silent for a short time and stared at Yoshio.

Mikizo said, "If you want me to go home first, I'll go …"

For a short time, Mikizo hesitated like he was thinking. He seemed more wounded than frightened and in a quieter voice said, "But why are you here alone in a place like this? Please tell me."

"I don't have any reason, so please stop asking. It makes me sad when you do."

Yoshio asked not to be forced to tell Mikizo because, in his heart, he knew all about Mikizo's crime and would never say anything to his face.

"If it's too hard for you to tell me, let me try to explain," said Mikizo. "Until now, I was afraid to hear the reason. But now, I'll stop asking. Despite being brothers, we are uncomfortable together and are slowly drifting further apart, but both of us know that's no good … I think you came here alone tonight to meet Kitako.'"

"Mikizo, please stop. You're scaring me."

"I'm sorry. I'm not trying to scare you. You're misunderstanding me if you're afraid. You may think Kitako's spirit is lost in this world, but that's not so. She didn't die leaving memories in this world. I've wanted to tell you that."

"But no matter what you say, I can't erase the doubts deep in my heart …" Yoshio wanted to answer but only answered in his heart.

"I guess you doubt me. What about her death was suspicious? Tell me what doubts are in your heart. Please be frank so I can understand you. By exposing our true feelings, misunderstandings will disappear. Please, Yoshio, don't hold back and tell me what you think is strange. Why do you think Kitako didn't die of intestinal catarrh?"

"Ah," shouted Yoshio from his heart. Did Kitako lure him to this spot tonight to catch Mikizo, who followed, and have Yoshio question him about the crime in her place?

All of this was nothing more than his baseless fanciful ideas of his suspicions so far. Kitako worried about a division between the brothers over an unimportant misunderstanding. Did she bring them together here to reconcile their relationship as brothers? In any case, Yoshio felt that Kitako was sticking by him.

"Mikizo, I'm not suspicious about that anymore, but I'm confused by the injection you gave her the day before she died. After that, she got sicker so fast."

His brother's mouth smiled, but his eyes reflected surprise. He stood like he was trying to peer deeply into the truth from Yoshio's silhouette in the night's darkness.

"What was strange about that injection? That was not her first injection. Any doctor would give that injection to cure an anemic patient. The injection was not mysterious at all. Although she died soon after the injection, that often occurs with acute intestinal catarrh, as I said earlier. Her sudden death had nothing to do with the injection.…"

"No. Kitako-san didn't have catarrh. The poison arsenic was put into that injection."

He felt clever like he finally said what he'd been thinking and had a hunch when Mikizo heard that, this would not come to an ordinary end. Yoshio tossed out these words as his spirit became confused like everything in front of his eyes was chaotic and blinded him.

"Arsenic?" said Mikizo, he looked like he was about to draw his last breath.

"Who told you that? Arsenic must be mixed in. However, arsenic is a commonly-used medicine for anemia. There's nothing particularly suspicious about it."

"But I heard from a pharmacy student a large amount must deliberately be used to kill someone. And he said the person dies in exactly the same way Kitako died. Doesn't the poisoned person gets diarrhea and end up turning white like milk?"

Yoshio wondered if his brother would topple over backward like he had been shot through the forehead by a rifle bullet, but Mikizo braced himself and let it pass.

"Hmm, really?" His shoulders trembled slightly, and he gave a mocking laugh.

"If you know that much, I have nothing more to say. But if you don't want to turn me into a criminal, don't say a word to anyone. If you keep that secret, I will dote on you from now on. Wouldn't that be to your advantage? And the two of us brothers will live together happily, right?"

"Yes, I think I'd like that. But if you regret it from the bottom of your heart and apologize to Kitako ..."

"I am remorseful. I will burn an incense offering every morning and apologize to Kitako."

"You are truly remorseful," said Yoshio.

He felt a weight had been lifted and leaped at his brother with joy. Mikizo was tricking him. He was careless and planned to kill Yoshio in this lonely field. That thought surfaced as if someone whispered it. With this spirit, he peeked at Mikizo's face. He cheered up and laughed heartily to keep Yoshio from grasping this.

"Oh, you're right. I've been a terrible older brother. I'm sorry for making you worry. I understand now, so can't we get along better? I've been slow on that front. Let's get home quickly, you're shivering. All right? Take my hand. This way."

The proof Mikizo wanted to kill Yoshio was he went in the opposite direction to going home to Hara-machi and down the hilly path on the stairs with the poor footholds towards the cliff. Mikizo talked sweetly to Yoshio to lure him while keeping a tight grip on his wrist as they walked. However, Yoshio increasingly believed he could hear a laughing voice in the darkness when they came to the bottom of the stairs. Mizue was waiting for them at the top of the hilly path.

"Yo-chan, you and your brother have made up. That is wonderful. I was worried so I came. Be careful don't tumble down, the footing over there is horrible."

As she spoke, Mikizo pulled Yoshio out front, and he followed. At that critical moment, he placed Yoshio between himself and Mizue so he couldn't escape. Yoshio felt they planned to attack him once they reached the top. Would his life end here?

Can Kitako protect him? There's nothing to do now. As these thoughts crossed his mind, his steps on the rocky path shrunk. The hem of his kimono drenched by the light rain, still falling, coiled around and clung to his knees. He supposed this made it harder to walk and kept him from escaping. Is he going to kill me now? Wait! Could they have already done it? He shut his eyes and kept walking. The blades of pampas grass wetted by dew on the roadside often stroked his collar giving him a chill that made him gasp like there was no space for the living.

When he took a step and reached the top of the hill, Mizue said, "You've reached the top," to signal Mikizo. Yoshio immediately crouched down in fear and forgot his resolve to this point.

"Oh, Mizue help me! Don't kill me!" shouted Yoshio

with all his might, knowing he was watching a dream. He still could not open his eyes. Of course, he had a fever and slept on the futon, not getting up. His head felt weighed down.

Mizue said, "Yo-chan, I'm here."

He gradually realized she was shaking him awake. With the sudden sensation of being saved, his eyes popped open.

"Yo-chan, what happened?" asked Mizue. Yoshio looked away from the electric light and blinked a few times.

"Huh?"

He was surprised and embarrassed. He moved his face into the large dark shadow made by the head of Mizue seated in front of the electric light beside the bed and talked nonsense. He looked up timidly like he was trying to read her like a puzzle. She seemed not to notice and smiled sweetly.

"What's wrong, Yo-chan? Did you have a bad dream?"

Her face was in shadow. She smiled brightly to hide the secret in her mind from others.

Yoshio sighed and placed his hand on his chest ringing from the palpitations echoing throughout his body. He rolled over to the right to avoid Mizue's steady gaze that bothered him. His ear on the pillow amplified the thumping. His brain pounded with echoes, like the Earth's surface being hit by a hammer, and grew numb.

From beneath the ice bag slipping off his brow, he looked past the futon spreading out flat like the ocean and across the tatami grains to the thick paper on the sliding doors at the end of the room. There sat Mikizo, dressed in a summer yukata, sitting erect with arms crossed, and eyes aimed at him.

Yoshio wondered if he hadn't already died. His face

was pale, not very different from the night he saw Kitako's corpse. Like cat eyes, his eyes became white and did not move. Finally, Mikizo spoke.

"Yoshio."

Like a curse had been broken, he let both arms hang from his shoulders and sidled closer to the side of the bed.

He asked in a calm tone, "How do you feel?"

He folded his arms and took a deep breath to calm his stomach and seemed to be thinking about what to do next.

"How do you feel?" he asked again and forced a creepy, weak smile like he did when they met in the dream. His smile moved slightly as if carved in wood and looked frozen between his cheeks.

Yoshio glanced over to see an injection needle, which he hadn't noticed earlier, shining between the fingers of his right hand. The needle trembled with his hand. A spider dropped a thread from the ceiling and hung above Yoshio's face.

"Yoshio, I'm going to give you an injection tonight.… It may make you feel better …"

This froze Yoshio's blood, and he lifted his head. After the sensation of burning, like his spirit was ablaze, he felt cold like the hot material burning on his skin was replaced by ice. He remembered Mikizo's slow approach from one side toward his hand and leg. The fear in his eyes contained animosity that surprised even him.

"Mikizo, I'm sorry but I don't want a shot," he said with all the determination he could muster and glared with hate at his brother.

"Why? What's wrong?"

The muscles in Mikizo's face stiffened in anger. His usual weak smile was still carved in his cheeks. Only his eyes gleamed with bloodlust. When he spoke, his hoarse voice echoed with melancholy. The sound of his voice made Yoshio more resistant. Yoshio spoke as he writhed in agony as if awakened from a terrifying dream.

"Mikizo, please have mercy and stop. I don't want to die...."

The room was quiet for a short time. The laugh lines in Mikizo's cheeks twitched. A strange flash flew out from deep in his wide open, dumbfounded eyes, then out of nowhere, "You idiot!"

Mikizo's face was savage, he thought about screaming at Yoshio. In reaction, he lost awareness of himself, and his lips lost color. His fingers lost their grip and dropped the injection needle.

FOR JUST A MONTH from the following day, Mikizo was not seen in Yoshio's sickroom. He gave orders to Mizue and a nurse to give Yoshio his medication. As July came, Yoshio's gradual weakening was visible so Mikizo had to come again. He often came to examine Yoshio and limited the conversation to the examination. Mikizo left the sickroom right after checking Yoshio's pulse and temperature.

Mizue wasn't as kind as she used to be talking about what Mikizo thought was the best treatment and only played that role sometimes. After returning home from the hospital in the evening, however, Mikizo was found only at Yoshio's side and probably thought he was sicker.

Mikizo seemed disgusted by Mizue's going to Yoshio's room. For a short time, she didn't notice him in the hall outside the sickroom.

"Mizue-san," he said quickly, facing the sliding door. If she were inside, he would come behind her. Each time he doted on her and neglected Yoshio more and more each day. He could not accept not being with her, whether it was to eat or take a bath.

On a quiet, muggy night two or three days ago after the long rainy season, Mikizo and Mizue, Rokuji summoned by telegram from Kobe, Miyamoto Ryuko, Aunt Hirosawa, and many others gathered in hushed silence at Yoshio's sick bed.

In his mind, the faint sounds of the ice melting in the ice bag resting on Yoshio's forehead sounded like far-off objects heard by his ears. Similar to the melting ice, Yoshio knew he was in critical condition and on the verge of the end of life.

He was no longer saddened or afraid. He contemplated various misfortunes, such as dying at the young age of fourteen, a short life in which he tasted the harsh feelings of only being suspicious of people and devoid of pleasant thoughts, and no longer worried about wanting to live more. Of course, when death approaches, people slowly resign themselves and feel able to easily leave this world.

"Yo-chan, don't worry and don't lose hope," said Ryuko and moved closer to his bedside. Yoshio smiled with sympathy for her words.

"Thank you, but Neesan, dying isn't painful. Please don't worry," he said and stopped smiling. A solemn expression rose on his face, white like a candle. Only he understood he was going to die now.

His eyes appeared to be watching some precious sacred object. For a long time, his eyes were opened wide and happily watched. Everyone was sure only Yoshio was watching the sacred object. Through his eyes, all their eyes overflowed with divinity, firm in that belief.

"Yo-chan, everything is all right, don't worry. Mikizo said you'll get well if your mind stays sound."

She tried to console him. Mikizo seated beside her timidly said, "Yoshio, be strong. You're still okay."

Yoshio's eyes fully expressing divinity suddenly looked at Mikizo. He seemed to see the precious sanctified object deep in Mikizo's face. Mikizo looked down like he was hit by that power so the secret still in his heart could not be read. However, more than mocking his wretched vain efforts, Yoshio was ashamed of his miserable narrowness of spirit toward his brother. In contrast to when Kitako died, he was now tolerant of people and overwhelmed by the need to apologize to Mikizo.

"Niisan, Niisan," he called to his brother and extended his thin wrist. "Niisan, I've been terrible. I'm praying for your happiness. From now on, please care for Neesan and live a happy life together."

"Thank you," said Mikizo and Mizue. Yoshio's sleepy eyes were closed, but he heard their voices. Yoshio sensed he was passing down the peaceful road with no worries that Kitako passed down before him. This time, he firmly believed he would soon be with her spirit he truly longed to see again.

4. GOLD & SILVER

One

Aono should have ridden the electric streetcar to the last stop in Dozaka. Why did he jump out of the conductor's cab when it arrived at the stop in Nezu? At that moment, he brushed past a man boarding at the driver's platform. Aono was relieved when he spotted the back silhouette of a man wearing an Inverness coat and a white bird-hunting cap who was hanging onto the strap in a crowd a distance away on the train.

He thought, I'm sure that's Imamura. That was lucky. He probably would have caught me if I stayed a little longer.

Aono felt he escaped the jaws of death. Last year, he told Imamura he was going to the summer costume ball and borrowed Imamura's overcoat and Satsuma kimono. He pawned them that night and disappeared.

Aono knew If Imamura caught him, he would get a beating. He'd heard rumors about Imamura's public declarations, whether on the train or in the middle of a major street, where he'd march up to someone and publicly shame him. The newspapers exposed Aono's notorious reputation several times. His friends ostracized him. But he was shameless, and his sole fear was getting beaten up.

Today marked one year since that day. Maybe, Imamura has forgotten about the summer costume ball, obtained a new Inverness coat, and walks around wearing it in triumph. Given his peaceful life on easy street despite being robbed, Aono envied him no matter how safe he felt. Aono thought, If Imamura was wearing that fine overcoat when he saw me, he'd have no reason to beat me.

Selfish thoughts rose in Aono's head. The pawn shop only paid me five yen for the coat last year, but this new one is probably worth ten. No, Imamura probably didn't see me. When I hurried to get off in front, he glimpsed my face from the corner of his eye and deliberately boarded on the opposite side. Depending on the situation, Imamura has no intention of fighting me.

More humiliated by this situation than his fear of getting beaten up, Aono realized his face was red. This encounter worried him a lot every time he went out. It would be a load off his mind to get caught sooner rather than later and pummeled.

"What a fool! Will I have to run away? It would be better to get beaten up," he said to himself but loud enough for passersby to hear. Unfortunately, I can't help it if others see me as a low-life, a disgrace, and ridiculous. I have the foolish notion that if I were a man of Imamura's stature, had a friend like me, and beat him up in the middle of the street, I would be exhilarated.

In fact, Aono was well aware of his rotten nature and thoroughly disgusted with love and hate. Despite his disgust, he could never alter his nature and had to live chafing against life.

Self-mockery was the escape route he allowed himself.

If not, he would have no place to put his body. Nevertheless, he couldn't stand it and was revolted by walking with a depraved man like me. He often wanted to dig out his terrible nature, fling it away, lament over, pity, and make fun of it. In that way, he thought his character improved temporarily.

"If everyone in the world threw me away like Imamura, I could live my life in peace and quiet. However, making a living would be hard without him. If that happened, what would I do?"

It's not a case of "if that happened," too much has already happened. Except for Aono's close friend, Okawa, not one charitable person would save Aono today. All those old friends became Imamura's allies and were only a gang that would have no problem striking the side of his face once or twice with a fist. They would happily carry out the better idea of tying him up and not turning him over to the police. In this case, if he were thrown away by Okawa and still alive, whether he liked it or not, he'd have no alternative but to become a thief or a beggar.

As Aono lazily walked through Nezu in the direction of Tabata, these thoughts coursed through his mind, assembling and unraveling endlessly. He occasionally stopped, like he regained his senses, to scan the passersby on this day in early summer. He took in the stunning, clear blue sky, the newly green trees in Ueno, and the roofs and ground reflecting a brightness that opened his eyes. The scene struck him as especially beautiful. How happy would he be if he could stand here forever and gaze at this view?

Five or six years ago, before his present ruin, the natural beauty of a river basin of the Ganges River in India, where he stopped for a short time on his way home to Japan from France, floated before his eyes like a mirage. He recalled dim memories of the mysterious colors of dreamlike cities of towns like Benares, Delhi, and Amritsar; the temples and religious buildings resembling the crystals of jewels; and the curious clothing of the people from fairy tales who lived in these places and the pilgrims passing through. From these scenes that faded deep in his memory, his brilliant eyes were struck by the fine radiant details in the real world he witnessed once in his life and the baffling products of his imagination.

Aono couldn't believe the scene now vividly expanding under the blue June skies as if he had been transported to a province on that continent. No messages on where and how to search were exchanged between the man of the generation that stepped foot on a land resembling a spectacular embroidered picture and the man in this state of misery passing through Nezu.

He tilted his head to look up and seemed to yearn for his home far away as he studied the colors in the sky, and then hurriedly walked on.

He headed to Okawa's house. He suddenly noticed his hunger and fancied eating meat or Western food, something greasy, food with some nutrients. Maybe it's because he deliberately went out without eating lunch. If he sees Okawa, he'll assess the situation, if favorable, he'll broach the subject as a joke.

"Ah, I'm so hungry. Shall we have a beef dish?"

Okawa will say, "That sounds good," and quickly order one and a half to two pounds of sirloin.

I'll place a chunk of meat cooked to a dark brown on the iron kettle of a water cooker on my tongue with warm rice. It'll be delicious, I'll pant like a horse, and chew so thoroughly the food will become mush in my mouth. Then my stomach will be so full I'll feel sluggish. If my belly becomes round and expands like a rubber ball, how much will that make life worth living?

Just these thoughts brought on an assault of the aroma of beef stew to his nose. He quickened his pace, turned right on Dozaka, and entered a quiet town on the outskirts of the city.

The tidy homes in this pleasant neighborhood were surrounded by photinia hedges. Stylish wooden slat fences enclosed large gardens similar to those found around elegant buildings like the retreat of a tea master or the second home of a wealthy merchant in the city. The scent of the wood of new construction wafted by, seemingly in battle with vivid sprouts of green trees glistening as if coated by oil. All the homes smelled of sukiyaki, further stimulating Aono's appetite. If he became the owner of this sort of mansion, he would lead a worry-free life of leisure.

All the gentlemen living here probably hold outdoor summer parties like Imamura. They're probably tired of eating beef. Those guys have gorgeous, fashionable wives like the women in ladies' magazines. Of course, their fortunes are considerable. The one or two hundred yen a month for pocket money flows like water.

Okawa, who Aono was on his way to visit, was one of those fortunate people. He and Okawa graduated from the same art school; Okawa surpassed all but two or three in success. If things had gone well for Aono, he certainly should have been able to reach his status. If assessed at the time of graduation, Aono was at the top of the class.

Needless to say, the crime that created the madness in his situation lay in Aono himself. His entire mental attitude was abysmal. For that, thanks went to a scandalous, innate affliction of corruption, enough shamelessness to amaze himself, and the absence of qualifications that should have made him a leading public figure in society.

When he saw the brick wall surrounding Okawa's

estate on Mount Tabata, Aono felt he came to a place of dread. The thumping of his heart rose with each cowering step.

He could say Okawa was always generous and kind to him, but how dare he knock on his gate? If only his visits were genuine, and not, depending on the circumstances, pleas for money. What facial expression should he assume to bring up the subject? So far, he has tricked Okawa too often by using a smiling amused face. He couldn't be obvious by crying and begging.

Okawa nearly agreed in a letter last night to loan him money in good cheer, but there's no chance he'll say nothing and toss a wad of bills to Aono. Okawa, the good-natured scion, probably would not hide his displeasure and, for a time, fail to hand over the money. In his heart, Aono did not feel it was too much to break through the reluctance to come and coerce money only from Okawa. This was the only crime he thought was more merciless than stealing Imamura's coat.

There's a saying, *Speech is silver, but silence is golden*. In contrast, someone should proclaim, *Talent is silver, but genius is gold*. As for our talents as artists, you and I are the difference between gold and silver. From the beginning, I understood I was silver and you had the precious-ness of gold. I knew you were superior to me. I will revere you to the end....

Okawa should not have lost the sentiments in this letter he sent to Aono. On this day that proved Aono's complete lack of character, Okawa cherished his artistic talent.

Aono's greatness was wrapped in a kind of pride he feigned being ignorant of. When Aono's masterpieces displayed in last fall's exhibition were ignored by all the artists and connoisseurs, only Okawa said, "I'm not jealous." He admired the work from the bottom of his heart and did not spare his praise. Beginning with the judges, all the senior artists and friends criticized Aono's work out of hatred of his past immorality. When they did not show a sliver of sympathy, Aono wanted to cry out of gratitude for Okawa's open-mindedness. Compared to his personality that was rotten to his bowels, Okawa's purity could be seen in the nobility of "I'm not jealous."

At least from now on, Aono pledged to abandon his dishonorable behavior. Nevertheless, in the future, how much gratitude to Okawa will he hold, or will he add to his disgraceful behavior and take advantage of Okawa's kindness?

He came to borrow copies of medieval religious paintings or famous Renaissance paintings he could not buy in Japan and said he'd bring them back in a few days. Over some unclear period, he sold them for fifty yen to a second-hand bookstore. Okawa found out he had been deceived. Since that wicked deed, others were repeated countless times.

If he had only stolen the overcoat, Imamura would have reason to beat him up. If Okawa sent a letter to break off their relationship, he would be in a messy situation but couldn't complain.

Of his old friends from art school, Okawa was a unique rival who had to compete with him in terms of talent and inclinations as well as being the one who secretly prayed the most for his downfall. Okawa longed for the same romantic world as Aono and sought the vision of beauty with the same state of mind.

Of course, he envied Aono's extraordinary natural gifts and derived intense pleasure from his adversity. Okawa pretended to be kind to Aono more than anyone else and acted with generosity but jealousy burned wildly in his heart.

Others didn't understand Aono, but he thoroughly understood him. Okawa's overprotectiveness of him was not the result of kindness. Deceived by his jealousy, he harbored groundless suspicions. His oversensitive morality was coupled with a selfish nature. He was driven to rescue his rival from great poverty because this jealousy disturbed him.

Aware of his cowardice, Aono had no choice but to attack that weakness and make a nuisance of himself. Of course, he had no focus in his ways to pester Okawa. Although Aono aimed to borrow money, in some sense, his discovery of a strong man in his patron brought a measure of joy to this shameless man.

He tended to look and speak triumphantly while being cursed with awful stubbornness and thinking about begging forgiveness from Okawa which he could not stand and found galling.

Along with exposing his weakness, his rival's weakness was also discovered. He had no idea how much Aono hated to swindle money. He may have praised himself when he gave to an old friend reduced to poverty and stimulated his nerves for noble generosity. But in no time, the hypocrite pitied himself and realized his rival was testing him.

His response to an amiable request from another person, unless that person was Aono, could be said to be the benevolence of a friend; however, no magnanimity welled up in either one's heart.

A man who should have deep compassion and great morality was, in fact, a narrow-minded man jealous of another's talent. The spectacle of his rival taking advantage of this was revealed here. Of course, with this exposure, he no longer cared about giving up on Aono. That was Okawa's unwillingness to admit defeat combined with his upright character. Despite his trace of jealousy toward Aono, his art did not surpass Aono's, and Okawa certainly had no reason to abandon him. Conversely, hardening his determination seemed to make the flames of jealousy burn brighter.

As society put Aono on a shelf and he suffered life's hardships, he continued to paint in a second-floor room resembling an attic. Each time Okawa looked at Aono's recent works created there, he felt threatened by his abundant talent that pioneered new mental states and finally realized Aono was a powerful rival.

Despite falling into poverty, Aono would be recognized again by the world; his reputation would survive. Even if an incident arose between Aono and him after death, his jealousy shouldn't change. Aono vividly saw that these thoughts built a nest in Okawa's mind.

True artists always feel the jealousy gripping Okawa. They are well aware of jealousy that is precious and deserves respect. Nonetheless, Aono would persist in pestering Okawa forever by manipulating these vile feelings. Compared to his own depravity, he had no idea how heartbreaking or how laudable was Okawa's hypocrisy? This Aono scolded his own body despite being on his way to Okawa's home.

"All right, only today, I will happily enjoy beef, not talk about money, and go home. I'll give him peace of mind by forgetting about the business in last evening's letter. Even if the meal is lost and I starve to death, it'd probably be better than making Okawa think this way ..."

Aono passed in front of the side gate once then went back and forth a few more times. Distressed by deep misgivings, the pangs of hunger he had forgotten worsened again as his stomach seemed to tighten. The treat of meat became as urgent as the gift of money.

Two

When a student escort opened the door of Okawa's study, Aono pushed the money problem aside, gathered his resolve, and cheerfully walked into the room.

During his wait alone for only thirty minutes, he rehearsed internally what he intended to promptly say with a grin when Okawa came out.

"Ah, last night's business is finished. I wandered around today and ended up here. I'm terribly sorry, but could I impose on you for a beef dish? Lately, I've been surviving on tofu and miso soup."

For a short time, he rested his chin on his hands on a rosewood desk in the center of the room and gazed out an east-facing window overlooking the brim of a hill to the suburban fields spreading out like the ocean.

Forests and houses dotted the plain bathing in the sunbeams close to midday. The fluttering lace of the white curtains sparkled in the distance. The blast fired from the noonday gun reached the room painted a deep indigo blue. As he looked, echoes spread to the far-off corners of the field. Faint booms bounced back countless times in all directions from the horizon. Steam whistles from the factories in Senju and Mikawashima sounded like voices in an ambush.

The student brought in food and placed it on the desk.

"Excuse me, Sensei is working. Please, enjoy the meal while you wait a little longer."

Aono's face swelled as he watched.

Although not the beef he longed for, a large pottery bowl of *donburi* and a small plate of pickled foods adorned with raw slender radish slices were placed before him. He looked wistfully with a side eye at the container he imagined held a *tendon* rice bowl and an eel dish. At least, there's eel. These were his momentary thoughts. After the student left, he reached for the donburi bowl. Before opening the lid, he immediately knew the sort of tendon from the batter bulging out from below like scrap paper.

"Aah, is it tempura?"

He quickly said to himself without thinking. His disappointment nearly brought on tears.

He thought about the student's words, "He's working." Okawa probably shut himself in and had been painting since the morning. The rumor mill said he's gradually preparing works to be displayed in the fall exhibition. This news appeared two or three days ago in the newspapers, so he might have started painting.

Okawa hated others seeing his work and took extra measures to keep them hidden from Aono, in particular, Aono could not easily enter his studio. Sometimes, Okawa made him wait thirty minutes or an hour. Today, however, Aono felt a long wait today would not be out of the ordinary.

He couldn't avoid confused thoughts and unfounded suspicions and imagined Okawa saying, "You've come again to shamelessly hound me for money. The fact is your situation is dreadful. It's gotten out of hand, but this time, I ask you to forgive me. I've had a change of heart while you waited and would like to ask you to go home without a meeting."

Aono's eyes felt like they already saw Okawa's cowardly expression worsened by this problem from the ill-humored letter written last night by him.

Today, I won't be made a fool of by Aono. Even if I

lend him the money, I always end up feeling like he's made a fool of me. There may not be a subtle way out this time.

Aono frequently turned his ideas of Okawa's thinking over and over in his head. The thumping in his chest intensified in vain. When he thought about losing his temper, Aono was exhilarated like he couldn't stand the wretchedness. A good person without sin feels displeased with his perverted nature, finds it particularly shameful, and becomes angry with no rival.

"Okawa-kun, excuse my intrusion. I'm disgusted and you're probably disgusted, too," muttered Aono with sincerity. Mysteriously, the feelings of disgust gradually strengthened. More than this disgust, he was less insistent on the peculiar conclusion that begging for money is better than his earlier brave readiness to abandon begging.

"Ah, forgive me for keeping you waiting," said Okawa, feigning calmness as he entered the study. He lacked the courage to announce his readiness to play along with the sham.

The moment he faced Aono, Okawa fought to calm himself and seemed revolted by his total inability to stand firm. He swallowed hard, wet his lips, and looked like a beast facing an enemy. He appeared as he did in the past in this sort of situation but didn't seem hostile or agitated like today.

Aono couldn't laugh to hide his embarrassment. If he nonchalantly said, "Let's not talk about money," it would sound unnatural. His face was so tense Aono feared further angering his companion. He swelled with nearly indescribable anxiety and anguish.

"I'm sorry it's been so long.… I am shameless and have no sense of decency showing up here to see you, but there is the request I made in last night's letter. I have no excuse for such brazenness."

This is all Aono could say. It was natural and appropriate in this situation. He kept on talking with this slightly exhilarating feeling in his chest that didn't stop and disappear. Only dark servile, mean-spirited, shameless determination stuck in his head, even he would say, with stifling tenacity. He endured this pressure, and his palpitations intensified for a time. He felt sicker until queasiness brought up a burp of the shrimp tempura he just ate and led him to desperation.

"I've been thinking a bit about this occasion. I thought I'd ask for your help one more time because I was pushed to a hard-to-reach place and had to come."

Okawa sat at the other side of the desk and stood a cut Western cigarette between his index and middle fingers like a chimney. He fixed his eyes on a narrow line like smoke from an incense stick rising from its tip. The trembling excitement of his fingertips reached the ashes on the cigarette's tip gradually forming a tower about to topple over.

"Well, what will you do? You have no reason to listen to me. Like I said in yesterday's letter about my situation ..."

"Well, I've never denied your requests. Only this time, in particular, it will be strange not to listen to your request ..." Okawa's voice trailed off.

"So I will listen to you. Specifically, looking at last night's letter, the money this time has a different meaning than the usual money. This money is not to save you but must be lent to save your art. Saying it this way makes it difficult for me to refuse. You adeptly targeted a vulnerable spot."

A slight smile rose for the first time as he spoke. Aono found the smile more unsettling than a frown and could only look down.

"You make all manner of specious arguments to

squeeze money from me. Now, you don't have funds to paint, and your job has become borrowing money from me and avoiding repayment. You seem to be more interested in this than putting all your efforts into your work. What I'm saying may anger you, but today, I will speak the truth."

His tone that sounded like he had reached the end of his rope suddenly returned to life. He leaned forward and looked straight into Aono's eyes.

"To say this loan is for your art is not a lie. Even a shameless man like you who lies about anything will use your art, a unique asset you should be proud of, to deceive me.

"You have been temporarily ousted from society but for you to bloom another flower in this world or sweep away hardships to bequeath, with some higher aim, a monumental work of your pure art to this world for eternity, I am obligated, as your friend, to help.

"Therefore, if I rejected your request for expense money to buy supplies for painting, rent a room, and employ a model, I would be the bad guy. At least, that's what you thought. If I rejected your request for money only this time, you would criticize me and accuse me of being jealous of your work."

"Hmm, I don't need to be that suspicious of you. Even a depraved ingrate like me is grateful from my heart for your past kindness ..."

"No, as I said earlier, today I'll be frank. My honest wish for you may be an unreasonable demand. I only ask you with all sincerity to listen to my words without artifice."

Okawa's arrogant eyes were bloodshot like a madman and his face, pale. Aono couldn't understand why he was this excited.

"You thanked me from your heart for my kindness? Even if your gratitude is genuine, you surely never consider being kind to me.

"These days, I don't even think about being kind to you in dreams. As you've guessed, I envy your talent. If I'm jealous, I understand your disgust with the awfulness of exposing that weakness. I'm sure this is it.

"From the beginning, however, I was not as jealous of you as I am now. At first, I was as kind to you as I would be to any friend. I'm appalled by your predicament. Out of sheer kindness and warm friendship, I helped you as much as humanly possible.

"Even when I was recklessly scammed and harmed for your sake, I didn't get angry but pitied you. As you know, I was born into a wealthy family and am gullible and timid. That makes me meticulous about my righteous or wicked behaviors but generous to others. Until now, I've never felt the slightest anger or irritability about your behavior.

"However, since I began associating with you, I discovered an ugly part of me hiding deep in my heart. While I was oblivious to this, at some point, I became aware of the jealousy provoked by your attitude.

"You once taught me something, you said, 'Your behavior is not kindness. I call it jealousy.' You didn't say it explicitly, but that meaning slipped through. As you crudely exposed your decadent character to me, I gradually competed with you and became disgraceful and unworthy along with you. If I may say, the fact is I can't stand unpleasantness. I have a hunch your scams are serious."

"The tricks were pretty bad," Aono said. "Of course, my attitude may have been aroused by your jealousy. However, I was aware of this from the beginning and made plans that were better not to adopt. First of all, what did I gain by acting like that? If I, who benefited from your kindness and made you jealous, wouldn't I be hurting myself?"

As Okawa spoke, Aono was not a man drawn to honesty but inadvertently carried away by his words. Aono visited his house intending to borrow money. He never forgot that. Despite his intention to be indignant, suitable lies emerged with ease from his mouth.

"Enough of this tedious discussion. Tell me now, are you going to lend me the money or not?" Aono would have simply asked this if he candidly spoke from his gut.

"You're still lying. I've refused your request but have not said I won't lend you the money. If you want money, I will lend it. Because I will lend it, I ask you to stop lying. For peace of mind, I will give it to you first."

Had he prepared the money in advance? Okawa took out a bundle of two hundred yen in bills from his pocket and slammed it on the desk. Then he flung it onto Aono's chest as if tossing a bone to a dog.

"That should be enough. You probably have no complaints. Today is different from usual. I'm growing angry. You also opened your heart a little and were candid with me. I'm not loaning this money. I'm buying your honesty with this money."

"If I got angry like you, I would be weak. I don't think I lie, perhaps, I lie unwittingly. Because my lying is already chronic, this illness can't be treated...."

As he spoke, Aono's chest seethed with animosity and self-hatred. Bleakness coursed his body like heavy fatigue and sorrow were mixed fifty-fifty with eating too much of a bad thing. Thinking about it, his one friend, Okawa, stopped being his friend today. He's simply a man who sends food to the enemy to conceal his jealousy. This was only an inconvenience to him.

In exchange for his gift of money, this man showered him with insults and contempt. Aono had to resign himself to listening to rude and bullying language neither a parent nor a judge would dare say. In no time, Okawa wielded power over him. Anyone given this total power would probably use it.

Okawa gave him money but did not see it as the result of friendship. Aono did not feel indebted. How did their relationship become so troubled? Both aspired to follow the same artistic path but only associated with each other to fight over the problem of lending and borrowing money. He and Okawa never argued with such agitation or intensity over artistic problems. If money were not involved, the two would face the dilemma of ending their friendship. Aono was fine with things as they were.

Aren't I to blame for dragging in Okawa? Would it have been better if I gave up on these money problems? Did I feel this horrible because I wanted the money? Why didn't I throw back the wad of bills? But I have no choice but to borrow this money. I was probably born amoral. While I'm alive, instead of behaving terribly, I will leave behind magnificent works of art for future generations because this is my unavoidable fate, thought Aono and sighed in relief. He timidly placed his hand on the bundle and quietly set it on his knees.

Okawa said, "I'll be honest with you, but that doesn't mean I'll be a virtuous man. If I'm a wicked man, then being wicked is good. You asked me to confess and conceal nothing. Until now I also hid my jealousy behind kindness.

"I confess I would like you to be open and tell me, what do you get out of our relationship? I have no idea how long the rotten connection between you and me will continue. Every time money problems occur, these unpleasant thoughts are unbearable.

"If in the future, a wicked man is wicked, a virtuous man is virtuous, and he acts accordingly, our relationship will be a little more agreeable. Similarly, I believe talking about borrowing and lending money will become smoother and more enjoyable…. Don't you think so? I'd like to take this opportunity today to discuss this with you."

"But you never take candid talk from me well," said Aono with resignation and a cold, eerie smile. "The mutual pleasure of frankly speaking one's true feelings is only an interaction between gentlemen of goodwill.

"Stirring up the five flavors of sweet, salty, spicy, sour, and bitter fermenting in my stomach produced nothing more than the release of a foul stench. I can't stand that smell, so a virtuous man like you would be disgusted. I am perplexed why a lowlife rogue like me was born an artist. I have a dishonest nature but also have the courtesy to not force a stranger to smell that horrible breath …."

"How awful a stench is acceptable? If the stench is known, I have ways to prevent it, but I rashly hide it and will be infected in a short time. For example, you intend to use my jealousy and concoct schemes to borrow money from me. You associate with me for that alone.

"If your attitude is so extreme, from now on, I can expose my jealousy and be in contact with you. I can't decide to behave meanly, leave you to your fate, and not help you out of jealousy. Instead, I delight in being used by you, pity your selfishness, and will be used as much as my heart allows.

"I will compete fair and square with your art through my work. You will use. I will be used. That will be our sole association.

"You and I aren't friends and will stop being connected by money issues. If that is the agreement, the decisive feeling is welcome. I give out money to satisfy my conscience, not out of obligation as a friend. Given this real-ization, I'll have no reason to get angry no matter how much you deceive me.... That will no longer be an impediment."

"Your words pain me, but ... I'm not the sort who shows my troubles on my face. If I follow what you say, I will use you for now."

"Please do," said Okawa in a deliberately hearty tone, folded his arms, turned away, but blushed redder.

"... Well, this talk is over. If you take the money and have no other business, please go home now. I'm busy today."

"I'm terribly sorry for the intrusion. I'll go, but one last thing. Please listen to my true intentions."

Instead of saying, "All right. I'll listen," Okawa nodded. His eyes glowed in reflection, and he impatiently flicked the ashes of his cigarette into the ashtray.

"It's odd to say this again, but I thank you. Whatever your motivation for saving me, I can devote all my energies to art thanks to you. If this happens, I will be reborn as a serious person.

"Although I'd like to interact with you as a friend, how hard will it be if that's impossible? Please try to imagine my distress. The man here is vulgar, selfish, spineless, and not the real me. Please understand my art to understand the real me."

While he spoke, Aono thought several times about returning the two hundred yen. How painful could it be? It would hurt but wouldn't returning the money be best? Even if I can't see how troublesome it would be to change my life, if I tossed back this money in my pocket, could I still become a serious man?

His conscience chastised him. Nevertheless, he couldn't bring himself to let go of the money.

Okawa said, "For you, nothing is without trouble. Although I regret asking for this from a friend who is a serious artist with your talent, I have no choice but to say that. I accept the exchange of one jewel in your belly rotted like a garbage dump. If I agree, I'll be jealous ..."

Both men felt tears blur their eyes and hurriedly lowered their heads as if they settled an agreement.

"But you're a living man, somehow, I can't bring myself to respect you. Your talent will not be recognized until after your death. When you die, not just me, many will respect you."

A sudden terrible thought entered Okawa's mind. After Aono and he leave this world, Aono's genius will be recognized everywhere. At the same time, my name will probably be transmitted throughout the world as an artist jealous of his talent, viewed as an enemy, and mediocre and commonplace.

"Okawa was an awful painter. Although he created inferior paintings, he believed he was competing with Aono's genius and often gave him money."

These rumors will last for one thousand years and ridicule him as a fine example of an ordinary artist.

"While alive, you don't only think about art, seek the fame I desire, and have my ambition. Therefore, I will always be jealous of you. If you create a finer work than I, I'll only feel displeasure. I pray that is not so. Although I provide economic aid, like a man, I declare here we are enemies in art. Try to remember this."

"Thank you for saying that. Of course, I have total faith in my art. However, when cast out from the world and persecuted, occasionally, I can't help but doubt my ability. The complete rejection by the world of my works, despite my confidence in them, gives rise to the bias that my art has no value. Moreover, this rejection is not necessarily caused by repulsion to my immorality.

"Your jealousy eliminates that bias and doubt. It's all right for you to be jealous of me and see me as the enemy. I comfort and encourage myself with those thoughts.

"Although I say this and listen with cynicism, please don't take it the wrong way because that's never been my intention. Everybody will not reconsider their abandonment of me, you alone recognize my talent, but I don't understand to what degree this is due to kindness."

Aono spent the whole year lying and could barely tolerate the awfulness of sporadic honest confessions. His cheeks blushed like a virgin's.

WHEN OKAWA RETURNED to his studio, "Sensei, today's visitor was Aono-san?" asked Eiko, sitting on the couch in a corner of the studio. Her toes covered by a white *tabi* sock and resembling a flatfish played with a half-on slipper.

She was eighteen or nineteen, a woman with a slender build and flexible, like springs were inside her, suitably tall, and buxom. Her arms and legs looked seductively supple and limply hung down as if she were lifted at the middle of her torso like algae being scooped up from underwater. The wavy ends of her parted hair, probably crimped by a hot iron, hit the cheeks of her oval face. Turquoise earrings, unusual for a Japanese woman, twinkled in her earlobes peeking out between the wavy tufts like rocks obscured by waves and swung like the bronze wind chimes that decorate the eaves of temples.

"What happened? Did you quarrel with Aono-san? You don't look well? Yoo-hoo, Sensei!"

In the midday silence, her vibrant, shrill voice echoed

off the four walls of the studio and could be heard two or three times. Still sullen, Okawa entered and sat down without answering.

She rattled the lid of a sandalwood box for rolled Indian cigarettes and took one out. Her lips pursed and made puffing sounds as she drew in the smoke. Her eyes followed Okawa as he walked in circles for close to five minutes.

Aware something was wrong, her innocent eyes widened as they shadowed his odd movements, but a sinister expression crept over her face. Eventually, her appearance changed into gloom in contrast to moments ago. There was no deeper cause, somehow, Okawa's mood infected her.

The serious Eiko always looked sly, eerie, and morose. Despite her looks perfect for a model for Western-style painting that depended on the curves of her body made for endless flirting, her brilliance embodied seeds of malice and anguish and often depended on her pleasant features, seemingly bright but rich in complex shadows.

Her contours looked strangely polygonal and refracted light similar to jewels. Dazzling beauty filled her entire body. Although a point-by-point inspection of her face would uncover many flaws, if her unique beauty were set as the standard, she felt like an immobile object, and her skin looked strangely translucent and bruised with coldness resembling frosted glass.

Her appearance was unsettling as though she was painted by some strange glossy, thick paintbrush. Was she aware of this? She was proud of never having to wear ordinary face powder and her dry bare skin. Because she came from a poor family, other than her treasured earrings, she did not adorn any other part of her body. Her clothes looked drab, grimy, and old.

"Sensei, Aono-san came to bug you for money?"

She flopped back on the sofa and blew smoke rings toward the ceiling.

Okawa stopped and curtly said, "It doesn't matter. Today, I have something to do and must go out. No time to play today, so please go home."

He stared at her body and seemed to be thinking, This woman resembles Aono. She has a beautiful body like Aono has genius. Both are also well-matched in having low character.

"I'll go, but I need to talk to you."

"What? Is it money, again?"

"No, it's not. It's about Aono-san. He sent me a letter saying he was about to begin a new painting and asked me to model for him one more time."

"What did you do?"

"Of course, I answered and refused."

"Why? Why did you refuse? Wouldn't it be better to do it?"

Okawa's brow darkened. He marched out with a glint of fear in his eyes that she didn't notice.

"Lately, he's run out of money and is in a fix. Has he become a man who goes around cheating his friends and is out of control?

"Has a depraved man like Aono wronged you?"

"Aono-san is a terrible man. I've been corrupt for some time. Associating with a woman like me is fine but getting deeply involved is not. What would I do if I had money?"

"But this time, isn't it better to do it for the money?"

"I don't know what will happen if I do. He's so poor."

"No, it's all right. This time, he has money."

"What? So you lent Aono-san money. I wonder how much he has now," said Eiko sounding interested, perhaps on to a good thing.

"You shouldn't leave Aono with one *mon*. Well, I guarantee it, so it's all right to model for him. It's all right if you only come to my studio in the morning. In the afternoon, your body will be free to play, okay? Aono said he will use you as a model to finish this masterpiece."

"This time, no one will compete with Aono-san's painting, and no rival models will be asked."

Her words didn't seem to enter Okawa's ears. He was too deep in thought. With arms folded, he lunged forward circling the room with his reddened eyes focused on his toes

Finally, I must compete with Aono. Why must a good man like me be forced to follow the same artistic path as a depraved miscreant like Aono? My mind and his mind exist in the world of the same dream and drift to the same visions of beauty, for instance, the choice of Eiko here with me now.

My eyes were quick to spot her dancing on stage as a lowly actress in the opera wing of XYZ Theater. At least, that was my intention. Soon after, Aono noticed her and was the first to ask her to model. Mysteriously, no one other than Aono and I recognized the strange beauty possessed by this amoral, shameless, audacious, and crazy fool of a woman.

Now, four or five years have passed. When I finally thought about searching for her to hire her as a model, Aono set his sights on her. I'd have no trouble getting in his way and monopolizing her, but I would never behave that despicably.

In that case, I will oppose him and persist in the competition to see who truly understands the beauty of her flesh and has the power to create art. Yes, that's what I'll do.

"Hey, I'm asking you to model for me instead of Aono. Go to his studio. Not going would cause me problems."

Okawa raised his head and sounded determined.

"If Aono doesn't have money, I'll pay you later."

"That's wonderful. In that case, I'll go."

"Aono probably has no idea you are modeling for me."

"I don't understand," she said. Her mouth hung open, shocked by his threatening look.

"Very well. Please do not tell Aono about our arrangement. Not one word. I have my reasons."

As he repeated himself to make sure, he stared at her face with a cursed look in his eyes.

Three

Aono stared at the vision before his eyes, more vivid than reality. He did not know what city in what country he stood, but he must be in the center of a prosperous, stately street. The prosperity of the street was reflected in the curtains of embroidered fabric flowing down like a waterfall of gold and silver threads drawn to the right side of the room.

He looked at the hazy view far beyond the veranda behind the curtains to see the calm, deep blue sky resembling a lake nestled in the mountains. He nodded, knowing he could not see everything on the Earth where people live.

Below the floating wisps of golden clouds, the towns of this city formed vast links. The landscape of towns was bewitching and magnificent. Aono mused over the scene, unable to pull away his spellbound eyes.

The spotless, spectacular streets were not outdone by the eternal beauty of the blanket of blue sky. He was sure his hand could pick up the round roofs of the shrines and temples rising sporadically in the view, the soaring spires, and the columns in the marble colonnades or the stone steps, surging one after another like waves.

The setting sun bathed the tiled roofs and walls of the towns with a calm light, quiet and cold, bluish white like mother of pearl. It was reminiscent of the color of the cheeks of a dying precious queen and looked noble and awe-inspiring.

Aono's line of sight drew back from the distant view and its nearly transparent brightness. His eyes frequently and enthusiastically surveyed the interior of the room in the dim foreground.

The melancholy, stifling atmosphere of a cave filled the room. The darkened room resembled the shade of dense trees in June but the dark gloom had a mysterious soft, deep lustrous black velvet. Likening this darkness to the pupil of the human eye may be accurate. The phenomenon inside the room where darkness drifts lies inside the cool pupils staring at the beautiful woman and has a complex dynamic as if the world reflected on the surfaces of the dark eyes.

For instance, Aono keenly observed everything, the Persian rug spread on the floor, the bas-relief decoration carved into the milky-white stone of the pillars erected on the left side of the room, the blooming flowers of the water lilies in the shallow bronze bowl on the table inlaid with *aogai* mollusk shells, the white peacock spreading its silvery train and strutting around all flickered as red or white shadows in the pupils of his black eyes.

The faint scent of smoke meandered and danced up the curtain woven in a creeping grapevine pattern from the cloisonne incense burner beside the bed in the front of the room, assaulting his sense of smell. Perhaps it was Arabian myrrh, Indian cinnamon, or Smyrna rose? Like a cup filled with aromatic aged sake, Aono's soul had to be guided to the border of senseless intoxication.

At the same bewitching and eerie incense teased his nose, whispered tender words of love, like lines from Baudelaire's poem *Bien Loin d'ici*, slipped into Aono's mind, and his gaze lingered at the bed in the center of the room.

From the canopy adorned with crystals, pearls, and agate hanging from the ceiling, the dark green satin curtain with raised figures hung down like abundant hair gradually spreading out like the figure of a tall witch dressed in a priestess robe further darkened the area.

A woman stretching out her arms and legs on the bed turned to lay on her back. If the entire interior of the room was in a human eye, radiance beamed like a dream from the woman's body with limbs twisted in the dim shadow of the curtain. Transient dazzling luster like flashes from a sea snake diving through seaweed or jewels buried in tufts of black hair occupied the centers of the pupils.

Carvings, embroidery, mother-of-pearl water lilies decorating the four walls of this room, and the towns in the city expanding far off beyond the veranda in the silvery wings of a white peacock were only a rainbow that appeared to praise the stealthy flirting of this woman.

Ah, did she come here at last? Aono couldn't help thinking this. His eyes narrowed and the ends of his eyelashes fluttered as if he were praying to praise the golden Buddha in an ancient miniature shrine for giving thanks.

His optic nerve watched her body, seemingly formed from shadows in light inside the Buddhist altar light, and sensed slight movements of a sapphire light pattern on her skin. These lights shined on the surface and threw brightness like the moon's halo from the hair of the woman inlaid with several emeralds one would suspect were the incarnations of fireflies from the ruby bracelet bursting from her wrist like beautiful swellings, from the diamond headdress like evening dew placed on a marble staircase linked to the woman's chest, from the metal rings shining like a dragon's hoof on both of her ankles, and, finally, from the silk gauze, thin like fog and light like the Milky Way, tied around her delicate torso and hips.

More mysteriously, her flesh and skin lived and squirmed under innumerable ornaments. Inside her, the lowliness of a human called *flesh* and *skin* transcended and weaved together the dreadfulness of a ghost and the luster of a fairy.

However, if the helpless fatigue spilling from her hands and feet as she lay listless on her side on the pillow and the greed for lust that knew no fatigue in her eyes were visible in the nasty sneer on her lips, she blew air from her chest to lighten the incense smoke and felt Aono could hear the gentle sweet-smelling sigh reminiscent of white lily flowers withered in the twilight.

Aono stared a long time at that vision. He forgot about himself as he stared at Eiko's nude body lying on the model's platform. His soul pushed into a fantasy world as a haze that passed through Eiko's flesh far away and spread out inside her. His paintbrush moving on the canvas only copied the figure of the phantom floating out before his eyes without painting Eiko.

This woman he painted now was someone living in a city somewhere in the world at some time. How often had she visited his soul? When he thought this, Aono's vision shattered. He was startled and returned to his senses as when waking from a dream. Eiko jerked up her plump legs.

"Hey, what happened? Please be patient for a little longer," said Aono in a pleading tone.

"Aah."

Eiko yawned, looking troubled and irritated.

She shook her head and again positioned her body in lazy disapproval. Like baiting a fish, her feral eyes, with a tinge of gloom, studied Aono's behavior.

"This ... this face. This face sends her spirit to my heart."

Again, Aono sighed in grief, drawn in by Eiko's expression. At the end of June, Aono used a portion of the gift of money from Okawa to move into this house with a studio. Although an improvement over the attic where he used to live, it was only bigger but not equipped or furnished to match its designation as an artist's studio.

The house was built between rice fields and a thicket of trees on the outskirts of town near the Mejiro train station. The studio was little more than an empty storage room. The house lacked an entryway, living room, and kitchen and was merely a workplace resembling a shack only built for use by a sculptor named B, who lived in Koishikawa and commuted here daily.

B traveled to the West at the end of last year. For ages, the For Rent sign remained stuck on the desolate house with no tenant until Aono was able to lease it from B's family with Okawa acting as his guarantor. That was just two months ago. Since then, Aono has lived in this room day and night. His life could be called confused and dirty. His situation could be guessed at a glance.

Like the storefront of a curio shop on an ancient road in a dilapidated section of town, dusty and shabby furniture was strewn everywhere on the rugless floor in the cluttered room. The dust clinging for many years reflected a black light. Cotton and straw flew out through scattered tears in the silk damask.

The only stylish object in the room was an old chair

with fringe. The varnish peeled off the warped planks of a wobbly round table. A stylish group of three complex goddesses was set on the table. In the past, hands raised each of these candles to shine from seats during a night-time event in an embassy somewhere. Now, they're used as lamps at night in this storeroom not equipped with electric lights.

An enamel washbasin speckled with clay resembling bird poo, an earthenware teapot, chipped tea cups, and several Western-style plates holding the remains of chewed-up tomatoes, salad, and grains of boiled rice seemed to be parting gifts from B's time here. The squalid bent-wood stool might have been stolen from a Western-style restaurant.

The heap of trash included a thick broken galvanized steel pipe filled with chimney soot from the stove removed from a corner when the previous resident moved out, two or three large sheets of charcoal paper with rough sketches on their fronts and backs rolled up like chimneys and propped against the side like lumber, and beside them various articles that seemed to be the bedding used at night by the current resident. Items like an old mosquito net like living seaweed, a ripped threadbare cover like a cloth wrapper so dirty it was nearly the same color as the mosquito net, a pillow stuffed with rice husks and wrapped by a towel with a distinct black head-shaped dent resembled the remains piled on the roadside after a major house cleaning.

The objects that seemed to play the role of decorations in this room were cans of cheese and sausage and bottles of peppermint and brandy on a shelf along the side. Although not intended as decorations and placed for the sake-loving Eiko who enjoyed a cup or two during breaks while working. The surrounding colors were muted, but those two glass containers sparkled blue and yellow like a huge emerald and topaz in the trash pile.

Other than these bottles, one magnificent ornament remained in the room. The magnificence of Eiko was not forgotten. When night came to the owner's bed along the eastern wall, the figure of a woman beside a pillow to her north on a couch of lacquered willow was fitting. Her figure could be pulled up if Aono saw a vision, most likely the bewitching beauty of a temptress. Today, it was probably her having drunk a large quantity of sake. Her skin radiating drunkenness had a sweaty luster and color of the silk of a fishing rig.

She was innately melancholy, wicked, weak, had a defeated appearance with dull, cloudy, and often sleepy eyes, and an element of dread. Her face seemed to flow like it was melting. If the peppermint and brandy bottles were likened to sapphire and topaz, comparing the woman's refined beauty to a sleeping leopard was not an exaggeration. At least, only Aono felt that was an exaggeration, or he still lacked the proper metaphor.

Every day, Aono focused his gaze on Eiko's flesh and the vision hidden in her. Unknowingly, his obsession with creating the work began after seventy days passed unnoticed. The time was the middle of August. He expected to finish this work by the end of the month.

From time to time, he had to think about this piece during his work. As an immoral man, in the fervor of creating a work, he wanted the people of the world to realize he's not a lowlife. If that's not possible, he'd like god's approval. He will do things that are bad and selfish in society. However, this was not his true wish. He wanted to have far more wins than the good people of the world.

Aono's mind filled with thoughts that boiled up not just this time but every time he created a piece.

There is a precious state of mind unknown in my dreams that I can't understand. The art world has value difficult to replace even with all the objects on Earth. I can't shake the feeling somehow it exists on this planet forever as a transient vision. In that case, can I, a man called bad in society, can I enter this art world and be happier and greater than all the other people? Instead of ignoring this scandalous bum, the affectionate mother of art pities him more, hugs him at her warm breasts, comforts him, and gives him kisses bursting with love.

Aono's heart heard the whispers of a woman's voice.

"No matter how must the world rejects and scorns you, never lose hope, never be discouraged. I understand your talent. Only you will be shown in your body a beautiful country never seen by outsiders. So you shouldn't curse or mourn your fate. You are a precious child."

Those caring whispers made him want to live and not kill himself in this unpleasant world full of contradictions and anguish. Everyone stared with disdain and suspicion repeatedly to apply pressure through judgment on numerous vices like fraud, embezzlement, big talk, flattery, and skipping out at night. Even today having fallen into circumstances so shameful and pathetic, he couldn't go out in public and walk the main streets.

When he shut himself up in this room and gripped a brush, the people of the world united, clapped their hands, sneered, and felt the courage to want to do the opposite and smiled with pity. Even when he recalled Imamura's expression as he slowly beat himself up and got angry, and Okawa's situation of always treating him as a scoundrel while posing as a moralist, he unknowingly lost the power to control himself and became small like a bug in a far-off world.

But these days, Aono felt the roots of mysterious

anxiety and terror spreading in his chest swell with pride and delight like a king who conquered the world. Maybe, he should die at the same time he paints this picture. For this last painting, perhaps he should consume his last bit of energy.

From the excess of love from the art god, he saw a precious beautiful world not seen by others. The secret of this world was discovered by everyone. Would he suffer divine punishment for this and die? This premonition accompanied the gradual approach of the time he would finish his work and slowly dominated the depths of his mind. This thought came to mind again. Depending on the situation, would I be killed out of jealousy?

Even if I announced this new work only to be ignored by many critics, would at least two or three true artists fear my talent and be jealous? Could they remain silent about my being the sole recipient of special caresses and revelations from the goddess of beauty? If my life and my art threaten their existence, wouldn't they consider killing me? In the rare event, this happens, the one to kill me would have to be Okawa, the most hostile to me among them.

Aono could not believe that supposition. The rich boy and his good-natured patron, Okawa, would stealthily come to kill him was a groundless fear to be treated with contempt. Somehow, that action was too obvious to him, like a natural event. He was fooled by indescribable excitement and fear.

"Idiot! I don't know that I'm not crazy."

While scolding himself from the pit of his stomach, he abruptly stopped working and frantically paced the room.

From anguish, fear, pride, and delight, each day he finished his work. In both happy times and scary times, Aono risked his life that would not continue within this fear and happiness. He simply thought it best not to die before he finished his work.

After he finished working hard for half of a long summer day, he'd recline his exhausted body in an armchair and say with relief, "This was a good day. I was safe today." However, his work was not over for the entire day. In the evening, he waited for one more risky job.

At first, he was tempted by Eiko. Aono thought she seduced him. Perhaps she became his model because she had designs on him from the beginning. This insecure, loose, and self-destructive woman was out of control. She should not have agreed to the one-time payment for the bothersome modeling job.

Sometimes, smart-aleck critiques came from those with superficial knowledge, post-impressionists, and pre-Raphaelites but she was never a woman with an understanding of or compassion for art.

Her six-month relationship four or five years ago as an actress in operas put on by the XYZ Theater resulted in her current sporadic jobs as a dancer on the stages of small theaters near the park. Her hidden motive may have been for her figure to appear in oil paintings to be shown in exhibitions. She should have understood the total ineffectiveness of work created by an unpopular painter with a dismal reputation like Aono as an advertisement from the time before she became a model.

More than that, she was interested in seducing Aono and extorting money. From experience, she knew Aono was fascinated by her flesh and raged with cruel violence. Of the men who only knew her, none worshipped and yearned for her flesh as much as Aono.

When the two started working together a few years ago, Eiko saw most men like Aono were conquered by the lack of resistance to her seduction. At that time, she was already promiscuous. Although she was a young woman no older than sixteen or seventeen, she could not stand toying with an artist nearing thirty years old with a stubbly beard and recently back from studying in the West as if he were a doll.

Before Aono dealt with her, he had no drive, lost the ability to tell right from wrong, and wondered how far he would become demented and descend into endless depravity for her sake. Aono's propensity to criminality forced him to raise money to buy her favor. His situation of going from one vice to the next startled the eyes of Eiko, a genuine delinquent young woman. She was slightly unnerved and had half-baked thoughts of running away.

Nevertheless, for a year, the two slowly rubbed each other the wrong way. He felt she was the type who enjoyed pranks and watched Aono's degradation with amusement. Witnessing the gratifying success of her seduction and making a fool of him bit by bit was a mysterious enticement she found unbearable. She was like a cat swinging a mouse's corpse from her mouth. This tore at Aono's heart. He had neither forgiveness nor compassion for that much violence. His joy seemed to come from the gradual death of his soul gasping for breath.

"You probably think I'm an utter fool and have never met a man who's a fool for women like me. That is my sickness. A man with this peculiar lust of mine is known in the West as a masochist."

He often grimaced as he offered his awful defense. In the next instant, he exposed his stupidity. Aono was unqualified to be a public figure and a man unable to savor pure love. Like he defined his friendships through money, he could not understand anything other than lust in a rela-tionship between a man and a woman. On this point, he agreed with her and thought, She may intend to corrupt me. But the truth may be I will corrupt her.

While they lived together for less than a year, how large was the total sacrifice he made Eiko pay? Sooner or later, Aono's social standing, reputation, and trust would plummet even without having a relationship with Eiko. She did not count those things, only objects, and money. Nevertheless, she didn't know they were worth several times more than her income as an actress.

At that time, her lover was a young man among her actor friends, but she craved only money. Western-style clothes, rings, and wristwatches bought for her poured out everywhere. Even if she had to shake him upside-down to get his money, her pursuit of the obsessed Aono until he spent his last mon ended when she disappeared with a lover.

After this, Aono felt refreshed. Feeling drained like his gut was weighed down by eating too much greasy food, he was sad and regretted cutting off the relationship with her. With no reason to completely forget her, the charm of her flesh dominated Aono's mind for a long time and gave birth to endless fantasies.

Like many masochists, he was dissatisfied with real women and longed to love an illusion. Aono could gaze at the beauty of the woman long after she left. The Eiko who appeared in his dream had little of the coarseness, shame, and filth of the woman Aono saw before him. At that time, she was complete like art.

The woman envisioned in his head was the true Eiko. He wondered, Was the woman living in this world a poor imitation of the true Eiko? The woman born as a human is shameless, greedy, and nothing more than a poor girl, but she shines in this imaginary world. She felt like a bewitching female entity with eternal life.

At some time, Aono found the object of beauty he yearned for in the vision of her. If that's wrong to say, his vision of her perfectly matched this object. Each time the appearance, posture, and contour of the Eiko idealized in his mind emanated brilliant light onto his eyes, Aono did not prevent the boiling up of strong artistic emotions.

One or two years after breaking up with her, finally, that vivid vision was drawn in Aono's mind. Centered on her figure, the amazing artistic realm was slowly built in this place. The city in the beautiful dream spread over the domain.

When spring comes, plants alone in the natural world bud and bloom flowers. Like them, what could Aono not do? He is equal to the natural world in his head. A beautiful world far better than this was shown to people. In addition to the truth of the natural world, one more hidden truth was deceived by the desire to communicate to this world using the power of his skill. The coming summer would provide the chance to realize his desire under the protection of Okawa.

However, Aono did not know what would be the best subject for this painting. The strange beauty in the customs and manners that appear here, the building, and the vision of a woman could not find an equal in this world. However, if compelled to find an equal from this domain that once flourished on the Earth or from gods, demons, or humans who live in the domain, this was the legendary world of ancient India Aono always admired.

The closest in this world were the long-ago country of Magadha where Shakyamuni Buddha turned over the teachings of Buddha to Jetavana Monastery and the country of the enchantress Matangi who became immortal in the scripture based on the sin of falling into the darkness of prostitution with the disciple Ananda.

Several years ago, Aono returned from Europe after visiting the remains of these legendary places. Still, each time he imagined the colors of the earth and sky, the ruins, the forests, the non-Buddhist shrines, and the circumstances in the towns, he sensed the realm of Magadha where Matangi lives. At least she and the world she inhabits were the flowers that bloomed and the fruit borne in his head.

Mysteriously, he always suspected this woman was Matangi when he considered Eiko's eyes burning with the light of evil thoughts and brutality. For that reason, Aono called the subject of the painting he would paint using her as the model, *Matangi's Boudoir.* Of course, the elements of the composition were products of the imagination woven through his dreams and not based on the customs or manners, and legends of ancient India.

Aono did not discover the disharmony and contradictions in this theme. To Aono, the name Matangi and Eiko's body were not in the legends and not in true human form but were the name of a goddess and the flesh enshrined in the altar of his innermost thoughts.

This time, however, Aono will create serious works. Will Eiko somehow understand this? She only knew Aono as a weakling with no self-control and a lack of moral sensibilities that surpassed her own. She only thought it acceptable to treat him as an inferior. This time, by crying to his benefactor, Okawa, who, fortunately, could be led around by his nose and would give him free money for his request for a model because he seemed to have a little money.

While scowling, spewing curse words, and sometimes whimpering like a dog whose paw was stepped on, he will slowly catch her in a net. In the end, he will see her crushed like a slave kissing the toes of the queen. These thoughts, half in jest and for mercenary reasons, were more intrusive than when she came to work in his studio.

He well knew her heart of hearts. From the beginning, he knew there was no technique to overcome seduction by the new goddess Matangi.

Aono reviewed the noble artistic desires and the bizarre sexual impulses in his heart. If he must throw out one of these two, and if the only person who lives in art truly gains eternal life, naturally, anyone would toss out the latter and want to do the former.

Aono, in particular, was only a weak-willed man compared to many people, a man afflicted with corruption who is hurt and useless despite living in this world, and troubled by the whip of a shameless, miserable sex drive. He desired to become more determined and enthusiastic but as this desire approached realization, the two goals eventually clashed. The result could only be doubling or tripling his agony and pain.

"Did I call you to model for me? Please behave and be patient. I feel like I'm going to have an attack of cerebral anemia and will faint. Beginning tomorrow, I'll no longer be able to paint," said Aono, placing his hands together to beg. To the end, Eiko understood his peculiar fetishes and psychological actions. She realized when he said that, she trapped him.

She said, "You stupid, stupid, stupid fool! How dare you say that? The nerve! Aren't you my slave? It'd be best if you do as you're told."

Like a naughty child, she called him awful names. Then a dazzling seductive smile swept over her malicious eyes and lips. Oppressed by her air of triumph, Aono lapsed into near ecstasy like his wish had come true.

"Are you trying to be bold? You sissy! You punk! I will seduce you to the ends of the Earth. I couldn't care less if you stopped painting. And if you want me to be patient with you, if you want me to put up with you, give me money!"

After this, Aono gave her an envelope containing two, three, or five yen every day. If in the middle of work, she became disagreeable, got off the model's platform, and couldn't make him give her sake or money, progress would not be smooth.

"You stupid, stupid fool!"

Occasionally, her sneering voice stuck in Aono's ears. He thought nothing was stupider than he.

Why don't I have self-control? Why can't I drop my devotion to art? How funny would it be for an ignorant and lowly young woman like Eiko with nothing more on her mind than the payment of money or carnal desire to receive this level of contempt? Will I forget my essential art? How should I think about sublime, magnificent art? Is it sublime? Is it magnificent? Do you think about exchanging something that good for a temporary despicable desire? He turned these thoughts over and over in his mind. His reflection ended up being fruitless.

At the same time he yearned for the Eiko of his dreams and praised her, he couldn't help rejecting and hating the actual woman and himself. Why are people subjected to these torments and must live with contradictions?

Since they are born into this imperfect world, humans are destined to be incomplete. Of course, I'm the most imperfect fellow of them all. If a person could ideally carry out his will, he would not be born to humanity in the first place. He eventually had these thoughts. He strove to reveal himself to be a man who has resigned himself to an unavoidable fate and, at least, had a reason for living in the midst of suffering. Summer deepened to the extreme heat of the middle of August.

The four walls of the studio enclosed by the flimsy boards of the painted Nanking shutters were illuminated by an earthenware hearth. In the middle, Aono struggled with frequent bouts of dizziness. Days were dedicated to art and nights to evil, an exchange between spirit and flesh.

After Eiko got drunk every night and went home by the final train to the outskirts of town, her leaden limbs carried her inside the mosquito netting like a corpse. At the base of his head numbed like a cavity with no ability nor determination to think about anything, his thoughts stagnated only at inexcusable remorse and animosity towards Eiko.

The next afternoon, however, the woman who invaded his studio again in high spirits washed away the maliciousness and wickedness of the night and had the vibrant freshness of newly caught fish. Aono's head numbed by this sight and throbbing with pain reminded him of his aching joints. His eyes shifted to the bookcase. He worried they would darken and no longer see.

Four

One morning around ten while Aono was sleeping late in the futon, someone was whispering at the door of his studio where visitors were rare. It was a little too early for Eiko. Who could that be? Has someone come to collect the rent? Aono pretended to be sleeping as he assessed the situation.

"Aono-kun, are you asleep? It's me. Okawa."

Did Aono hear his voice? As he ripped the cover off his head, he heard Okawa's voice still calling to him a few more times. What's Okawa doing here at this time? What business brought this man who had never visited him once? I've visited him, but he should have no reason to come here. Maybe Okawa came to see his painting? He knew this house had no rooms other than the studio. Why is he here? Did he come to get insight into my creative designs?

"Aono-kun, please wake up. It's me. Okawa. I have a little favor to ask you."

Aono jumped out of bed like he was irritated. His lumbering footsteps on the floor boards approached the door. He inserted a key in the keyhole.

"I was asleep, and the door's locked. Wait a minute while I open it."

Okawa, standing in front of the door, moved his mouth closer.

"Don't bother. I can talk from here," he said. "... This house is only the studio. If I go through this door, wouldn't I see your work?"

His mood wasn't his usual rebellious irritation as when he lent money to Aono. His considerate tone exposed his meek and timid nature like he feared being misunderstood. Aono could be ashamed of his benefactor's absurd doubts.

"It's all right. Come in. There's no reason to stand here talking," said Aono with a touch of pity. At last, his rival seemed ashamed and whispered.

"But before I come in, I have one request. There won't be any objections if I glimpsed your painting? I have no particular business here, but today, I came to see if you would show me your painting...."

Aono was shocked. At the same time, Okawa's kindly tone now sounded sinister. Outside the door, his rival's eyes brightened with excitement, and his breaths shortened.

Aono stopped to think. When we became artistic rivals, he made a clear declaration to me at the time, but the stubborn, nervous man abandoned his integrity and came to say this. Isn't that the same as surrendering to the enemy? Is he that interested in my painting? Am I that threatening? I wasn't in the habit of stepping one foot into his studio, but because he constantly helped me with money, I often went whenever I had a request. If I refuse, will he go home?

Aono remembered he recently borrowed just fifty yen. Eiko cheated him out of more than half of the two hundred yen he borrowed. After four or five days passed, he had no way out. If Aono didn't humor Okawa, he didn't know how much of an enemy he made. If he willingly listened to his request and all went well, that would break the ice.

"It's fine if you see it. I'm not keen on people seeing my work either."

Aono assumed an unconcerned look when he opened the door.

A couple of poplar trees grew on both sides of the stone steps at the entrance. Hydrangea bloomed in their shadows.

Not even a hint of wind blew since the morning. The blazing sun brought concerns about the daytime summer heat. In the brightness beaming on the red earth torched by sharp rays of light, Okawa was smartly dressed in linen and wore white shoes. He carried a cane made of coffee tree wood propped on his shoulder and stood like he was leaning with both hands on the door. He looked pathetic and timid, like someone begging for help at the gate.

"That may be so. I never let anyone come into my studio...." he said and hesitated to cross the threshold. His white, genteel, oval face looked straight at Aono. A combination of heat and shame flushed his cheeks cherry-blossom pink. He didn't look thirty-one years old. Strangely, his demeanor as a rich boy made him adorable.

"Depending on the situation, I thought you might refuse. Although it would be better to not come and interfere with your work because I could see the painting when you finished, I happened to hear something troubling the other day. By chance, you and I are painting the same subject. We're using the same model ..."

"The same model? You're using Eiko?"

Aono felt like he was doused with cold water. Okawa, who was secretive about everything, would never leak his model's name and couldn't suppress the feeling of being tricked. What did she say to Okawa? Did he know she toyed with him many times and made a fool of him? The claim "for my painting" he used until now to borrow money had been exposed.

If she had a relationship with Okawa other than as a model ... no, even if there was no relationship, if the secret of his sexual desires were known and not just his money problems, he'd feel indebted to Okawa even for his relationships with women. Thinking about this embarrassed and angered him. He wanted to crawl into a hole.

Okawa mustered the courage to say, "I must explain to avoid misunderstandings."

His tone was calm. He leisurely took a silver cigarette case from his pocket. He lit a Three Castles cigarette cut at both ends and tossed the burning match on the ground. The immaculate white pants covering his long thin legs, still standing straight at the entryway, glowed in the sun and formed a sharp crease at the border between the two faces.

"I have no reason to use that woman to disturb your work and force a competition with you. The truth is, this time, I hired her before you. You went to Eiko's place to ask her two weeks after me."

"How do you know that? Eiko probably told you."

While speaking, Aono tried to hide his irrepressible anxiety. After not bathing for a few days, his dirty fingers scratched his hair full of dandruff.

"Probably so.... If I confess, when you asked Eiko, I told her to refuse. However, I was not satisfied with that and, in the end, persuaded her to get your consent. Although I say this, I don't intend to convince you to do me a favor but, at least, want you to understand I'm not ashamed.

"Or you may wonder why you weren't told. But you probably know I usually maintain absolute secrecy about the model who will be the subject of my paintings. This time, I had no reason to hide the model because she is Eiko."

"That may be so. I am quite aware of this point. I didn't know you recommended me to her. I must thank you," said Aono. He dropped his head in a bow with a displeased, unhappy look on his face. His gratitude was genuine, but he knew his words were sarcastic.

"This misunderstanding may happen again. Don't I have a relationship with that woman?"

Okawa interrupted him to show his reaction to his companion's expression. But Aono's head stayed down. He didn't react or speak.

"Even if you're a little suspicious of me, I must be excused."

"No, there's no need for that."

This time, Aono blushed and raised his head.

"If you happened to have a relationship with that woman, you don't have the right to criticize me about this," he said with no hostility.

Of course, no relationship was much better. But if one existed, he would not be particularly jealous. He, who never savored the meaning of true love, never experienced the jealousy that springs from love. His anger was only his concern of Okawa not grasping the important secret of his own moral bankruptcy or being warped in his sexual desires and the secret of horrible rumors and, more than this, a shameful and infuriating secret.

"But whether you're suspicious or not is a serious problem to me," said Okawa, changing his tone slightly. "When I lent you money this time, I declared we would be artistic rivals. I will persist in being jealous of your talent. I probably prayed your work would fail in the end. You must understand that the meaning of those words at that time had to be artistic jealousy and did not emerge from some foul motive.

"If I have a relationship with Eiko and that makes me jealous of you, more than anything, I fear the groundless suspicion that expresses malevolent feelings under the pretext of art.

"Of course, I also recognized Eiko's beauty enough to ask her to model. When you and I first saw her dance, I recognized the mysterious beauty of her flesh at the same time as you. However, happy or unhappy, I don't care to love an ignorant woman like her.

"If I knew nothing about the past relationship between you and that woman, I might have become curious and saw her as a plaything, like now, and had a fling with her just once. In the end, what relationship would result? What would we experience? How much would we have to sacrifice? I've watched your previous examples and understand them well.

"You've probably guessed I'm not a bold enough man to have a relationship with that sort of notorious bad girl. While I simply use her greed and pay double or triple the ordinary modeling fee and flatter her, I am using her.... You certainly don't doubt me about this."

"I don't. There's nothing I can do about the doubts mentioned earlier."

While Aono spoke with his usual indecision, he smiled

for some unknown reason. Deep in his eyes, he seemed to be troubled by some other matter.

"I'm worried because I have no choice. I want you to believe in my innocence."

"I believe you.... But I didn't say I love her. Although I am hiding and remember speaking to you a little at one time, because I lean towards my innate masochism, I was troubled wondering whether she would mention that to you.

"I behaved stupidly with that woman. I acted bizarrely in that case. More than being called amoral, I was terrible. If you heard something from her, I would feel better if you didn't tell me. Please stop talking about Eiko."

Aono didn't intend to say this but felt like he was on a boat barreling into the open sea and spoke carelessly. He smiled a strange grin as his cheeks burned like they were on fire.

"All right, I'll stop."

Okawa's embarrassed eyes sparkled, but after a short time, he clumsily spoke in a comforting voice.

"Stop that talk and get back to your problem. You choose the same subject as me and are painting the goddess, Matangi."

"Yes. I know I am using the same model and the same subject as you. Nevertheless, I didn't change my initial plan. I decided just how far I'll compete with you. Until yesterday, Eiko came to my studio every morning then went around to your studio in the afternoon.

"Sometimes, however, she told me about your creative work that slowly intimidated me. This is the third time you and I happened on the same goal. When our works were displayed in the same place at last year's exhibition and two or three years earlier, I was consumed by jealousy and hostility toward you.

"Perhaps if I hadn't placed my work beside yours, or if we hadn't been students at the same school, I probably would have come to worship you. Plainly speaking, until now, I may have been incapable of being jealous of you. I don't know if worship is natural.

"Although until now, happily, your unpopular work has been ignored and only mine, celebrated. If this major piece is exhibited and is a success, how much will the world hate your banality and decide to stop ignoring it?

"In the rare chance, society loses interest and investigates your immorality, even if they vilify and persecute you, under these circumstances, my reputation will improve. So my jealousy and insecurity will not diminish.

"From the beginning, I intended to be fairly confident about my work this time. My enthusiasm would resist you.

"I don't know how often I thought it doesn't matter to me if you exert the strength only you have. But when I imagine the scene where my work using the same model and theme as you hangs near your work in an exhibition hall, I'm assaulted by obsessions. A great distance remains between you and me. Despite thinking I don't see it, I do see it."

Okawa breathed with difficulty. He removed his hat and wiped the sweat from his forehead.

Without knowing it, his eyes became bloodshot and his skin paled. Was it too much smoking and a distended stomach? Often during long conversations, he had a painful hacking cough like painful vomiting with his mouth hanging open like a yawning dog.

Okawa said, "I can't be called a virtuous man but am more particular than the average man about right and wrong in my behavior. Also, strangers see honesty and cowardice as kindness. Many think I'm a good man. To the world, I carry the moral influence opposite to yours.

"But even I wanted to be an artist more than a virtuous man. For example, even a man like you wants to create good art. I don't want to think my moral nerves are sensitive, but my artistic senses are dull. When I found out my art would be exhibited alongside yours in the same venue, if I have even the slightest artistic conscience, how could I blithely continue with my work?

"If a homely woman brazenly comes out before the beautiful woman, she wears heavy, thick make-up. If she boasts that I'm better looking than her, then that woman is, no doubt, an idiot and insensitive.

"My situation is identical. I'm called a rich boy among friends and said to be gullible. I strongly feel I would say that, too. Even in art, I don't want to be the gullible rich boy. For now, if I expose my inferior self to the public and make a show of competing with you, what will sensible people think in their gut? As an artist, I don't think I'm too much of a disgrace. We have a curious relationship.

"The public vaguely knows I befriended you and help you financially. That alone intensifies my humiliation. I don't want to be such a shameless person."

While listening, Aono was elevated to a high position in no time by his companion. Okawa's words of fearing, pitying, and believing him would strangle his listless soul and make it soar to a far-off sky. Truth overflowed in Okawa's confession and concealed his passion. Were these eloquent words encouragement? Were they fawning words of gratitude? Aono felt intoxicated.

"I'm grateful for that much of your recognition," said Aono with a distracted expression as if recalling a dream. What could he say to comfort Okawa? If he used obviously modest words, would Okawa get angry?

"This time, following your example, I'll do my best. I understand you deliberately came to me because of the question of how serious will you be about your creation now.

"If that's so, do you know whether your paintings are inferior to what is expected? You shifted my mental breakdown these days. I'm immersed in too much work and a little excited. So I worry."

"That may be so. But anyone in my position would probably become excited and suffer a mental breakdown.

"As long as you haven't shown me your paintings, I've become unable to work. I have a favor to ask. Please let me see your paintings."

Okawa spoke in an intense, frantic tone like a man short of breath and asking for a cup of water on the brink of passing out.

"I know you're ashamed to ask this while you proclaim we are rivals. However, compared to humiliation before the public, I can brave this. In front of people who have a talent surpassing one's own, it's not a bad thing despite bowing your head like a man....

"If I say this, you, in contrast, will decide to become better. When I think this, my jealousy worsens and I'm determined not to weaken. I will endure the intolerable aspects so I came to make this request.

"All in all, you and I differ in ordinary characteristics like black and white. Nevertheless, our art tends to be similar. Why do our paintings always collide or coincide? Both of us believe we cannot coexist. As a result, the one of lesser talent must perish. Victory will shine on the man of genius. I fear a speck of me won't exist."

When Okawa said this, an invisible dark shadow passed before the two. As though they agreed, both stopped talking and looked at the other's icy expression.

"All right, given all that you've said, I have no objection to showing you."

After a few moments, Aono said in a gloomy tone, "Excuse me for saying, but what will you do after seeing my work?"

"Compare it to mine. But if my painting doesn't reach your level, I think I'll withdraw my painting from the exhibition."

"If you don't withdraw even after seeing my painting, it will be an acknowledgment of extraordinary confidence in your work," said Aono as he pursed his lips in a malicious twist.

"You laughed at my cowardice, and I saw your success and declared my rivalry with you. I pray for understanding that my painting will not be an embarrassment compared to yours as well as for confidence.

"But I feel like I understand the general result before looking. Is self-confidence awakened after being shown another's work? If I had true self-confidence at the outset, I would never come here."

"If you must abandon exhibiting your painting, what will you do? Wait, will you abandon your perpetual competition with me?"

"Of course. Being shown your painting will inspire me. I'll say, 'This is stupid,' and you'll slap my head. If this year's painting is bad, then I'll be sure to fix the painting by next year. I will compete with you to the very end."

"Please wait. We can talk after you see the painting. Depending on the design, until you complete your painting next year, I will not exhibit my work ..."

"What?!" said Okawa.

During his moment of surprise, Aono wondered what he was thinking and immediately felt weird. His faint sleazebag smile floated up as when he pestered for money.

"No, I'm not saying that out of friendship for you. Because I'm not a man with friends, rather than think that, the circumstances are not right. The truth is, as usual, I've already run out of money. So you won't exhibit your work until next year ..."

Okawa became distressed as he watched Aono's face mumbling these words and a cunning expression surface. Okawa didn't feel his temper unsteadily rising and was overwhelmed.

"Saying that is strange, but you can buy my painting. If you did then never exhibiting my paintings ever again would not be a problem. Why my paintings? You're the only one who praises me. No one who came to the exhibition venue will criticize me. Although you call it selling, there's not one buyer. Unlike other people, I don't feel grateful for my reputation when my works are displayed in exhibitions. I'm much more thankful for money."

Okawa flatly said, "If it's money you want, I can give it to you. Money and paintings are different problems."

"Instead of borrowing money from me, you will postpone exhibiting your work until next year. If you do that, I'll be unhappy. You must exhibit your work this year."

"I guess that's how it has to be. But you'll really give me money? What do you need? Even one hundred or fifty yen would help for a little longer."

In his gut, Aono felt that went well. Other things can be done to borrow money. If he wants to look at my painting, go right ahead, look as long as you wish.... Now, I'll make Eiko my companion and dream a funny dream.

"You stupid, stupid, stupid fool. Aren't you my slave?"

He imagined her mocking face baring teeth as she spoke. She was gorgeous like the hydrangea blooming at the entryway.

Five

Bang! Bang! Okawa came to live like a beast in a cage near the rosewood desk in a corner of the eight-tatami studio. Arms folded, head hanging down, his eyes stared two or three feet in front of his feet. Now, a dangerous light, a crazed light, filled his eyes.

After leaving Aono's house in Mejiro this morning, he had no idea which roads he travel or when he arrived at Tabata. Perhaps he was swept away by a storm and sent flying from Mejiro to here in one leap.

He lacked the courage to enter his study and face his painting. Alone in his head, the painting *Matangi's Boudoir* Aono showed to him earlier hung like a rainbow in a vast sky filled with splendid colors, a rainbow beyond his power. When he stared at the rainbow, brilliant light rays like sunlight stole his vision and his courage, and, eventually, stole his soul. He felt faint, awash in disappointment, and fell into a deep, dark valley of melancholy.

"Aono-kun, you are a genius. A formidable genius. My competition with you is the height of absurdity," he said and prostrated himself before his rival. He often recalled the shock of that moment, the hopelessness, and distinct words sounding like delirious babbling.

If the gods showed their two figures in shadow, how the gods would laugh at, have mercy on, and pity him. No, gods are the allies of genius. They wouldn't give him a second thought.

If the gods abandon me as an artist, I no longer need to live in this world.

Unlike Aono, I inherited a fortune from my parents, have social status, and a fine reputation. If I want to throw art away and travel the world, I will pass through with ease.

But what is the value, what is the meaning of living that kind of life?

I may be an ordinary man but cannot become that mediocre.

I know there's no path to live forever outside of art. If I can't live forever, ... if I can't ... it would be best for me to die.

Okawa stopped as if he came to the edge of a cliff. The room shut tight around two in the afternoon was so stuffy, breathing was a chore. What would the world think if I were strangled to death in this room?

Okawa took his right hand out of his pocket, lightly pressed an artery in his throat, and staggered out.

So if I decide there's no hope in art, I'd rather die … in that studio. Should I write a will to shred my paintings and endorse Aono's genius to the public, then die in this room by strangling myself or gulping down poison? If I do, my name will spread for one thousand years in connection with Aono.

I have too much attachment to art and a yearning for genius. Only my heroic will and vigor will remain in this world. I don't know whether the futile competition with Aono and becoming a laughingstock in the world will be satisfying. In that case, suicide is the best option.

But if I died, would I die over my agony related to art? If I could commit suicide over one painting, would I be insane? ... There's nothing wrong with being mad. It's reasonable for me to be driven mad when the madness was caused by agony. I would be grateful to go insane. In the end, this would prove the sensitivity of my artistic conscience was a consequence of insanity. Just like a soldier dies honorably in battle, I will go insane honorably. If I'm this serious, I will die. I can die. I will definitely die. I'm already insane!

But to die in peace, I must think about it once again.

Other than killing myself, is there no other way? Have I truly been abandoned by the gods? No matter how much discipline I muster, no matter how many years pass, will I never possess Aono's genius?

To this day, I still have regrets about my talent. I don't believe I have absolutely no talent. My suffering now may be proof of my genius. Losing hope here and throwing away my life, or gathering courage and breaking through hardship may be the turning point between genius and ordinary.

I don't know if I will be tested by the gods without being abandoned. If that's the case, it would be awful if I thoughtlessly kill myself. It would be a colossal failure. Well, it's probably best to keep on living.

The more I think, the less I understand. Although I'll live if I can, I can't live like this. I must discover the way out of only living in life. Depending on whether I discover this escape will determine if I can become a genius.... It'll be no good without courage. I won't be rash and seriously reconsider life. From the beginning, I lacked courage.

Aono caused my loss of courage and plunged me this far into this abyss of despair. No, the causes are my fear and jealousy of Aono rather than him. For example, Aono and I aimed for the same art. If the times or our inclinations are different, I did not easily take these blows. That fellow and I always trace the same path in art, like two men from one soul. I also paint the themes he paints. In an instant, his eyes are attracted to the model I sought out.

When the completed paintings are compared, I lose decisively to him. I feel I could be called Aono's shadow. If two artists express the same beauty, one does not need to survive.

From the moment I realized this, I was warped by jealousy. Aono hardly noticed. The more I saw him calmly continue to work, the more I felt threatened by him and envied him. I obsessed for a long time. If he is gold, then I am silver. He is a genius, and I am ordinary.

Of course, he is a genius, but I will not play his enemy. But some people are precocious, and others are late bloomers.

Although I turned thirty-one this year, I don't have the talent of a genius. Who can declare this? Shouldn't you know after reviewing a life of hard work whether you're a genius or not?

My inferiority to Aono is not inferiority in talent but slower maturity. The proof is my advance in the same direction as Aono. If I hone my talent, I may become gold. If so, why does my confidence sink? Why is my courage lost? Why am I intimidated by Aono?

If I could be said to have the talent of a genius, could I eliminate my uneasiness with Aono? Perhaps not. But I probably could curse him.

While he continues to run the course with the same artistic inclinations as mine, no matter how time passes, I will feel threatened by him. As I advance a foot down this path, he covers three or four feet. His conceit is he discovers that path and walks ahead. Again I feel like I go by only clinging to the tracks he leaves behind.

My hostility toward him is not simply jealousy. Uneasy self-awareness comes when an artist identical to oneself lives in this world. He inhabits this world of imagination I inhabit. He also creates the works I will create.

When I look at his painting, I discover the birthplace of impatience my soul will reach in time. In the end, the threat I feel is identical to the menace felt by Poe's William Wilson tormented by his doppelganger. Who in my position would not be harmed? Who could be untroubled?

The source of all of this is found in my loss of courage and the sluggish growth of my ability. If Aono did not exist, my talent would shine. I may have already become fine gold.

As far as Aono is concerned, I would be said to be like Aono. But I would say, Aono is like me. At least, I'm said to resemble Aono and have no reason to change the direction of the path I've traveled so far.

I contend my art comes from an unstoppable desire in my heart. I firmly believe it's not fake art and is not easily changed. Otherwise, I was not qualified to compete with Aono from the beginning. Weren't there objects demonstrating talent and others that were crap?

However, if I stress the individuality of my art, Aono would probably make the same declaration. If I'm unable to change, Aono probably can't. Then the opportunity to eliminate the anxiety and stress I feel will never come. Naturally, my disappointment will cause me to lose hope and feel threatened. Nevertheless, if I must live, what should I do? Where is the path to save me from a fatal destiny? I exist, and Aono exists.

Where is the road to compromise? If I concluded there is no road no matter how much I thought about it, do I have to die? Will Aono's genius eventually defeat me? Laugh or cry, was I abandoned by the gods?

There is absolutely no road to compromise! It's wrong if Aono must be in this world when I will live, mature, and stretch into the realm of the genius. As long as he exists, my prospects are dark.

Somehow, I must kill myself. But if I commit suicide, there's no reason for Aono to live.

"Yes, that's it. I have no choice but to kill Aono," Okawa feebly said without thinking.

He rushed over to the bookcase to look at his face in a

small mirror leaning there, interested in seeing what is a man's expression when thoughts like this arise. Only two situations existed. Will Aono die? Will I die?

If I die, Aono's art will evolve. If Aono dies, my art will be saved. Although immoral, is killing Aono more immoral than killing my art? I want to be faithful to myself before being faithful to others. If my art is saved, I can live forever. If the will that lives eternally in qualities held by humans is most sacred, what sacrifices should be endured to penetrate this will?

I have courage and the feeling of only enduring that and, for the first time, will become a genius. If so, even the gods will not abandon me. Although people may not understand my crime based on an earnest and solemn motive, the gods will approve.

Did anyone in the distant past kill with my solemn motive? Has anyone been as faithful to his art? I have the impressive qualifications of a genius with only that motive.

That's it. Without the qualifications of a genius, how could someone kill for art? I had this thought because I am a genius. I reserve the right granted by genius to kill Aono! I can kill gold based on silver killing gold.

If Aono no longer exists, the god of beauty who loved Aono will love me. Yes, that's it. This is my escape. I passed the exam given by the gods. Not following the exam at all is identical to abandoning the right of the genius. Where is the need to hesitate? Doesn't flesh kill flesh, and spirit kill spirit?

It's not a battle against greed in this world but a battle with eternity! Very good! I understand!

Okawa jumped for joy in the silent room. The happiness of a child when rewarded by its mother sent a shudder through his body.

"I'm saved. I won," he shouted again and again to himself.

If done well, no one will suspect me. I pass through this world as a timid man rich in sincere, deep friendships. Today, in addition to being Aono's patron, haven't I witnessed his many troubles?

My friends know this. The appearance of a generous god is confirmed. The world's ordinary people do not believe my art is inferior to Aono's. Nobody knows even in dreams that I'm jealous of Aono.

News is exchanged between the two of us only through Eiko. Does that woman understand the conflicts in art? If I'm in a relationship with her, I suspect the result may be jealousy borne from love. Although it would make me happy, I did not touch her. Despite her making me a thing and seducing me, I was not trapped.

I mediated for Aono and asked her to model.

I won't have the flaws of my crime being sniffed out by anyone for any reason. All these favorable circumstances are proof of heaven's blessings on me.

If skillfully and secretly implemented so as not to be seen by anyone and not leave any traces, I will live a safe life.

Today, Aono lives alone in an isolated house on the outskirts of town.

He's made no friends other than me. The only person who goes in and out of his house is Eiko. Every afternoon, she goes to his studio and returns home during the evening or late at night by midnight. So I'll have ample opportunity from midnight until daybreak. During that time, I can act.

Okawa stayed calm despite these thoughts. His mind was as composed as possible and as perceptive as a scholar's brain.

With patience, I must establish a meticulous plan that

doesn't leave behind the tiniest shred of evidence, such as a strand of hair.

"Stay calm. Always stay calm."

While repeating this in his heart, he smiled broadly to display calm behavior to others. If he smiled, he felt he became an admirable man. Then he carefully went over to the ashtray, held the ashes at the tip of the cigarette for five minutes, and then let them drop.

Although insignificant, an extreme calm swept over him. He lay face up with one hand under his head to sleep and stared at the ceiling.

"Strictly speaking, every action of a person always leaves a trace in the world."

However, detectives like Sherlock Holmes or C. Auguste Dupin exist. If a rigorous investigation is conducted on whether I smoke or don't smoke, would they be fooled by something like that?

First, I'll wipe out the ashes from the ashtray with something. How would I get rid of the dust cloth or paper scrap used? If I burn the rag or paper to make it disappear, that will create ashes. I'll open the hibachi and mix in these ashes. The large ashes should stick. Next, where should I toss out the cigarette butt? If I throw it out this window, it would be immediately picked up.

I smoke Three Castles, I would easily be found out. I could slip the butt and the burned match in my sleeve, walk far away, and throw them out in a grassy spot on Ueno mountain or the paving stones on Ginza Boulevard. No, it's better to burn a bunch of rags.

No traces remain in this room today of my smoking Three Castles. If my other actions are carried out in absolute secrecy, which famous detective would find it difficult to get me to confess the truth?

I shouldn't be surprised if someone says, "You have the

habit of smoking, so while cooped up in this room for several hours, you can't say you didn't smoke one cigarette during that time. You're certainly a smoker."

I'll explain it away.

"As you've said, I smoke, but lately, I've been smoking too much and my thinking dulled so I had to cut back. Because I would say I didn't smoke one cigarette, there would be no mystery."

How would that work?

He could say, "However, you smoked."

"I said I don't smoke, but what are you saying?"

If I'm determined in my resistance, they'll probably get worried and be at a loss for words.

In his novels, Conan Doyle gives three qualifications for detective work. The first is observation. The second is knowledge. And the third is deduction. If sufficient power in these three is reached, the origin of the crime can be uncovered. Is there a margin to apply observation, knowledge, and deduction somewhere for this smoking incident I imagined? Even if provided with such fine abilities, are they ineffective if no traces remain of the behavior that's the target?

Strictly speaking, it can't be said absolutely no traces remain in the case of cigarettes. But for now, I'll get up and stand before a different shelf. I'll see a face reflected in the mirror propped up there. Then as before, I'll sleep again.

Detectives will invade this place to search for what I've done. In this case, will the detective see through what I saw in the mirror? Perhaps unless he's a god, he wouldn't perceive that. In the two states of being asleep from the beginning and waking up for a time to look in the mirror, what difference is impossible?

My behavior in front of a different shelf and copies of my previous position leaves no traces. Of course, because only my face is reflected and should not be touched by my hand, evidence should not remain in the mirror.

Only god knows my behavior. God even sees the thoughts churning in my head. To him, I should not conceal anything. A unique fearsome god of suffering may become my ally.

How will god love my genius and approve of my committing murder? If god is excluded, I can fool ordinary people in this world. I can execute the job with the skill that will make it unseen by others.

In short, killing a person is a single act, like smoking or looking in a mirror. The last two acts can be done without leaving traces, it's unreasonable to be able to kill a person in this way.

If this fails, it will be the result of my inattentiveness, so I won't get excited. To the end, I'll be cool and collected. My brain must have keen perception.

"What would be the best plan? Finally, I will be disciplined and work out a plan."

Okawa slowly stood and resumed plodding back and forth in the room.

Six

Half past midnight on September 3, according to the calendar, should have been a moonless night. A black seal stamped a page of the calendar hanging on the wall of Okawa's heart at that time on that day. Every day, he fixated on the stamp and waited to peel off each page. He didn't wait in vain with arms folded. When seven pages covered the stamp, exactly a week before the day the incident should happen, based on the existing plan, he moved to his preparations.

The paintings he intended to show at the exhibition

were nearly finished, so Eiko no longer had to come after September began.

Nevertheless, he always shut himself up in the studio in the afternoon. While his fevered eyes concentrated on the canvas, Matangi's figure vanished in an instant from the canvas and only the black calendar seal spread out. He fervently moved the brush.

Of course, he had no lingering attachment to that picture. He was not confident enough to believe the result would improve slightly if he played around with it a little more. Instead, he wanted to rip it to shreds. However, if he didn't exhibit this work with his usual confidence, the world would be suspicious. He calmly thought this through and appeared to be hard at work. This was the first stage of his preparations.

Secondly, he always went out alone for a walk after dinner. He wandered home between ten and ten thirty and again shut himself up in the studio and didn't go to bed until after two in the morning.

His home was divided into two wings, the main wing and the studio. The main wing was a one-story building where tea was made and where his parents and younger sister lived. Other than his three appearances each day for meals, the bachelor Okawa usually spent his days in the spacious studio. For that reason, a study, a bedroom, and a student's room were added beside the studio.

After returning from his nightly walk, he immediately went to the studio after a brief visit with his parents in the main wing. Sometimes, he didn't visit but left the gifts he purchased. At breakfast the next day, he'd take out the gifts and innocently say things like, "I bought these last night when I went to Ginza. I returned home around eleven, but you were already in bed. The people in this house are early to bed."

Okawa was scrupulous about these things and acted so it didn't seem staged.

A student lived alone in the student's room in the studio. From six in the evening, he attended night school in Kanda to learn French and returned home at ten. The student forced himself to stay awake until Okawa returned from his walk. Okawa usually returned home later, passed through the studio to have the student make a cup of tea, then immediately sent him to bed.

Based on Okawa's experiments, the student never woke up until the next morning or at least until two or three while Okawa was awake.

So after eleven at night, Okawa was doing something in the studio that no one in the household knew anything about.

The student might have thought, Every night, Sensei is studying. To encourage that conclusion, when the student came to make him tea, he always had books opened and spread around.

The thick volume called *Chinese Porcelain*, which is not a frivolous book, was wide open on the desk. Piled high was the complete set of books about Chinese porcelain called *Ceramique de L'Asie centrale*. He looked to be absorbed in research on antique arts and crafts of Asia. Once in a while he bought a celadon porcelain vase or a seven treasures incense burner at a secondhand shop and set them beside the ornate books.

The thought in Okawa's gut was, I can't believe seven days from now I will kill a man. I must carry on naturally as on any normal day.

He believed he could tell the student he stayed up late each night to study porcelain.

"I suddenly stopped but began the hobby of pottery around this time. My hobbies have no limits," he said to himself. He considered discussing his porcelain hobby with the student a few times. But he rarely spoke to the student because he was unremarkable and of no use. Okawa felt these discussions would be too unnatural.

For seven days, he worked hard to methodically repeated the three actions of creating in the morning, taking an evening walk, and then staying up late each night to do research.

His typical work time was in the morning. In the evening, his habit was to go out for a walk. He should not have started the late-night reading and the porcelain hobby now. As a man with a deep love for his family, buying gifts for his mother and sister was not extraordinary. This also seemed natural. And he continued to have objects he ordered delivered.

"Everything is fine. Nobody fixes their eyes on me. Nobody who lives here watches me. The people living in the house believe I'm in the studio alone until late at night every night. Making them think that was essential," he muttered to himself and celebrated his thorough preparation.

On the off chance, after he returned from his walk, let the student go to bed, and snuck out of the studio, someone realized he disappeared somewhere for two or three hours. Even if this weren't so, the members of Okawa's family aren't the sort of people whose hands would touch the door to his studio without permission. Although they come to this part of the house as little as possible during the day, after midnight, someone may peek into the studio. Okawa prepared for that time on that day to be an absolute secret.

As the number of days decreased by one for seven days, Okawa was confident of success and felt a lightness of body and spirit. His feelings night after night when he swung the coffee-wood cane and went out a walk were not those of a person with a diabolical plan near at hand.

On the night of the first day, he aimlessly wandered Ginza Boulevard while drinking fresh plain soda from Shiseido. As it did every night, the flavor stabbed his wet tongue and seemed to penetrate his cold, refreshed chest. Then he went to Cafe Giana and bought a cream puff for his sister. On the second night, he went to Asakusa, watched an operetta and a moving picture, and ate Western food at Chinya Bar.

How could he make this decision with ease? How did the serious incident of taking another's life change him into a person with a slightly different life? Were his nerves always insensitive to crime? Is the truth I'm much better than Aono at wicked deeds? Okawa was an enigma.

Until now, I've been the most gentlemanly among my self-destructive, depraved artist colleagues and should be a good man. Nevertheless, the thought of killing a man pops into my mind, and I act with calculated coldness. Is madness driving me? I don't seem the least bit excited, but in fact, is overexcitement making me lose all reason?

Being this calm in this situation is not normal. How have I come to this? Perhaps, this sprouted from my genius qualities. In no time, I have become a formidable genius. I don't know whether my brain tissue has undergone a radical change. In that case, what a delightful event!

As Okawa mulled over this, he acted while remaining calm.

Have I become a genius? Have I gone crazy? There's no way other than moving forward to the destination.

On the third night, he went out to the edge of the lake from Dozaka-shita, crossed Kangetsu Bridge, and dropped in at Seiyouken for ice cream. Each time he ate something cold, his head cleared, and he felt refreshed and a strange joy. When he left Seiyouken that night, he window-shopped at the Hirokoji night shops. Dahlia pots hung as decorations.

On the fourth night, he hunted for secondhand shops along Hongo-dori Avenue from Komagome. It was still too early to go home, but he had nowhere to go. He got the idea of visiting his friend K in Morikawa-cho. It was probably important to appear to be behaving normally to others. As he walked a couple of blocks to K's house, he changed his mind.

"Not going may be best," he said quietly to himself.

"Don't I normally visit K at times like this? Wasn't it my custom to not meet with my friends as much as possible while I create my work for the exhibition every year? I'm at peace like nothing matters. My constant nature is not changing. But isn't deliberately going to see a friend proof of something? If I saw him, my unnaturalness dressed as naturalness would be exposed. An insightful detective could grab the tail of a thoughtful criminal who takes many precautions. Haven't I been discreet with my words even to the student in my home?"

This would be no good. Carelessness would lead to immediate mistakes and, eventually, people would sense the secrecy. I must be smarter, he thought. Okawa cautioned his heart.

In fact, he may have planted the seeds of suspicion so that no one would fixate on him. Okawa thought he couldn't be happier Eiko no longer came to the studio.

The fifth and sixth days ended without incident. At last, the seventh day, September 3 came. The weather was good that day and for the last week. The sky with the blazing sun was true blue like waters in the deep sea. The intense heat of late summer pounded the ground.

Okawa opened his morning eyes, opened the window

of the bedroom, and gazed enchanted at the flowers blooming in the back garden.

The zinnia and Chinese aster flowers that bloomed this summer tirelessly withered and crumpled like cigarette butts and faded to pale yellow. Beside the wilted flowers, fresh tampala and sunflowers were bright and beautiful, like they had bathed in water. Yellow flowers blossomed yesterday on five or six stems of Canna lilies and fell off. This morning, a sole deep red flower opened in the center. His eyes fixated on the crimson color. He thought, Like that flower, I will succeed in a splendid, beautiful, and innocent way. Creativity fills my mornings. I take walks in the afternoon—I choose Hibiya Park for today's walk.

Light from arc lights shined under the wisteria trellis at the edge of the water fountain. Like a moonlit night, the shadows of new leaves delicately rustled in the cool breeze. A stream of groups of citizens passed before him as he lazily relaxed on a bench and listened to their lively footsteps. Young couples quietly and happily cuddled. A group of geisha passed by dressed casually in seductive silk crepe *yukata* summer kimonos. Their footsteps, solemn and bewitching like night elves, made them appear and disappear in a thicket of planted trees. A middle-school student came singing *Lorelai* in a low nasal voice. A Westerner wearing a gold necklace was dressed in pure white clothes like a heron. Their figures were reflected and disappeared in Okawa's eyes like a revolving lantern.

Warm light overflowed from the balcony of the Matsumotoro building. The whole building was designed to sparkle like a gigantic beehive made of jewels.

Meanwhile, the beak of a bronze bird in the water fountain sprayed incessant rain aimed at the sphere of the arc lamp and formed a rainbow. The spray babbled constantly and choked on tears in quiet weeping.

Okawa rarely had the chance to visit this park. He found the scenery poetic and invited sweet and gentle sentimental feelings. He thought, Everything is beautiful. It's like a dream. The people move around like shadows in the firelight. The water echoes. Leaves rustle in the trees. The evening is like music.

He boarded the train at Hibiya around eight-thirty and got off in Jinbocho in Kanda. He thought about buying *The Short History of Chinese Art* by Hugo Munsterberg in a secondhand bookstore in Imagawakoji before it disappeared.

The proprietor and clerks in this store were familiar faces, and Okawa chatted with one about art books for fifteen minutes. He was well-informed and remembered discussions comparing the ideas of Fenollosa and his art historian colleagues on Eastern art. Later, he bought a couple of ribbons as gifts in a notions shop and returned to Tabata by ten-thirty.

The rain shutters of the main house were closed, and the household had retired to their beds.

"Hey, Michiko, are you asleep? I bought these lovely ribbons for you," he said while walking towards his sister still awake under the mosquito net, and placed the gifts at her pillow.

"Oh, those ribbons are so pretty. Thank you so much. When I go to Enoshima this Sunday, I'll wear this one. I'll wear Western clothes and tie my hair in a braid," said the smiling Michiko, rubbing her cheek against the pillow. The three ribbons glistened like toffee.

"Who's going to Enoshima with you?"

"Father and Mother are taking me. Will you ... are you coming with us?"

"Well, I have work to do for the exhibition and can't go.

If you go to Enoshima, you'll have to buy me a souvenir," he said, not wanting his mother to hear.

Their mother joined their conversation. Okawa implied that he had to study tonight in the studio until after two. To endure, he needed a lot of perseverance. After his mother said a few words, she ended with "Goodnight."

Okawa rushed back to his studio and let out a sigh. A couple of minutes later, sleepy as usual, the student carrying the tea tray opened the door. As he poured the tea into the teacup, he looked amazed at the illustrated book of art history opened on the desk. But within one or two minutes, he felt Okawa had been a little too quiet for too long. His silence was unusual.

"It looks like you found a good book...." the student said without thinking. He already finished pouring the tea and bowed to leave the studio. Okawa endured until then but could no longer take it.

"Yes," Okawa said, looking pretentious as always. A cheery smile appeared on his face. The student felt strangely happy.

"Sensei, what is this a photograph of?"

"The carvings of Buddha at the temples at Longmen Grottoes in Luoyang, China. They're from the sixth century, the end of the Northern Wei Dynasty. Interesting, isn't it?"

"Yessir. Very interesting. Sensei, are you researching ancient Asian art?"

"Yes, I research until two every morning."

"Oh," said the student, sounding discouraged. Like he suddenly remembered his drowsiness and was embarrassed for a short time. He gathered himself, said, "Goodnight," and quietly left the studio.

"I've done too much acting. I talked when not talking

would have been better. I research from around two every morning.

"Why did I deliberately dismiss the student? He's absent-minded and disorganized. If he were sensible, wouldn't he immediately suspect something?"

He thought, Until today, I took great pains through ingenuity to get this far with ease but blundered in the end. Even if that weren't so, my preparations are done. I'm worried this was a bad start.

Despite no fear of the crime being exposed by this, his smooth control lost a bit of its spring. However, he was not overcome by regret.

"But I can only take a brief break. From here on, I will pay attention to what's ahead. Without being particular about smoothness, I will be bold."

Okawa listened to his gut and rose heavily from the chair.

A half-hour after the student left the room it was exactly eleven-thirty.

He collected a costume secretly in the dead of night over the past few days. A toupee and a fake mustache were in a Chinese trunk in a corner. He got used to wearing everything a few years ago and only used them as parts of a costume for costume parties.

Not buying anything new was Okawa's idiosyncrasy. For example, if the toupee, fake mustache, and a strip of cloth were dropped at the scene of the crime, someone could ferret out the owner.

The suit was made from black twill wool. The texture and colors were ordinary and tailored in a conventional style. When Okawa returned home from America, he had the suit made to replace the tuxedo as his dining clothes on the ship. The name of the American tailor sewn into the back of the jacket was cut out. If clothes shops anywhere in Tokyo were asked about this suit, none should know its origin.

The toupee and the fake mustache were souvenirs from the player of a scientist in a comedy show put on a few years ago by amateur performers of school alumni. A friend borrowed them from an actor in a new theatrical troupe that has since failed. Their props had been borrowed and forgotten long ago. No one would know Okawa had them. He saw that wearing that toupee and mustache changed his appearance completely. His face transformed into that of a melancholy student. He ripped the lining with the brand name out of his hat, a brown fedora also bought in America.

A gentleman about thirty with neatly parted long hair and growing an unfamiliar thick but finely trimmed mustache briskly walked down the hill from the back gate of Okawa's residence. In the main house and in the student's room, everyone was enjoying a pleasant sleep. He repeatedly looked back at the window of his studio as he descended the hill. The light from electric lights glowed red behind the meat-colored curtain. He escaped his desk but, today, as usual, was up late at night studying Asian art.

He climbed Dozaka and went out to the crossroads on top of Hakusan. Customers enjoying the cool air of early evening approached the displays in front of the makeup shops and haberdasheries on both sides of the street to admire the lights.

The streets were still as busy as early evening. From inside the beer halls hanging out Gifu paper lanterns floated out raucous *nagauta* songs played on out-of-tune gramophones.

There, Okawa called a carriage to rush him to Iidamachi Station. When he crossed Suido-bashi Bridge and turned onto a lonely back street in the shadow of the embankment of the railway line to the outskirts of town, for the first time, his body and spirit were wrapped in the pitch-black darkness of night.

After leaving the carriage, he loitered in the area of a parking lot for a minute or two and then sped by taxi to the vicinity of Mejiro Station. So far, he followed his plan exactly.

After the taxi crossed a bridge over a railway on the outskirts of town, Okawa said, "Stop here," opened the door and energetically jumped out.

He was near fields skimmed by chilly autumnal winds. Insects buzzed in thickets of grass on the bank along the railway.

The lights of the parking lot shined dimly under the far-off bridge. Elsewhere blackness spread endlessly and even embraced the dark sea.

"Thank you. You can go," said Okawa and rushed off. His back was lit for thirty-five feet by the band of light inside the taxi then swallowed by the curtain of night.

He listened to the groggy-sounding echoes of the taxi slowly driving away. Not a single building was on either side of the road for seven or eight blocks.

On a moonless night, the sky, quiet like death, passed over, clear as it was earlier in the day. The stars twinkled in a plane.

It may have been Okawa's imagination, but innumerable stars clustered in the skies directly above Aono's studio in the shadows of trees along the way and seemed to glitter and shine.

Many stars gathered in this part of the sky. They appeared to shine brightly all at once. As smoke spread out from the chimney, the stars gathered densest above Aono's studio's roof and gradually dispersed thinly in all directions. Almost all of them dazzled while backlit by the studio.

"Look at that. Look at the sky above the studio. It's a marvel for a house where a genius lives," he whispered. Maybe he heard me, thought Okawa, a little frightened.

"You will cowardly kill that amazing genius. No one should know this secret, but the stars are watching.

"He blinked at the twinkling in the skies above the studio that played the role of the night guard. This proves the soul of the genius called Aono fell from the world of the stars and is not of the human world."

But what is that called, thought Okawa. If he's a genius, and I kill him, the stars in that big sky will twinkle above my studio, and the backlight will shine from my studio. I will be exposed. No, depending on the circumstances, tonight, countless stars will gather above my house at the edge of the fields and await my return.

He pulled himself together and swaggered down the forest road not like a thief but like a government official on his way to an inspection.

When he stepped a foot on the front stone steps of the studio, he pulled gloves from his pockets and put them on. As he removed his disguise toupee, the fake mustache, and lightly rapped on the front door, he called out several times, "Aono-kun, Aono-kun." His tone seemed to command latent energy.

Aono seemed to be in a deep sleep and did not respond. Okawa went around to the north-facing window and pressed his forehead against the glass to peer inside. The interior was as pitch black as it was outside. He grabbed onto the frame somehow fastened to the sliding paper shoji at the window and pushed it up. He twisted his body and forced his way into the room.

First, he groped for something around his waist and

loosened the flexible cloth band fastened around his waist outside of his suspenders.

His initial plan was to see his acquaintance Aono. After struggling with his painful inner feelings for a time, he would aim into space and wrap the band around Aono's neck. However, he could easily sneak in and deliberately call to him.

These thoughts flashed into Okawa's mind.

That's it. Secrecy is important. If something is hidden, hiding it from Aono who is going to die is safe. The most disagreeable element would be for Aono to know about my crime more than anyone else. Even if Aono dies, his soul will live and know about my evil act for eternity. That was even more unpleasant. But he was careless and slept with an unlocked door.

Thankfully, I could kill him in a breath while he slept peacefully. I'm a lucky guy. I will achieve my objective.

In an instant, his plans changed. He put the mustache and toupee on again. Even if Aono opened his eyes, every-thing would be fine.

After putting just these things on in the dark, he struck a match to light the room. He wondered if the small flame shimmered and brightened the ends of the toupee on his face. He put out the match immediately and lit another.

This time, the match burned until it burned itself out. However, this sliver of light only illuminated blackness found in a cave. With a third match, he slowly walked tracing a circle. Shigishima cigarette butts, wax remnants, rags, and paper scraps were strewn all over the dusty floor. The last few candle stubs were burned out. He picked up the longest one and moved the light. The corners of the room grew dim like a horrifying cave. The shadow of Okawa's long, narrow back as he stood there zigzagged on the four walls and the ceiling to become five or six gigantic pillars.

He nearly squealed in surprise when his nervous gaze fell on a woman's face drifting at the edge of the darkness. It was the figure of Matangi drawn on the canvas.

In an instant, Okawa wondered what was Eiko up to lying down and smiling. Under the quivering weak light of the candle, flare-ups of the soot made her features reflect bright red into the empty space. Vigorous blood coursed through her cheeks. The tips of her eyelashes of her cool eyes faintly trembled.

Okawa pledged in his heart, I will not see this painting again until I overtake Aono. Unexpectedly, a mysterious door in the inner hall opened before his eyes. A radiant yellow light stung his eyes.

"This painting is immortal art made by the hand of a true genius," said a voice from somewhere and struck Okawa's ear like thunder. He threw himself prostrate onto the floor. He found it difficult to stop the praise and wonder storming through his mind. This disturbance blocked and strained his eyes but did not blunt his determination. The more threatened he felt only served to strengthen his resolve.

Aono's bed was positioned along the wall opposite this painting. It was called a bed but was a futon flung over a raggedy old sofa. A Japanese light yellowish-green mosquito net hung over the bed. Candles stood on the desk beside the bed.

Okawa guessed he was breathing peacefully in his sleep. His left hand firmly held the band wrapped around his palm. He deliberately wound the mosquito net around the sleeping man from his head to his chest.

Aono stayed sound asleep. He lay sleeping face up. His mouth hung open, and his reddish neck rested on a pillow.

His breaths flowed peacefully from the dirty nostrils of his thin nose with long hairs at the same rhythm echoed quietly by the breaths of Okawa who stood beside him.

He lifted the mouth of the sleeved padded nightwear to expose the thin flesh of his thighs in his poor sleeping posture. He looked pathetic, almost like a corpse.

Okawa rested his hand. He started to wrap the band around Aono's neck.

Suddenly, Aono's lips wiggled loosely in a panic. His eyelids fluttered and moved like a flying moth.

In the next second, Okawa put all his strength into strangling Aono and roared like the howl of a fierce beast. A swift creature jumped up like an insane cat from the bed and unwound the band.

"It's you. You. Of course, you came to kill me! Okawa-kun!"

Okawa began to cry as he howled. Okawa didn't have the sense to quiet his mind to serenity.

It was simply controlling frenzied cold-bloodedness. Aono leaped from the bed and straddled his rival's body. He intended to violently shake off the band as he lifted his head like he was emptying a glass of wine. But as Aono shook and rose, he bit his rival on the left wrist and wouldn't let go.

The two fell off the bed and rolled around the floor, limbs entangled. Okawa's right hand happened to grab the long iron fire tongs beside the stovepipe.

Aono resisted with all his might until that point, then his throat shut several times, and he dangerously stopped breathing. It was no good. No one can help you anymore. Again and again, Okawa's spirit shouted, "I can kill!"

Aono tried with all his might to valiantly fight the arms and legs of his rival. A sudden blow from the side knocked him to the ground.

Thud!

He felt his head numbed by a heavy object like a huge rock. Again, thud! He was paralyzed. He could hear a deafening echo like the rumbling collapse of a mountain.

The floorboards under his face sunk to the depths like the bottom of a ship. His body seemed to be dropped headfirst like a weight was fastened to his neck. An unknown substance perhaps mud or lead flooded from his eyes, nose, or mouth to fill and clog his brain. His consciousness faded away.

Like a fly whacked by a fly swapper, or like a human turned into wastepaper, his corpse became frighteningly stiff and no longer moved.

IT WAS a little after two in the dead of night. In front of a police box at the corner of the Sugamo Mental Hospital, a lone gentleman with a neatly trimmed mustache, dressed in a black suit, wearing a brown fedora strolled in the direction of Shinmei-cho in Komagome. When a police officer called from behind to stop him, he docilely returned and presented a business card from his jacket's inside pocket.

The card read:

Matsumura Toshio, Professor of Education
Tokyo Imperial University

Without hesitation, he answered fluently, "I was playing a game of Go until late at the home of Dr. XX in Hara-cho, Koishikawa. I'm on my way home to Komagome."

"Oh, all right. Everything seems to be in order," said the officer, politely.

Okawa had no fear of being questioned by anyone and disappeared through the door of the Tabata Library. He had his business cards printed with a plausible name in preparation for this situation.

Seven

The calamity at Aono's home was discovered the next morning by Eiko. The room in shambles like a garbage dump had been overturned into chaos. Aono's body lay face up, knocked over like the smokestack, amid the overturned chairs, bed, and desk.

He was not a total corpse. Aono regained consciousness around dawn, lost all his memory, and was frighteningly lightheaded.

"What did you do? Try to kill yourself?"

While speaking, Eiko moved to his side and stroked his forehead. From below, Aono stared up with distrust and saw her frozen expression. From time to time, his lips trembled faintly, but he made no sounds.

THE DETECTIVE CONDUCTING the investigation scoured the scene for evidence, but no traces of a criminal remained. He found no clues that conclusively determined the method of entry from outside as the first proof. Of course, nothing seemed to have been stolen. Only the painting *Matangi's Boudoir* on its side had been bounced around, trampled underfoot, smeared with mud, and ripped to shreds.

From the beginning, no clues emerged from the knife that tore up the painting, the iron smokestack that smashed the victim's head, or objects in the studio handled by the villain.

Eiko became the suspect, was arrested, but was released within half a day.

Okawa was simply investigated as his guarantor. In the end, the criminal could not be discovered. The only option was to wait for Aono's mental faculties to recover.

The incident soon became the seed of rumors among his young artist friends. These were their explanations.

"He swindled people again and again and hurt most of his friends. Someone must have nursed a grudge and wanted revenge."

Others said, "It's awful. To gain sympathy from society, he faked suicide."

Another opinion was "Perhaps he became obsessed with Eiko and went mad."

Whichever it was, people thought this sort of thing was Aono's fate.

His dementia worsened as the days wore on. The doctor confirmed hope for a full recovery was lost. Okawa, his sole guarantor, had him admitted to the mental hospital in Sugamo. From time to time, he visited.

"Aono-kun, do you know who I am? It's me, Okawa. Have you forgotten the past? You used to be an elite artist. An extraordinary genius."

When he peeked into the madman's eyes, Okawa's always pale face had a smile that seemed to twitch. The following deeply meaningful enigma shined in the idiot's eyes from deep inside his eye sockets like the broken mechanism of a dark and dismal gadget.

"Yes, I'm a genius. Even now, my soul plays in a world of fine art. I simply cut the nerves that transmit the inner soul to the flesh on the outside. The connection between the flesh and the soul was severed. The people of the world call this person an idiot. Maybe, you know the joyous state of mind of a man called an idiot."

∾

THE FACT IS Aono's brain never died. After his soul lost the connection to this world, he rose higher and higher in the world of art he aspired to and saw a figure of eternal beauty.

His eyes could not reflect the colors of the human world but reflected the light of the truth that becomes the source of those colors.

In the time he lived in this world, the various visions that occasionally appeared in his head now became the reality of living in this world of beauty.

He thought, When my soul was still attached to the flesh, I often imagined this reality and dreamed.

He was sure he had returned to his hometown.

Even among these many assorted visions, the bewitching woman who often visited his mind—the figure of that beautiful Eiko—created dignity like the queen of a gorgeous country more perfect and more dignified than what appears in an imaginary world. Seated on a throne in a palace far more mysterious and beautiful than Matangi's boudoir, while she stroked the neck of Aono who was kneeling at her feet and kissing the hem of her white gown, she sweetly consoled him in the morning and evening.

"Surely, you frequently saw me until now. The woman called Eiko lost you when you lived in the floating world and Matangi who floated into your vision are my shadows.

"I praise the heart that longs for your beauty, from the realm of truth to the realm of the fleeting, my figure appeared as a phantom, the way the light of the moon in the heavens falls to a valley stream.

"Only the truth surpasses the shadows. Only in that, I surpass his women. You, who worship the transient vision of Eiko in your heart, may serve peaceably in my palace. Regret and agony covering this world of humans forever wiped out traces in this country."

The tears filled in the appreciation for something on the cheeks atrophied to sharp angles of the idiot Aono were silently connected like evening dew. Okawa's works exhibited in the fall exhibition were presented in newspapers and magazines as splendid masterpieces. In addition to the critiques of expert writers and art reporters, brash accounts of the hardships told by Okawa were published. The words *Matangi's Boudoir* were talked about by people like the title of a play. The highly favorable reviews not only puzzled society, but Okawa's conscience was also deceptively satisfied.

Someday, Okawa thought, the man Aono would not be that celebrated. If looked at now, his hatred of Aono was nothing more than overestimating him.

Clearly, his talent was not the least bit inferior to Aono's. If he hadn't stolen the artistic life of Aono, he might have never been able to drive away the obsessive thoughts. This means he succeeded in killing Aono.

Okawa thought, Of course, Aono's body is still alive.

But what became of the idiot's body? Without a doubt, he was killed.

I was formidable. Of course, I became a genius in his shadow.

With this thought, confidence and resolute bravery boiled up in Okawa's heart.

In the summer of the following year, *Matangi's Boudoir* he painted to be shown at the exhibition was superior to Aono's painting from last year, not inferior. Without a doubt, Okawa already surpassed Aono. The gods of art who loved Aono now bless and favor Okawa.

Silver became gold.

Eiko's reputation as the model created more clamor than the rumors about Okawa's painting. She returned to her life as an actress. When she appeared on an opera stage in the park, she was no longer a backup dancer.

Every young man in the capital attracted to her delicate figure like a rainbow or dazzling costume like a Chinese phoenix fought and rushed to this theater.

All the guests were duped by the charms of her flesh stuffed with garish appeal. No one pointed out her clumsy technique or awkward dance moves.

However, as she flew wildly about in the light of the footlights, she imitated the figure of the queen of an eternal country but was nothing more than an imperfect shadow. Aside from the idiot Aono, did anyone else know?

5. ALONG THE WAY

Around five one evening in the last few days of December, Yugawa Katsutaro, a lawyer at Tokyo TM Corporation, walked aimlessly to Shinbashi over Kanasugi Bridge along the streetcar tracks.

"Excuse me. Excuse me, but aren't you Yugawa-san?"

Someone called from behind when he was halfway across the bridge. Yugawa turned to see a stranger. A gentleman with a fine appearance approached and greeted him with a polite doff of his derby hat.

"Yes, I'm Yugawa ..."

Innately good-natured, Yugawa's small eyes blinked rapidly in dismay. He spoke timidly like he was talking to his company's director. The man's demeanor was dignified exactly like his company's director. He glanced at the man as he wondered who was this rude fellow calling me on the streets and pulled back. In spite of himself, he revealed his nature as a salaried worker.

The fortyish, plump, pale man wore a black overcoat made of wool tufted like the coat of a Spanish Mastiff with an otter-skin collar and striped pants, most likely, morning pants, beneath the coat. With every other step, he thrust forward a cane capped by an ivory knob.

"Please excuse my rudeness in calling to you in this sort of place. I received a letter of introduction from your friend and colleague in law, Watanabe, and just visited your company," said the gentleman and handed him two business cards.

Yugawa took them and examined them under the light of the lamppost. One was unmistakably the business card of his good friend Watanabe. On the front of the card, the following was written in Watanabe's hand.

This is Ando Ichiro. We've been friends for many years, as far back as grade school days back home. This gentleman wishes to investigate the background of a certain employee at your company. I'll leave it to your discretion. Thank you.

He looked at the other business card.

Ando Ichiro, Private Investigator
3-4, Kakigara-cho, Nihon-bashi-ku
Tel: Naniwa 5010

"So this says you're Ando-san."

Yugawa stood there and looked over the gentleman again. A private investigator is a rare occupation in Japan. He knew about, perhaps, five or six agencies in Tokyo, but this was his first time meeting a private eye.

Yugawa thought the Japanese private investigator looked more elegant than those in the West. He believed this because he liked moving pictures and had seen them in films.

"Yes, I'm Ando. As for the matter written on the business card, fortunately, you work in the human resources department of your company. If possible, I'd like to have a meeting with you at your company soon. I realize I'm imposing on your busy schedule, but would it be possible for you to find the time to see me?"

True to his occupation, the gentleman spoke crisply in a powerful, metallic voice, but the detective's words relaxed Yugawa.

He said, "Well, I have the time so that's not a problem … If I understand what you're asking, what can I do to satisfy your wishes? Is your business urgent? If you're not in a hurry, is tomorrow acceptable? But today is fine, too. This is an odd conversation for the middle of the street …"

The gentleman said, "I understand, and the employees will be off tomorrow. I have no reason to visit your home. Excuse the inconvenience, but we can talk while walking around this area. Don't you always take strolls for leisure? Ha, ha, ha."

His animated laugh was often used by men acting like politicians.

Yugawa looked troubled. His monthly salary and year-end bonus he just received from the company were tucked away in his pocket. The amount was not small. He was secretly happy that night.

They walked to Ginza. Along the way, Yugawa recalled a recent occasion. He bought gloves and a stole—a heavy fur one that complemented his wife's stylish face—after relentless pestering by her and rushed home to delight her.

Because he did not know this man Ando, his pleasant dream was ruptured, and a crack formed in his exceptional happiness that night. That was all right. He was alarmed by this Detective Ando who knew he enjoyed walks and tracked him from his company. He was unsettled by thoughts like, how did this man know what he looked like?

On top of that, he was hungry.

"How should we do this? I don't want to cause trouble for you, but do you have the time for a conversation? I'm asking to pry into the background of a certain person. Therefore, meeting you on the street is better than at the company."

"Let's go this way."

With no way out, Yugawa walked beside the gentleman to Shinbashi. The gentleman's stance was logical. Also, he worried about the problems a man carrying the business card of a private eye appearing at his home would cause.

Soon after their walk began, the gentleman, rather the private eye, took out a cigar from his pocket and smoked it but only smoked for the first block. Naturally, Yugawa got angry, feeling he was being mocked.

"What is the substance of your inquiry? Who is the employee you're checking on? If I know him, I could provide some answers—"

"Of course, I think you probably know him," said the gentleman then smoked a cigar for a few minutes in silence.

"Perhaps you are investigating his background because he's getting married."

"Yes, you've guessed right."

"I'm in the human resources department, and that's a common request. Who on earth is this man?" asked Yugawa, like his curiosity led to intense interest in him.

"'Who?' you ask. It's a little hard for me to say, but that man is you. I've been asked to investigate your background. I thought it better to bump into you to ask you directly rather than ask someone else, so I am here to ask you."

"But I … you may not know this, but I'm already married. Could there be a mistake?"

"No, there's no mistake. I know you have a wife.

However, you did not complete the procedure for a legal marriage. You should consider completing the process as soon as possible."

"Oh, I understand. It was my wife's family that asked you to look into my background."

"My professional duty prevents me from saying who made this request. You have a vague idea, so please overlook that point."

"All right, that's not important anyway. Ask me anything you wish to know about me. I feel better this way than the indirect investigation. I thank you for adopting this method."

"Ha, ha. Your gratitude pains me. I've always adopted this method to conduct background checks for marriages. When the subject has a suitable personality, a direct chance meeting is best because the problem of misunderstandings arises when the person is not asked."

"Yes, that's true," said Yugawa in happy agreement. His mood changed in an instant.

"Furthermore, I sympathize in no small way with your marriage problem," said the gentleman and glanced at Yugawa's smiling face and smiled, too.

"By enrolling your wife in your family's register, your wife and her family will reconcile one day sooner. If not, your wife will have to wait three or four more years until she turns twenty-five. However, more than your wife, you must understand this to reconcile. It's vital you do. I will also do my best, but for that to happen, please be forthright in your answers to my questions."

"Yes, I understand. Please, ask me anything—"

"Now then, you went to school with Watanabe-kun and graduated from college in year 2 of Taisho? I'll begin my questions there."

"Yes. I graduated in Taisho year 2 and immediately joined TM Corporation where I still work."

"So right after graduation, you entered TM Corporation. I'm aware of that, but when did you marry your previous wife? I believe it was when you joined the company."

"Yes, it was. I joined the company in September and was married the next month, in October."

"October of Taisho year 2," said the gentleman while counting on the fingers of his right hand. "You two had been living together for exactly five and a half years. That means your previous wife died of typhoid fever in April of Taisho year 8."

"Yes," said Yugawa, puzzled by this man who tells him he didn't want to investigate him indirectly but has investigated various matters. Yugawa looked displeased again.

"It seems you were deeply in love with your late wife?"

"Yes, I loved her. But that's not to say I don't love my current wife as much. When she died, of course, I longed for her. Fortunately, that longing was not hard to heal. My current wife healed me. From that perspective, Kumako, my wife now, is everything to me. Needless to say, you already know that. I know it's my duty to officially marry her."

"That makes sense," said the gentleman, avoiding his zealous tone. "I know your previous wife's name. Wasn't it Fudeko-san? I heard that Fudeko-san had poor health and frequently fell ill before she died of typhoid fever."

"You surprise me. Your official duties demand you know everything. To know that much makes it look like you've already conducted your investigation."

"Ah, ha, ha, ha. I'm sorry to hear you say that. We'll be sharing a meal, please don't browbeat me like that.

"Now, back to Fudeko-san's illness. Before she came

down with typhoid fever, she was infected once with paratyphoid fever.... That happened in the fall of Taisho year 6, around October.

"I heard you were racked with worry because she was seriously ill and lowering her fever was difficult. The next year, Taisho year 7, came. She caught a cold in the New Year and slept through to the fifth and the sixth."

"Yes, that happened."

"Like everyone else, she suffered bouts of diarrhea in the summer, once in July and twice in August. Of these three spells, she hardly rested for the two minor bouts. She was laid up for one or two days for the slightly serious bout. Now, the influenza epidemic spread in the fall. Fudeko-san contracted that a second time. The illness was light in October.

"The second time came in January of the following year, Taisho year 8. Her illness was complicated by pneumonia, and she was critically ill. The pneumonia was hard to manage, but she had a full recovery. Within two months, she died from typhoid fever. Is this correct? Is what I've said correct?"

"Yes," snapped Yugawa, looking down and in thought. The two crossed Shinbashi and walked down Ginza-dori boulevard decorated for the end of the year.

"Your previous wife was an unfortunate soul. For the six months before her death, she fell seriously ill twice and looked to be on the verge of death but frequently saw the terrifying danger. Now, about when did the suffocation incident happen?"

Yugawa was silent. The gentleman nodded and continued talking.

"For two or three days when your wife was getting better from pneumonia and seemed to be in recovery, the room was chilly, and the gas stove in the sickroom malfunctioned. It was the end of February. The gas stopper was loose. Your wife suffocated a little during the night. Fortunately, it didn't become serious, so your wife recovered two or three days later. And nothing like that ever happened before?

"On her way from Shinbashi to Sudacho by bus, she experienced a near miss when the bus crashed into an electric streetcar ..."

"Please, wait a moment. For a while, I've had a high opinion of your detective's eye, but how is this relevant? My guess is you're investigating from all angles."

"You're right. It's not very relevant. I overdo my detective's habits, investigate a little too much, and like to surprise people. Even I think it's a bad habit but can't stop. We'll soon enter the main topic. Please bear with me a little longer. At that time, your wife's forehead was injured by glass fragments."

"Yes, but Fudeko was fairly carefree and not terribly upset. Her injuries were scrapes and scratches."

"Well, I believe you bore some responsibility for that crash."

"Why?"

"You ask, 'Why?' Your wife was riding the bus. You ordered her to go by bus and not by electric streetcar."

"I may have said that. I don't clearly remember those details but probably ordered her. Yes, yes, I surely said that. That was the reason.

"After Fudeko suffered twice from the epidemic flu, at that time, newspapers reported on the human-garbage riders of the electric streetcar being highly infectious. I thought she'd be less likely to be infected on the bus than on the streetcar and was firm in her not riding the streetcar.

"Unfortunately, I never imagined Fudeko's bus would

crash. But I'm not responsible. Fudeko didn't think so and thanked me for the advice."

"Naturally, Fudeko-san was grateful for your kindness until she died. However, I think you were responsible for that bus accident. You said you were thinking about your wife's illness. That's true. Nevertheless, I believe you are responsible."

"Why?"

"You don't seem to understand so I'll explain," said the detective. "You said you did not think about the bus getting into a collision. However, that was not the only day your wife boarded a bus. After she fell gravely ill, she had to see a doctor and rode one every other day from your home in Shibaguchi to the hospital in Manseibashi.

"From the beginning, you understood she had to do that for about one month. During that time, she always rode the bus. The collision occurred during that time. Another warning was collisions often occur when the bus departs. Nervous people worry frequently about being in a crash.

"Excuse me for saying, but you are a nervous man. You made your beloved wife ride that bus often. At the very least, unlike your usual self, weren't you being incautious? If she went back and forth every other day for a month, she was exposed to the dangers of thirty collisions."

Yugawa laughed then said, "I see nervousness in you equal to mine. What you said is true. I'm slowly recalling that time. I was aware of all of that then. However, I considered everything. Which had the higher probability, the danger of a collision or the danger of contracting pneumonia in a streetcar?

"The probabilities of the dangers were equal. Doesn't either one threaten life? I thought about this problem and concluded the bus was safer.

"I asked why because as you said she went back and forth thirty times a month. If she rode the streetcar, I had to believe the pneumonia bacteria was present on each of those thirty streetcars. It seemed right given the infection rate was at its peak. If the mold were already present, getting infected there would not be accidental.

"Still, a bus accident is a disaster of chance. The possibility of a bus crash is reasonable. From the beginning, however, the causes of disasters are obviously different. Next, you mentioned Fudeko contracted epidemic flu twice. This is proof her constitution made her more susceptible than the average person.

"If she rode the streetcar, she must choose to be in danger among many riders. Nevertheless, I thought about the degree of danger. If she contracted the flu a third time, she would certainly come down with pneumonia and probably could not be saved.

"I've heard if someone contracts pneumonia once, they more easily catch it again. Moreover, my concerns were not pointless given her weakness after the illness and not having recovered fully. In the case of an accident, her death would not be certain.

"Unless it was the unluckiest situation, she would not be seriously injured. It's not rare for life to be taken by serious injury. That's why I felt this line of reasoning was correct.

"Please understand, although Fudeko met with one accident during those thirty trips back and forth, weren't her injuries only minor scrapes?"

The detective said, "Of course, what you've said is logical if that were the only reason for my inquiry. I listened like there was no way out. However, facts that can't be glossed over were in what you just said.

"That is, the problem of the probability of danger for a

streetcar and a bus. The bus has less danger than the streetcar. Although there is danger, the probability is lower. In your opinion, the riders equally shared the burden. But in your wife's case, at least, I believe one person was selected to face the same danger as the streetcar even when riding the bus.

"She should not have been exposed to danger equal to the other riders. When the bus crashed, your wife was positioned to be the first to meet with destiny and to be more seriously injured than anyone else. You didn't overlook that."

"Why do you say that? I don't understand."

"Oh, you don't understand? That's odd. But at that time you told Fudeko-san to always sit in the front seat on the bus because that was the safest seat—"

"Yes, that was for safety—"

"Hold on. That's what you meant by safety.

"Numerous flu viruses were in the bus. To prevent breathing them in, the preferred and logical approach would have been to have the wind at her back. Although the bus is not as crowded as the streetcar, the danger of flu infection is not absolutely zero.

"Earlier, you seemed to forget this fact. Later, you added this logic. A bus delivers few shocks to riders in front. Your wife was still fatigued after her illness. Little jostling of her body was preferred.

"You advised your wife to ride in the front for these two reasons. More than a suggestion, you gave a strict order. Your wife was an honest woman and would think it wrong to ignore it. Therefore, she did her best to follow your instructions. Your words steadily took effect."

Yugawa said nothing.

The detective continued, "Initially, you didn't take into account the danger of flu transmission inside a bus.

Despite not doing so, with that pretext, you convinced her to ride in the front. This is a contradiction.

"Another contradiction is your complete neglect of the danger of a crash in the first account. Riding in the front seat of a bus may not be that dangerous in a collision. In the end, that seat was chosen for its danger.

"Wasn't your wife the only person injured in that collision? Even in that minor crash, the other passengers were unharmed. Only your wife was scratched. If the accident had been more serious, the other passengers would have been scratched, and only your wife, seriously injured.

"In the worst case, the other riders would have been seriously injured, and your wife, killed. Needless to say, a crash happens by chance. But if one occurred, your wife being injured would not be by chance but inevitable."

The two crossed Kyobashi, but the gentleman and Yugawa seemed to have forgotten where they were going. They walked straight ahead while one spoke with fervor, and the other quietly listened.

"Thus, you placed your wife in danger having some fixed probability. You drove your wife into inevitable danger within the range of chance. This has a different meaning than the danger of pure chance. You don't understand how much safer the bus is than the streetcar.

"First of all, at that time, your wife had recently recovered from the second bout of epidemic flu. Thus, wasn't it reasonable to believe she was immune to that disease? I would say she was in absolutely no danger of contracting the disease again. Even the selected person chose safety. Someone who suffered from pneumonia once is more easily infected again for some period."

"But I didn't know about immunity. Anyway, she fell ill in October and again in January. After that, I thought the immunity was unreliable ..."

"The period is two months from October to January. However, your wife had not fully recovered and was coughing. Rather than moving away from people, she moved toward people."

"Well, the danger of a crash in this story was inevitable within the range of cases of extreme chance that the vehicle has already been in a crash. But isn't that extremely rare?

"The probability of inevitability and the probability of pure chance have different meanings. Much more, that inevitability is only inevitable injury and not inevitable death."

"However, you could say death was inevitable when an awful crash was inevitable."

"Yes, you could say that. But isn't it boring to play logical games?"

"Ah, ha, ha, ha. Logical games? I like them but was rude to carelessly push my luck too much. The time has come for the main topic.

"Before that, we will finish this logical game. You may laugh at me, but I greatly enjoy logic. I think my interest came from my field or my senior colleagues. Thus, I research chance and inevitability. When that is tied to the human psychology of an individual, a new problem arises. You probably haven't noticed the logic is no longer simple."

"Well, it has become much more difficult."

"Nothing is difficult. One branch of human psychology is called criminal psychology. A person will unknowingly kill someone by an indirect method. If the word kill is inappropriate, then cause to die may suffice.

"For that to happen, the intended victim is exposed to as many dangers as possible. To prevent the intended victim from becoming aware of the plan or having to guide the unwitting victim, the only plan is to select possible dangers.

"If some unnoticed inevitability is included in this chance, that's perfect. Doesn't making your wife take the bus match that superficially? I say superficially so I don't hurt feelings. Of course, I didn't mention the intention, but you probably understand the psychology of that sort of person."

"You are thinking about peculiar aspects of your job. Whether or not the methods match superficially, I have no choice but to rely on your judgment. If someone thinks a person can lose his life by only going back and forth on a bus thirty times over a month, that would be stupid or insane. Probably, no one depends on chance, which is undependable."

"If you board a bus only thirty times, the chance of getting hit is minuscule. However, various dangers are discovered from various directions, and many chances pile up for the person. The reason is the success rate increases several times. Countless possible dangers gather, a vortex is created, and the person is dragged inside. In that case, the danger inflicted on the person is not by chance but is inevitable."

"But what would that look like? Can you give me an example?"

"Well, for example, a man wished to kill his wife. He considered the climax to be her death. But the wife had a weak heart. The seed for possible danger was contained in the fact of her weak heart. To broaden the danger, situations to further weaken her heart were presented.

"For instance, the man got his wife into the habit of drinking by offering sake. Initially, he offered a glass of wine to sleep. The number of glasses gradually increased by always having a drink after meals. Little by little, she awakened to alcohol.

"She began as a woman who lacked a taste for sake and did not drink as much as her husband wished. Therefore, the husband added a second step and suggested smoking cigarettes. 'You must try one. Women seem to enjoy them quite a lot.'

"He bought imported cigarettes with a pleasant fragrance and made her smoke. This plan was a great success, and within the month, the woman became a true smoker. She wanted to quit but couldn't. Next, the husband heard cold baths were harmful to a person with a weak heart and made her take them. 'You easily catch colds and should take a cold bath every morning without fail,' he told his wife out of concern.

"The wife, who relied on her husband from the bottom of her heart, immediately did as he said. Meanwhile, her heart deteriorated unknown to her. This alone sufficiently advanced the husband's plan. After her heart became fragile, a shock would be delivered to her heart.

"This would be an illness with a constant high fever. He placed her in situations where she could easily contract typhoid fever or pneumonia.

"First, the man selected typhoid fever. He aimed to have her frequently eat foods contaminated with the typhi bacteria. 'Americans drink untreated water with meals and praise water as the best drink,' he said and gave his wife unboiled water to drink and raw fish sashimi to eat.

"And he knew raw oysters and jelly noodle strips contained high levels of typhi bacteria and made her eat them. Of course, the husband had to eat them, too, because they were his recommendation. However, he had an earlier bout of typhoid fever and was immune. His plan did not achieve the desired result but was seventy percent successful.

"That means although his wife did not contract typhoid fever, she caught paratyphoid fever. She suffered for a week with a high fever. Death from paratyphoid fever was around ten percent. Luckily or unluckily, his wife with her weak heart was saved. The husband gained momentum from the seventy-percent success rate and, subsequently, never failed to feed her raw foods. His wife often suffered from diarrhea when summer came.

"The husband nervously watched the course of events each time, she did not easily contract the typhoid fever he unfortunately ordered. Then finally, the opportunity he was waiting for arrived.

"Severe influenza spread from the fall of the year before last to the winter of the following year. The husband schemed to somehow infect his wife with the flu during this time.

"Early in October, she caught the flu. Why was she infected? At that time, her throat was worsening. Her husband ordered her to gargle to prevent the flu. He deliberately prepared a strong hydrogen peroxide solution and made her gargle it. This caused a build-up of mucus in her throat.

"At the same time, an aunt was suffering from the flu. The husband often visited her. Right after he returned home from the fifth visit, the wife came down with a fever. Fortunately, she recovered. Then in January, she contracted a more severe case that caused pneumonia."

As he spoke, the detective did something slightly odd. He lightly poked Yugawa's wrist two or three times like he was tapping the ashes from the cigar he was holding. He seemed to be urging caution in the silence. Just then, the two came to the front of Nihonbashi Bridge. The detective turned right in front of Murai Bank and walked toward Chuo Post Office. Of course, Yugawa went with him.

"This second bout of flu was the husband's work," said the detective. "At that time, the children in the wife's family were down with acute cases of the flu and admitted to S Hospital in Kanda.

"Despite not being asked, the husband made his wife nurse the children. His reasoning was 'This flu is fast-moving, and few people are available to nurse. My wife gained immunity from her recent bout of the flu and is best suited to be a nurse.'

"His wife considered that to be sensible but was infected again while nursing the children. Her case of pneumonia was serious, and she faced danger several times. This time, the husband's plan was more than enough.

"At her bedside, he apologized for this disaster caused by his negligence. His wife held no grudge and quietly died while thanking him for his love in this life. Her husband's heart probably saw this as a failure after so much hard work.

"Therefore, the husband committed himself again to the plan. He thought another calamity had to befall her in addition to disease. He used the gas stove in her sickroom. His wife was getting better, and the nurse was no longer present. Also, he still had to sleep in another room for about a week.

"The husband then discovered a chance. Concerned about fire while she slept, his wife slept with the gas stove turned off. The stopper for the gas stove was at the threshold of the sickroom to the hallway. His wife had the habit of going to the bathroom once during the night, and she always crossed the threshold. As she walked over the threshold, the hem of her long nightgown drags behind, and three times out of five touches the gas stove's stopper.

"If the stopper is already a little loose, it would surely come off when touched by the hem. The sickroom was a Japanese-style room, the joints were tight, so the wind did not leak through the gaps. The seed of danger was prepared in this opportunity. The husband noticed the advantage of adding the few steps needed to guide this chance. It was to further loosen the gas stopper.

"One day, while his wife took an afternoon nap, he secretly lubricated the stopper with oil to make it slippery. Although he should have done this with complete secrecy, unfortunately, unknown to him another person witnessed this act.

"A maid who worked in his house at the time saw this. This maid came with his new bride from the same town. She was extraordinarily attentive to his wife and a quick-witted girl. Well, that is fortunate."

The detective and Yugawa crossed Kabuto-bashi Bridge in front of the Chuo Post Office then crossed Yoroi-hashi Bridge. In no time, the pair walked to the streetcar tracks in front of Suitengu Shrine.

"This time, the husband had seventy-percent success and failure for the remaining thirty percent. His wife was in danger of being suffocated by the gas. She woke up before reaching the finale and set off an uproar in the night. How did the gas leak? Although the source was discovered in a short time, her negligence was blamed.

"Next, the husband selected the bus. As explained earlier, she went by bus to the doctor. He never missed any chance. When the journey ended without success, he grasped a new opportunity. The doctor gave him this chance. The doctor recommended she relocate to recuperate.

"He suggested a month-long stay at a location with fresh air. The husband informed his wife. 'Since you're always ill, we'll relocate for a month or two to a place with fresher air. I thought about the house in Omori because the move isn't too far. The ocean is near, and I could commute to work.' She quickly agreed with his opinion.

"You may not know this, but Omori is a land with mostly undrinkable water. Consequently, infectious diseases will never end—especially, typhoid fever. In other words, this man's calamity didn't happen, and he began to target illness again. After the move to Omori, he gave his wife unboiled water and raw foods more fervently. He also enforced cold baths and encouraged smoking.

"He maintained the garden and planted many trees, dug a lake, and provided a reservoir. He claimed the location of the bathroom was poor and changed its position to the direction facing the afternoon sun. This measure led to mosquitoes and flies in the house.

"There is more. One of his acquaintances contracted typhoid fever. Because of his immunity, he often visited his sick friend and, from time to time, in the company of his wife.

"He should have been patient. However, within one month, this plan rapidly exceeded all expectations and was effective this time. Soon after visiting his friend with typhoid fever, he may have put a sinister measure into play, but his wife caught that disease. This only superficially resembles your case."

"Yes, only superficially—"

"Ah, ha, ha, ha, ha. Up to this point, it's only superficial. You loved your previous wife, but the love was shallow. But at the same time, you loved your current wife behind your first wife's back for two or three years. The love was for appearances. When this fact is added to the previous facts, the extent the earlier case applies to you is no longer superficial."

The two men walked down a narrow alley that turned right off the streetcar tracks at Suitengu Shrine. On the left side of the alley, a house with the air of a business office had a large signboard reading Private Investigator. The brightness from burning lanterns lit the second and lower floors fitted with glass doors. When they arrived at this spot, the detective laughed heartily.

"Ah, ha, ha, ha. I can't … I can't hide it any longer. Haven't you been trembling for a while? This evening, your previous wife's father has been waiting at my home for you. It's all right. You need not be so afraid. Please, come in."

Without warning, the detective grabbed Yugawa's wrist while his shoulder pushed open the door and dragged him into the brightly lit house. Electric lanterns lit Yugawa's pale face. He staggered as if in a stupor and dropped his butt into a chair.

6. THE TUMOR WITH A HUMAN FACE

Recently, Utagawa Yurie heard several rumors about a horror mystery film she appeared in as the leading lady had been making the rounds in the seamy parts of Tokyo and screened in obscure movie theaters in Shinjuku and Shibuya. The film seemed to be one from her time in the United States where she acted in various roles as a contract actress with the Globe Company in Los Angeles.

According to someone who saw the film, a globe icon appeared at the end of the movie, and the cast was several white actors mixed in with Japanese actors. The Japanese title was *Obsession*, but the English title meant *the tumor with a human face*. Critiques called the long, five-reel film an extremely artistic, melancholy, and mystifying masterpiece.

Of course, the American films of Yurie have been shown in Japan's movie theaters; this was not the first time. Since returning to Japan, she appeared in five or six movies imported by the Globe Company. Though often ranked below European and American actresses, her sleek limbs and beautiful face seasoned with Western coquetry and Eastern purity were quickly noticed by connoisseurs.

The woman who emerged on the screen possessed the

courage and agility to be active, an unusual trait for Japanese women, and enchanted by her smile in the adventurous films. She specialized in dressing up for roles needing glamour and athleticism like women bandits, she-devils, and woman detectives.

In the film titled *The Samurai's Daughter* screened at Shikishimakan in Asakusa, a young Japanese woman called Kikuko is a spy. Disguised as a geisha, a noblewoman, and a circus stunt rider, she crisscrosses the East Asian continent in search of the military secrets of a certain country. The spectacular artistry displayed by Yurie in the role of the heroine Kikuko drove audiences of the screenings in the park wild.

Last year, she received an invitation to join Nitto Motion Pictures in Tokyo and returned to Japan after four or five years in America, no doubt enticed by an exceptionally high salary. That movie greatly boosted her popularity in Japan.

However, Yurie couldn't remember ever acting in a movie called *A Tumor With a Human Face*.

She heard detailed descriptions of the plot and each scene but couldn't imagine when it was filmed. Perhaps the incident in the plot originated somewhere in Nagasaki at a Japanese port facing the southern seas, as captivating as a Hiroshige painting.

When the story opens, she's Ayame, a high-ranking prostitute, who lives in the red-light district occupying the streets along the bay. This prostitute is praised in song throughout the town as a first-class beautiful woman. In the evening, she is enchanted by the sounds of a *shakuhachi* flute drifting in from out of the blue. Her beguiling figure, like the maiden in the Palace of the Dragon King, appears on the third floor of a blue brothel that commands a view of the sky over the bay. Enraptured, she leans on the railing and cocks her head to listen.

The owner of the flute is a shabby, lowly youth who begs for food and longs for her love. He wishes to receive the compassion of the prostitute for one night as his reward for being born a man and then leave this world without hesitation. The youth keeps this wish a secret in his heart.

He is ridiculed for his impoverished life and ashamed of his ugly face. Always under the cover of darkness, he wanders in the shadows of the wharf on the coast and enjoys catching glimpses from a distance of the prostitute's face during the serenade of his flute.

Not only the pitiful beggar's, she had also stolen the souls of many men. In the end, not one customer receives the reward of her true passion.

At the end of spring of the previous year, she signed a temporary contract with a sailor on an American merchant ship anchored at the dock and could never forget the face of this white man. While she waits impatiently for the fall of this year and the promised reunion, each time she hears the beggar's flute, she lazily watches the sails on the bay and falls deep in thought.

This is the film's prologue and moves to the time the American sailor returns to the port.

The white man is nearly drowning in Ayame's love and in a hurry to bring her back home to America. But he has no way to raise the large sum of money to buy her out of prostitution and plans to kidnap her from the red-light district. He will stow her away in the bowels of the merchant ship and smuggle her into America.

To carry out this plan, he explains it to the flute-playing beggar to bring him in as an accomplice. One night, the prostitute will sneak out the back door of the brothel. The white man will be waiting and put her in a big trunk, load it on a cart, leave the cart in the hands of the beggar, and then return to his ship with an indifferent look on his face.

The beggar's role is to pull the cart to an empty house at an old temple where he wards off rain and dew every night in a lonely place away from town. He puts the trunk holding the prostitute near the dais for the Buddha statue in the main temple building.

In the dead of night a few days later, the white man rows a lighter up to the water's edge at the bottom of the cliff where the temple stands, receives the trunk from the beggar's hands, and successfully loads it onto the ship.

The beggar is happy and agrees to the white man's request. At dawn, if the work ends successfully, he'll be rewarded with money. The beggar confides his ardent true feeling he's never told a soul.

"If I do this for the benefit of the prostitute, even if I throw away my life, I'll have no regrets. While I struggle with impossible love, I'll lend my powers to adore the prostitute even more and promote the love between you two. That is my kindness to her.

"But if you have a little pity on this beggar's inner feelings, while I happily hide the prostitute at the old temple, for only one night, please let me use her body as I wish. This is my once-in-a-lifetime request…," said the beggar as tears flowed. He repeatedly placed his forehead on the ground and pressed his hands together in prayer.

"After your ship left the port last spring, I hung around under the railing of her room every day and played the flute to console her heart. This request from a beggar like me is more than I deserve, but if she listens, I have this great hope even if I die. Even if the crime is discovered by chance, I will take all the blame for the crime. I'll help you in every way," he teased.

His pestering prevented the white man from flat out rejecting his wish. She is his cherished lover but is a prostitute who has given herself to many men. To reward the beggar for his kindness, he thought buying one or two nights of love would not be a problem. However, Ayame heard this story and shuddered, having glimpsed the beggar through the latticework.

This arrogant woman was cajoled by clients and behaved with complete selfishness. The thought of being touched by this filthy youth with the face of a demon was crueler than death to her. She conspired with the white man to trick the beggar.

They will load the trunk onto the cart. The white man will leave the beggar and return to the ship. After pulling the cart into the old temple, the beggar will want to see the prostitute's figure and open the trunk before the statue of Buddha in the dimly lit main temple. But the white man will not be able to open the strong lock of the lid and make opening the trunk impossible. During the night, the beggar will cling to the trunk and complain to the prostitute hidden inside about his anguish over the white man's distrust of him.

To soothe the beggar, the woman will say things like, "The white man is wicked and should not have deceived you. He was confused and probably forgot to give you the key. If he comes now, he'll open this trunk and keep his promise."

After two or three days passed, the white man rushed to the temple at dawn and repeatedly apologized to the beggar for forgetting to give him the key.

"The merchant ship will weigh anchor soon and set sail. Please forgive me, but there's no time for your request," said the white man and tossed him several packages. Of course, the beggar didn't seem happy to receive them.

"After this, I'll have to live a long time in a world where I won't be able to see her figure ever again. If I don't get my wish, I swear I'll throw myself into the sea and die. You were a rat to trick me.

"If the prostitute dislikes me, then my wish is a hardship. Instead, please let me see her face just one time for my memories of life in this world. At least, let my last kiss be to kiss the hem of her gorgeous kimono embroidered with gold."

He asked over and over, but the prostitute refused to consent. Her voice rose from inside the trunk to urge the white man to act.

"No matter what he says, do not open the lid of this trunk. Chase away this beggar soon and take me onboard the ship."

The white man gave a confusing explanation.

"This is hard on you, but I have no reason to disobey her. I'm sorry, but I forgot to bring the key to the trunk again today."

The beggar said, "That's all right. If that's your reason, I'm gonna throw my body into the sea right before your eyes. Even if I die, I will meet the prostitute. I'll meet her without regrets."

For a second time, from inside the trunk, she yelled, "If you die, die as you wish."

(In the movie, a longitudinal cut-in shot inside the trunk is projected. Her upside-down shoulders and her face becoming enraged are freely photographed.)

The beggar thought about saying, "If I die, my pigheaded idea is my ugly face will eat into the prostitute's flesh and cling to her side for life. When that time comes, I'll have no regrets."

Then he jumped off the cliff in front of the temple. The white man looked relieved for a moment, took a key from his pocket, opened the lid, and helped the prostitute out. They celebrated the success of their plan.

These events took place in the first and second reels.

The third and later reels tell the story beginning when the ship leaves Japan to their lives in the white man's hometown. The first scene is a longitudinal cut-in shot when the man leaves the trunk carrying the woman in a corner of the ship with miscellaneous cargo.

In preparation, water and bread were provided in the cramped trunk. She squeezed her body inside with her hands hugging both legs, and her head rested on her kneecaps.

After two or three days, an odd tumor erupted on her right kneecap and ballooned to a frightening size. The tops of four smaller tumors bulged out on its flexible, bloated, spongy surface. Mysteriously, the tumors didn't hurt, but she pressed her hand on them and poked her fingers at the swellings. Perhaps caused by the crushing pressure, the pliant surface hardened as the days passed. In contrast, the four small tumors slowly became more defined and resembled distinct curves.

The top two rounded like two spheres. The center one took on a long, narrow, vertical shape. The bottom one meandered to the side and was chilling like a crawling caterpillar.

The trunk should have been pitch black inside, but light passed through the small holes provided for air and floated dimly around her body. Particularly near her right kneecap, the light rays drawing a circle like a fairly bright halo of the moon blurred like a dripping water droplet.

One time, she closely examined the affected area and couldn't help seeing the two upper projections as the eyes of a living being. This time, the long, narrow center one was a nose. The lower one shaped like a caterpillar resembled lips. She suddenly discovered a full human face.

She wondered if her mind was confused but was sure she saw a human face. Despite being composed of simple lines like a cartoon drawn by a child, the worst part was the face looked like the beggar's. The moment of realization overwhelmed her with an indescribable, palpable fear, and she slumped forward, unconscious. Her head drooped down and rested on her kneecaps.

Meanwhile, the tumors grew with each passing second. The eyes, nose, and mouth were nothing more than simple lines. They gained color and shape as if they were gradually being inflated with life. Finally, the beggar's face came alive and turned into an actual human head. It was smaller than a real head, but an exact copy shrunken to fit on her kneecap and skillfully baked on.

The flute-playing youth's face wore this melancholy look when he threatened to jump into the sea. His expression was silent and forlorn like it was carved by the splendid hand of a master craftsman.

After this, that tumor with a human face carried out revenge in various forms against the woman. When the ship landed in America, she kept the tumor a secret from her lover. The couple rented a room in a seedy part of San Francisco. The white man set up house with her, quit being a sailor, and went to work as a clerk in a company.

He became suspicious of her recent sullen mood and wary of her. One night, he happened to see the grotesque secret and tried to run off. She fought fiercely to keep her lover and strangled him to death. (The vengeful ghost took over her body and summoned enough arm strength while she was unconscious.)

Before her lover's body, she stood in shock, like she was in a trance. Through the tears in the hem of her gown shredded during the fight, the tumor with a human face glimpsed the white man's body. Its frozen facial muscles moved for the first time and let slip an evil, chilling smirk.

After that, the tumor eagerly formed a full range of facial expressions. It showed joy, sadness, angry eyes, stuck out its tongue, wept bitter tears, twisted its lips, and slobbered. This was the first revenge. Later, her destiny became constant persecution and intimidation from the tumor with a human face.

After she killed her lover, her personality changed in an instant. She became a bold temptress with frightening amorous passion and good looks. Much more graceful than before, she exhibited more powerful coquetry. She deceived many white men, one after the other, swindled them out of money, and stole their lives.

The woman was occasionally tormented by visions of her crimes that interrupted her dreams in the dead of night, but she was somehow penitent. However, the tumor with a human face was always a nuisance and unknowingly amassed regrets for ridiculing her cowardice and making her commit crimes.

Sometimes, she became a prostitute and at other times, an entertainer. She led the luxurious life of a noblewoman, lived in a magnificent mansion, and rode around in an automobile. But when alone, her conscience always bothered her. As her troubles mounted, her flesh swelled with fat, and her complexion shined brightly. Finally, she fell in love with a young marquis of a certain country and succeeded in marrying him.

If she spent quiet years as the young wife of the

marquis, things would never go well even with the best luck. One night, the newlyweds hosted an evening affair with many guests. She exposed the tumor with the human face she kept hidden from her husband and everyone else.

She tightly wrapped gauze over the entire tumor, and no one ever saw it. That night, however, as she danced wildly in a trance around the ballroom, red blood traced a line on her pure white silk shoes and noiselessly trickled to the floor.

She was unaware and kept leaping around. The marquis was perplexed by the gauze always wrapped around his wife's knee. He approached and innocently examined the wound. The human-faced tumor's teeth devoured the stockings. A long tongue stuck out and loud laughter erupted while blood flowed from its eyes and nose.

That's where she lost her mind. She dashed to her bedroom, fell on her back onto the bed, and plunged a knife into her chest. She seemed to have killed herself, but the tumor with a human face appeared to be alive and laughing.

That is the gist of the story of *The Tumor With a Human Face*. In the end, the expression of the tumor was projected in extreme close-up to fill the screen.

Usually, the list of credits of the names of the writer and the director followed by the names and roles of the main actors scroll at the beginning of this sort of film. The names of the writer and the director were missing from this film.

Utagawa Yurie, the actress playing the prostitute, Ayame, has a bold introduction and first appears on the screen dressed as the marquise and the prostitute. Next, the Japanese man in the role of the flute-playing beggar, perhaps a more important role than Yurie's, is left out even though his face remains unfamiliar. Who is he? Where is he from?

Several patrons told Yurie how much they enjoyed the story because the movie captured the living form of the true person. She was definitely filmed somewhere at some time but had no memory of acting in this movie.

Normally, when a play is performed for film, the natural progression of the drama is not followed as it is in an ordinary play. The scene from the script is selected depending on which is best for the moment. Filming proceeds without regard to what comes before and after.

At the same location, two or three scenes in completely different stories may be shot at the same time. Often, a movie actress does not know the plot of the story she's acting in.

Especially at the Globe Company, which employed Yurie, the directors intentionally kept the actors from knowing the plot of the story. The actors didn't need to read through or rehearse ahead of filming. Oblivious to the full personality of the character, in a simple game, they mimicked the actions acted out by the director. While they cried or laughed as instructed, they made the movie scene by scene. Because this technique prevented wrong interpretations by the actors, the unnaturalness of the stage was avoided, and the performances were infused with energy. This approach was usually adopted by American companies.

Therefore, for most of the four or five years Yurie worked at the Globe Company, she was filmed in countless scenes but could never imagine what became of these dramatic elements or how various stories were assembled. In other words, she was a cog in a large machine that manufactured parts like gears or springs.

Of course, she recalled dressing up as a prostitute and

a noblewoman many times in the past. Because she specialized in being pirates and detectives, more times than she could count, she acted in scenes where she hid away in a trunk or toyed with or killed men. It was reasonable she had no idea which scenes became parts of the story of the tumor with a human face.

This drama on film employed advanced technical tricks to burn the tumor face of the beggar on her kneecap. It makes sense she had no memory of this.

Nevertheless, if she viewed the completed reel of film in the future and told the plot, most of the time, she suddenly recalled when it was filmed. It's outrageous that to this day, she had never seen this superb film, a standout among long films, or known of its existence. Also, she preferred watching her American movies. No matter how short the film was, she had seen them all.

After returning to Japan, she longed for the past in Los Angeles and did not think about the success of the films made by the Tokyo company. She would sneak off to watch the occasional screenings of her American films in a nearby park. Therefore, in no time, the movie of the heartless human-faced tumor was produced by the Globe Company and imported to Japan. This fact about *The Tumor With a Human Face* puzzled Yurie. The mystery lay in an artistic and brilliant film of that caliber not being recognized for a long time by the public and the film making recent rounds in the movie theaters in seedy parts of Tokyo.

When was this film imported to Japan and by what company? Where did the film premiere? Where had it drifted through before being screened in theaters in run-down parts of Tokyo? She asked actresses and several managers who worked for the same company but none of them knew.

If she had the chance, she'd like to see it one time and thought about going to a faraway town. But the screenings were always moving around, today in Aoyama and tomorrow in Shinagawa, so she always missed the opportunity.

Unable to view the film for herself, her curiosity grew stronger.

The Globe Company hired a technician named Jefferson who was skilled at the technique of *burning in*. He devised a wealth of photography tricks. She presumed the movie about the tumor with a human face used his technique to achieve the effect.

Thinking about Jefferson's energetic and funny personality, he might have executed the daring trick to surprise her.

Other than the tumor, she couldn't imagine where else he used these unimaginable, subtle tricks. To determine that, she had to see the film. Also, she was deeply suspicious of the Japanese actor who played the flute-playing youth.

At that time, only three Japanese actors worked for the Globe Company. One of these three actors was sure he never dressed like a beggar and stood in front of the camera with her with the backdrop of a harbor like Nagasaki. What Japanese man reluctantly left the permanent disfiguring scar on Yurie's beautiful kneecap? How much came from Yurie's imagination? Or did she feel she was the real Ayame and cursed by a suspicious Japanese man?

She wondered, Who understood the hard-to-solve puzzle of this film's history at the Nitto Motion Picture Company? Then a man called H popped into her mind. He was a high-level manager who worked for the company for many years. His job was in communications in dealings with foreign companies and translating English-language film magazines and plots. He probably has detailed knowledge about the years in which American films imported to Japan were produced, the import route, and the identities of the actors in the films. If she questioned him, what clues would she uncover? One day, she climbed the stairs to the second floor of the business office near the studio in Nippori and gently tapped the shoulder of H.

"... Ah, you want to know about that film?... I know absolutely nothing ..."

H was dismayed and looked at her with kindly eyes after listening to her question. He anxiously scanned the room. Then he closed the door Yurie left open when she came in and calmly glanced at her face.

"So even you don't remember making that film. That makes this strange film more mysterious. The truth is I have questions for you about that film, but I hesitate to ask. The story is a little disturbing, and I've had no opportunity to indulge myself by asking questions. Fortunately, no one is here today, and we can talk. But after listening, please try not to get agitated."

"All right. If it's a scary story, I want to hear it," Yurie said and forced a smile.

H said, "… That film is owned by this company and was leased to the usual outlying theaters for some time. It had been purchased by the company only a month before you returned from America. We did not buy it directly from the Globe Company. A Frenchman living in Yokohama sold it to us.

"This Frenchman obtained numerous other films in Shanghai and, for a long time, enjoyed them at home. Before the Frenchman bought them, they were exhibited all over the colonies in China and the South Seas and suffered significant damage.

"In society, however, your popularity has been amazing since *The Samurai's Daughter*. When you signed the contract to join this company, the film was full of scratches but was exceptionally clear. Its price was exorbitant because you were particularly attractive and your hair was dyed a different color in this film. Soon after the purchase, strange rumors about the film began.

"When that film was projected and watched by someone alone in a quiet room late at night, a frightening incident would occur that made it impossible for a courageous man to watch it to the end. That fact was accidentally discovered when a technician named M, employed by the company to check for damage. He was projecting the film one night in a downstairs room of the business office to correct the cloudiness in the film.

"At first, no one believed M, but later, two or three fans in several groups took turns watching the film. Upset after seeing it, they said, 'That spooky film is a monster.'

"Not only was it spooky, they believed the technician M gradually went mad because he felt threatened by the film and, a short time later, quit the company. In addition to M, groups who watched out of curiosity were tormented by nightmares every night, became dizzy and tired for no reason, and experienced inexplicable events.

"The current company president was another witness. A few weeks after seeing the film, he suffered from a fever caused by some unnamed disease and had a horrible time.

"As everyone knows, the company president is superstitious and high-strung. Later, he came to hate that film being owned by this company. Right after he recovered, he held a secret meeting. He presented two options: 1. Sell the film to another company and 2. End employment contracts with anyone connected to that film, even you.

"However, counterarguments to the president's options

were presented. A product bought at such a high price must not be sold unchallenged to another company to the detriment of our company. Also, nothing should be canceled while the contract with you exists and a huge advance for the film had already been handed over. The discussion was extremely contentious. In the end, a compromise was reached.

"The strange phenomenon in the film was only seen by one person late at night. Therefore, no one else has discovered this. There should be no opposition to screening this film for many spectators in public viewings.

"Although the president hated having that film in the company, for the time being, he supported renting the film to other companies and waiting for a buyer who would offer a suitable price. And there's absolutely no reason to cancel the contract with you.

"Of course, the questionable nature of this film spread far in the world. Jinxed by your popularity and the film's value, everyone kept the secret. For example, the company employees were not informed of the situation. His proposal was put into action. Today when terrible tremors passed through the lineup of employees and actors, reasonably, almost no one in the company knew the secret.

"At first, following the wishes of the high-level executives who attended the secret meeting, they considered renting the film at a high rental fee to a first-rate company anywhere. Lately, however, the competition and friction between the companies intensified, and it didn't go as expected.

"Without authority, they lent the film to small theaters in Kyoto, Osaka, and Nagoya. But without the involvement of exceptional promoters to place spectacular advertisements in newspapers, the film gained no traction anywhere. Around that time, it made the rounds in Kansai and was exhibited in the shabby towns of Tokyo.

"I heard talk from people who experienced the strangeness of the late night first hand but don't remember experiencing it myself. However, a company bought the film and previewed the film to the police and newspaper people, but only one person watched the entire film while paying attention to detail.

"At the time, I thought the strange element was the Japanese actor playing the role of the beggar. The main actors and actresses in the drama were people whose names were mostly familiar to me. The only actor I had never seen was that Japanese man. I should have been quite familiar with, at least, the Japanese actors working for the Globe Company when you worked there. I confirmed from my research that the other two actresses were E and O, and the actors were S, K, and C.

"Is that right? The Japanese man who played the beggar was neither S, K, nor C. Other than those three men, nobody else comes to mind. That's why I thought I'd ask you."

When H paused after this long story, she said, "Well, I don't remember anyone other than those three men. Did an actor unknown to everyone including me leave a lasting impression in my mind? That's what I think."

H continued. "I also thought about memories seared into my mind. After hearing about Jefferson, a man famous for trick photography, I wondered about him, but there were certainly one or two places where Jefferson was exceptionally skilled. If all of that was burned in, Jefferson only thought up supernatural, mysterious secret methods I found unimaginable. Because many of the various points were suspicious, I compiled these doubts about six months ago and sent a letter with questions to the Globe Company.

The company responded, but it missed the important points.

"In my position in the company, I didn't create the drama title *The Tumor With a Human Face*. But the scenes that appeared in this film have been used in different films. A movie drama with a plot mostly resembling this was certainly made.

"Did someone make forgeries by mixing other films into that film or cutting or burning in parts? I don't believe the actors exclusive to this company made this film secretly here. They worked in the studio every day and never had any spare time.

"Miss Yurie, while you worked at this company, the only three Japanese actors working there were S, K, and C. Two or three Japanese actors were employed before you. Recently, five or six more actors were new hires. Burning in a Japanese actor you didn't know at the company into your film was not ridiculous and, at the same time, probable.

"The burn-in was too difficult and unprecedented for this company, but this much burn-in was possible. Unfortunately, a clear answer was impossible because it's a company secret.

"If the film in question is a forgery, the company had no reason to throw it out. For reference, I'd like to examine the product by transferring suitable compensation to the company.

"The meaning is mostly what was said, but the true form of that film is still not understood. My best guess is someone created a filmed drama by splicing the film with a similar plot to various other films, skillfully restoring the film, and burning in. No one other than the talented Jefferson could have done that.

"Even if there were another expert, that complex job did not simply have the objective of making money. When

I think about the connection to frightening events in the dead of night, that is surely the origin.

"This is a little odd, but maybe you can remember someone from your time in America who holds a grudge. Can you recall a relationship with a man who despised you or was tricked by you while longing for you? I've always believed this is related to deep-seated hatred from a man."

She said, "Please stop. I don't recall any bad incident like a deep-seated grudge, but isn't the human face that becomes a tumor a story about a face or some hideous man?"

He said, "That's it. A frightening ugly man. This man may be Japanese or a South Seas islander with a fat, round face with blank, staring black eyes. He looks about thirty and about ten years older than you in this picture. Because you won't forget that face after one glance, if you knew that man, you would remember.

"No. Not only you, to this day, none of us knows who he was or where he came from. He was one million mysteries. Why? The role of the flute-playing beggar was serious. The actor capable of the melancholy and miserable expression after becoming a tumor and a match for this unknown actor was Paul Wegener, the star of *The Student of Prague* and *Golem*.

"The strangest aspect is the only Japanese man who had that appearance and craftsmanship, naturally, should have appeared in domestic and American movie magazines, but not even the name of the movie was published. To this day, that man is not living in this world and is simply a vision that lives on film. I have to believe that. The people who felt the strangeness of the film did not believe the man filmed in that movie was a human.

"They say, 'That man is a phantom. That actor should

not exist,' or 'If he's not a phantom, that strange incident should not have happened.'"

"I want to ask what is the answer? Although you've explained quite a lot in detail, I still haven't heard the crucial response...."

"The truth is you must not agitate your nerves and be calm. If the talk has come this far, it has already been said. I heard the most detailed account from the technician M, who later went mad, but in summary, the strangeness of that movie is the face of that phantom man.

"Based on the long experience of the technician M, the spectators actively watched the motion picture while listening to the music and the narrator for the silent film in the theater in Asakusa Park and felt jovial and exhilarated. However, a person alone watching the film projected in a dark, silent room late at night feels haunted and ill at ease.

"The film is quiet and lonely but has a spectacular banquet and fight scenes. Although the shadows of many people moved energetically, it is impossible to think of them as dead bodies. Instead, the viewer feels like he's being erased.

"The most unearthly element is the scene where the close-up of the human face grins. When that scene appears, the hand turning the projector's hand crank unexpectedly stops. In that case, the technician M often said the smiling face is scarier than an angry face."

He said, "I'm a technician, so it's nothing. But if a film where some actor's image appears and looks like me for me alone, what strange feelings will I have? Surely, I appear in the film, watch standing in the dark, and feel like a shadow."

"The feelings when one person watches *The Tumor With a Human Face* in the dead of night in an empty screening room of the Nippori business office could be imagined for an ordinary film. From the moment the figure of the flute-playing beggar appears in the first reel, you become aware of feeling like being stabbed in the chest or having water poured all over your body.

"The film was blurry and full of scratches, but they weren't the problem. Rather, they helped create a gloomy effect. Isn't that odd?

"You persevere and watch the first reel, then the second, third, and fourth reels. However, in the final scene on the fifth reel, when the wife of the marquis, Ayame, goes insane and kills herself, in the next scene, your eyes are subtly commandeered, and most people are overtaken by fear and temporarily lose consciousness.

"That scene projects a close-up of half of your right leg from the knee to the toenails. The tumor erupting on the kneecap has the gravest expression and a unique smile like it's crying while twisting its lips to clear away irrelevant thoughts.

"Suddenly, an almost imperceptible laughing voice was undoubtedly heard. The technician M thought this was extraneous noise and a little distracting. He had to listen carefully to hear the nearly inaudible voice. Depending on the situation, the laughing voice may be audible when the film is shown in a public screening and may have gone unnoticed by others.

"After hearing this story, you probably don't feel well. I forgot to tell you, but finally, the film was transferred to the Globe Company. A few days earlier, it was taken from the theater called Taishokan in Sugamo. A subordinate of mine put it on that shelf in this business office.

"Screenings inside the company are prohibited by the president, but that doesn't stop anyone from watching the film. What do you think? Shall we watch it? By only looking at the beggar's face, we may find the clues to solve this puzzle...."

H waited for Yurie's gleaming eyes filled with curiosity to agree. From five round tin-plated canisters stacked on the shelf on the side, he pulled down the canisters containing the first to fifth reels.

He removed the lids on the desk. As he pulled a long length of the film strip gleaming like steel, he held it up to the bright window to show Yurie.

"Look. This is the beggar," said H and showed the face of the tumor burned into her knee in the fifth reel. "As you see, it becomes the tumor here. I can tell this is definitely burned in. You've never seen this man."

She said, "I don't remember him."

She was clear without having to trace her memories. That was the face of the unknown Japanese man.

"But H-san, this is definitely the burned-in face. This man is somewhere. He's not a ghost."

"But there are bad spots in the burn-in. Please look here. This is the middle of the fifth reel. The leading lady stands up to the tumor. When the face weakens, it bites her wrist. The teeth clamped onto the base of her right thumb and then let go. You wiggled your five fingers in pain. This could not have been burned in."

As he spoke, H handed the film to Yurie, lit a cigarette, and walked around the room like he was talking to himself.

"This film will become the property of the Globe Company. What will be its fate? I think I'll make copies because it's a product of a shrewd company and sell them. Yes, that's what I'll do."

7. THE STORY OF MR. AOTSUKA

Yurako thought her husband, Nakata, died of lung disease. She still believes so, as does the world. Only Nakata didn't seem to think so. This is understood when you read the suicide note found in the sickroom of the rented villa in Suma where Nakata drew his last breath.

Before I present the will, I want you to know Yurako surely succeeded as a star actress because of her physical charm, but she also owed thanks to her late husband.

When she was sixteen or seventeen, Nakata quickly plucked her from among the many aspiring actresses when she appeared as an extra in a minor scene of a play. He used his position to gradually showcase her. This led to love between the director and the actress, a common occurrence in any movie studio, jealousy and malicious gossip among colleagues, and Nakata living with the eighteen-year-old Yurako.

In addition to her pure heart at the beginning, she seemed to rely on this man to help in her ambition to rise in the world. After they married, she never had an affair and was envied by others. Some gossips said Nakata weakened and died because she loved him too much. She was healthy and enjoyed sports. Robust vitality that could be called barbaric overflowed from her graceful body. The rumors were not unreasonable.

After her husband moved to Suma last autumn, she always visited during breaks in filming but not necessarily to nurse him. Despite his flesh wasting away as a patient, her husband's sexual desire flourished. Not only did he wait for Yurako's arms to reach out for him with no fear of catching his disease, but he was also grateful for her passion that drank in the pleasure of love to the last drop. These occasions piled up. In the end, Yurako had to admit they may have hastened his death.

However, her husband was happy and made that choice. Why should she object? She could do nothing else. Like her husband, she teemed and burned inside with lust. Although she would have been wrong to have an affair for that reason, she acted so that her husband would die the death he desired. She let the fire of her spirit kindle in the fire to be extinguished from this world and made the flames blaze to heights as high as she could imagine.

Nakata could go with no qualms to the other world. He lived a brief four years after marrying his love. But from twenty-five to twenty-nine for him and eighteen to twenty-two for Yurako, he enjoyed the most brilliant years of his life. Fortunately, he never betrayed or had a nasty quarrel with her.

When Yurako thought about her personality and future self, she felt his death was beneficial because her harmonious love with Nakata ended completely. If her husband had lived, how much longer could she have been well-behaved to protect him?

She had built enough of a reputation to not be easily

forgotten by her true fans, even without the loving protection of the director. A movie actress is beauty and body more than artistry.

As with any original work or any plot, she could not forget to show off a row of pretty teeth when she laughed, brighten her eyes with tears when she cried, and expose patches of flesh beneath her clothes when she acted out riotous scenes, especially in plays.

Although that actress was said to be crap and always chewed the scenery, the spectators enjoyed her. If she showed her naked body from time to time, their applause grew louder.

When Nakata painted her portrait, he captured her essence. For the director to nurture one woman, the woman he loved, to become a star, more than instilling technique, the director's pet theory favored understanding the merits of her limbs, striving to master each change in them, and developing the infinite beauty born there.

Director Nakata filmed her in several different kinds of films. More than drama, these films were nothing more than various poses stitched together to show her young body in flowing silk after rain in the rays of sunlight.

She impressed her body onto each frame of many feet of celluloid film. Nakata engraved various symbols on a stamp using her as the medium, closely examined the red ink pad, mulled over the positioning, and produced a vivid image on high-quality paper.

Although Yurako thanked her late husband for this kindness, if she recognized the excellent quality of the stamp medium and knew the ink, the positioning, and the paper quality were secondary issues, among the possible engravers, he was competent with the stamp medium if a mistake were made. Thus, more than dismay and anxiety with Nakata's death, her slight feelings of indebtedness intensified.

Seated beside her husband on his deathbed, the sigh she released carried something resembling the satisfaction of a person whose heavy responsibility came to a successful end. She sent her husband safely to the other world. Although she did not know his destination, she had no misgivings and saw his corpse white as wax as something noble and beautiful. She placed herself in the still inextinguishable love and could press her hands together in prayer before Buddha.

Yurako took the will mentioned earlier from a desk drawer while she waited for his cremated remains and left the rented villa. Four or five days later, she read the will.

She didn't realize the *kiku-ban*-sized book wrapped in old newspaper was the will nor expect this object to be her husband's written bequest. She tore away the starched newspaper to expose another layer of newspaper. Written on the newspaper with a thick brush was

Top Secret - Confidential
To Yurako

The object from inside the two newspaper layers was a notebook of about two hundred pages that looked like a bookkeeping register with a gold arabesque pattern inlay on the back cover. The details were written inside in pencil.

The sick man moved to Suma. For the year he lay down and got up while listening to the sounds of waves on the Monoui coast, at his leisure, he wrote a diary of his illness. In the extremely long volume, pencil traces faintly marked spots on the paper.

Yurako, who had no memory of this in her heart, was bedeviled by the puzzle of what her late husband revealed.

The will printed below related strange contents that made her shudder and the truth the dead man believed brought on his death.

YEAR YY OF TAISHO, Month MM, Day DD

Beginning today, I will write in this book the circumstances I intended not to reveal to you during my life. For that reason, I don't think I'm alive.

When you came home last evening, you gathered your strength to comfort me. I thought about this when alone and concluded my fate is following a straight line to the goal of *death*. That does not make me anxious, instead, my anxiety resembles a kind of resignation.

Dying around the age of twenty-nine is unfortunate, but the time your youth and beauty peaked became mine. If I thought about dying while this deeply in love with you, my life was not an unhappy one. To this, you may say, "I'm just twenty-two and have not passed my peak. I will become more beautiful, and I will love you more."

Here, however, I'm writing about the current situation. The fact is I will not die from lung disease but another cause. That fact has sickened me and robbed me of my strength to live. To me, that fact is *death*. Hearing that probably does not make you feel good. I'd prefer never having to tell you, but dying without at least appealing to you would have been pathetic.

Based on all of these thoughts, this situation, one man's death, becomes an absurdity. In any case, please listen to me. Try to understand, even a little, because this has an important connection to you.

This story happened a while ago. At that time, I

believe, around the middle of May of the year before last, I was still in good health.

One rainy night, I sat across from a lone unfamiliar man at Cafe Green in Kyogoku and poked at a plate of Western food. The day was the first showing of your film *The Woman Who Loves a Black Cat*. I dressed up and went with Ikegami Yano to see the film at Miyako Cinema. I often frequented this cafe when alone. I looked like a man who had gone somewhere else with someone else and parted company. The strange man arrived before me. By chance, I sat in the empty chair facing him.

For a short time, we sat in silence with the table between us. He stared oddly at my face, smiled from time to time, and seemed on the verge of speaking. He appeared to be a good-natured man but drunk on whiskey and snacking on cheese.

His behavior suggested he wanted a companion, so his expression was charming and innocent. Whenever I found myself in this situation, I was quick to talk, but that night I wasn't drunk.

The man was an elegant gentleman about forty years old, and I had no reason to rudely clash with him. His manner was fairly friendly but cowardly, bashful, and feminine in ways.

He smiled at me and was too reserved. Most of the time, he sat askew showing me his profile. A Snake Tree cane stood between his legs. Its grip propped up his chin. In that state he remained, not speaking until I was served my after-dinner tea. He gathered the nerve to speak, "Excuse me, but aren't you the movie director, Nakata-kun?"

I looked up at his face again and had completely forgotten about the conspicuous Cravenette collar standing upright and wet with rain and the Taiwanese Panama hat he wore.

"Yes, I am. Please, excuse me if I've forgotten. Have we met?"

"No, tonight is our first meeting. You were at Miyako Cinema earlier. At that time, I was behind your party. From your conversation, I guessed you were Nakata-kun."

"Oh, you saw that movie?"

"Yes. I've seen nearly all of Fukacho Yurako's films."

"I thank you and greatly appreciate it."

Unlike a middle school student, this being said by a stylish, discerning gentleman cheered me a little.

He said, "No, I'm the one who's grateful. If anything, I must be thankful."

A clean cup was placed with a clink on the marble table. The face propped on the grip of the cane looked at me up close.

"The world is that way, but I believe only your work among Japanese films is worth seeing. The Japanese people are prisoners of foolish sentimentality. Although things are often damp in plays and movies, your movies have remarkably clear skies and are hedonistic. In short, motion pictures must be that way.

"When I watch your movies, Japan seems brighter, and they bring me joy."

"It would be nice if there were only people who said things like that. But among them are the fault-finding critics who say the movies are copies of American movies."

"What? The movies have no difference in quality from American films and are funny. Although a poor imitation is a problem, you make movies with the same ideals and the same intuitions as an American director.

"If that's the case, an American viewer would never

feel they're ridiculous. What do you think? Will you show your movies to Westerners?"

"No. How could I? I'm still too embarrassed...."

"Don't say that. You're being too humble. I've been watching your movies more than recent Western ones. My impression is Western films are slightly inferior. Sometimes, I recall yours being more inspiring."

"Well, I wanted to … to tickle her."

I didn't understand his intentions, but his praise was over the top. I was a little depressed, but he didn't seem to be making fun of me. I only felt he was more intimidating than he looked. His persistent drunkenness gave him the glassy eyes of a heavy drinker. As he drank, his speech quieted, and his ruddy complexion paled. The ways he looked at me were mostly serious aside from a couple of sharp glances. The tone of his words was serene but unsettling and plodding.

"No, it's true. This is not flattery," he said with conviction. "But I can't say it's only your achievement. No matter how accomplished a director, it's hopeless if he can't find decent actors. In this regard, you've been blessed as a director. Yurako agrees exceptionally well with your tastes. She seems to have been born for your films. If that actress did not exist, you may not have set your sights on this profession. Excuse me, Miss ..."

He called to a waitress.

"Miss, two whiskeys, please," he ordered in hushed tones.

"No, thank you. I don't drink."

"It's all right. Have pity and drink just one with me. We'll drink to your film and to Yurako's and your health."

What on earth was this man's business? Is he a newspaper reporter? Is he a lawyer? He may hold a top job at a bank. Is he an idler with a lot of free time? At first, I had these cowardly thoughts, but as the conversation progressed, he seemed to be magnanimous and treated me as a child.

He was older than me and kindly like a good-natured uncle. While slightly perplexed, I couldn't resist and accepted the drink.

"By the way, who wrote *The Woman Who Loves a Black Cat?*"

"I improvised that. I always create in a rush and can't produce decent work."

"No, it's fine. It was perfect for Yurako. In the scene when she gets into the bath and the cat jumps in, that cat was well trained."

"He was our house pet and no stranger to Yurako."

"Oh ... animals are skillfully used in the West but rarely in Japanese films. As always, Yurako was superb. After the bath, only Yurako, a Japanese actress, would exude that impression when nearly half naked. She was bravely filmed," he said to himself while nodding.

"The censorship concerning that part was annoying but flimsy. My films were scrutinized by the authorities who said they were more indecent than Western films."

"Ah, ha, ha. I guess so. When she left the bath and went to the bedroom, she wore a sheer silk gown and was bathed in backlight."

"Yes, yes. Two or three feet were cut from that part."

"Her entire body appeared to pass through. Wasn't this the first time for that? I think that level of exposure occurred earlier.... That was certainly true of *The Dream Dancer.*"

"So you saw that one, too?"

"Yes, I did. It had the same scene but not in a bath. Yurako became a dancer and changed into a costume in the dressing room. But at that time, she was naked except around her breasts and hips.

"You didn't use the backlight then. An intense light flowed in from the side far below the angle of Yurako's right shoulder in a light streak down the outside of her leg to the heel of her shoe."

"Well, you have a fine memory," I said, a little stunned.

"Yes, I have reasons for remembering that."

He grinned with satisfaction and slowly leaned into the table.

"I believe you filmed two places on Yurako's body never seen before on film. In that film, you showed Yurako's belly button for the first time. Previously, I saw from below her breasts to parts reaching the pit of her stomach in *The Young Hag*, but her belly button remained unknown. I am so grateful to you for showing me that place...."

I remember people saying I filmed your belly button in the film *The Dream Dancer*. You probably didn't forget that. When I filmed you, what detail of your body was carelessly filmed? Even a crease arising from the twisting of muscles in motion appeared in the film. Nothing appeared by accident but was planned. If you twisted your body in any direction and at any angle, some number of creases were carved in different parts. The drawing of all sorts of lines was closely examined like assembling the plot of a complex story.

Of course, what this man said about that film and *The Young Hag* was true. Although I'm grateful to him for drinking in my hardships, he attentively watched only the strange. Instinctively, I could no longer stay there. However, he was unconcerned about the queer look on my face. He kept talking like he was proud of his knowledge of your body.

"The funny thing is Yurako's belly button is a deep innie. I hate outies. I've known that for a while.

"In *Love on Summer Nights*, didn't she come out of the sea in clothes drenched with sea water? From the clothes she wore, the dimple of her belly button is faintly seen. Did you deliberately dampen her clothes to show that indentation and filmed it close up? I considered you to be a cynical director like Stroheim.

"The belly button reliably seen in *The Dream Dancer* on her clothes was the imagined belly button."

"You're quite interested in belly buttons," I said coldly, but he was serious about all of this.

"Not just the belly button, I'm interested in all parts. The first part of *The Dream Dancer* has another place."

"Where?"

"Where? You should know."

"I don't know. There was that sort of place?"

"There was ... the back of the leg."

When he saw I did what was in my heart, he started laughing loudly.

"Ah, ha, ha. Well? Am I right?

"When a dancer dances in bare feet, she'll step on slivers of glass dropped on the stage. A cute dancing girl dances through the pain. Blood flows from the bottoms of her feet, and toe-shaped bloodstains dot the stage. These bloodstains look like she walked on the tips of her toes. The five toes leave tracks that spread out a little.

"Yes, I should have seen the toe prints of Yurako's big toes. And when she dances like that, she relaxes and falls with a thud. The actor in love with the dancer picks her up and carries her to the dressing room.

"Two chairs were next to each other. He placed Yurako on them and pulled out the glass. To examine the wounds, the actor took a lamp from the table and placed it on the floor to light the bottoms of her feet from below. At that time, the bottoms of Yurako's feet looked wonderful."

"What is it? Are you looking only at those places?"

"Well, yes. Is there some mentality for looking at that even for you? A man like me takes in your work through the same senses as you. If you're so thoroughly looking at Yurako's body, isn't that your hope?"

"It's so if you say so, but that makes you a little creepy."

At that time, a spiteful and crazy light shined in the man's drunken eyes. His complexion was paler than earlier, and his lips lost all sheen. I felt an ominous foreboding but was charmed by this man and could not escape. Naturally, I was also driven by curiosity.

"What is it? Something a little more spooky?"

"You'll understand in time," he said and called to the waitress. "Two more whiskeys, please."

He continued, "Do you intend to know more than anyone else in this world about Yurako's body?"

"That may be so. You may know that the actress I've directed for many years is my wife."

"Yes, you are Yurako's husband. Which of us, the husband or I, knows the geography of Yurako's body? I hope to determine who it is.

"You probably think what a strange fellow to have these odd thoughts. But I'm one man and a man who has never seen your wife in person.

"Simply through film research over the years, I went to see the close-ups five or six times of particular scenes to clearly identify every part of your wife's body, such as her shoulders, her breasts, her buttocks. Now, I know them so well and can close my eyes, and their visions rise in my head.

"If by chance, one night this man runs into the man he

believes is her husband, the curious hope he holds is natural."

"Uh-huh, so you are that man and talk about knowing my wife's body?"

"Yes. I know. If you think I'm lying, ask me anything."

While I sat blinking in silence, he didn't hesitate to speak.

"For example, Yurako's shoulders. They are plump and gently slope. Her neck is long. The continuous line from the base of her ear to her shoulder joint, if viewed from the side, is so gentle, it's hard to tell where her arm starts. Her neck is wrapped in rich fatty tissue. The bones and muscles of her throat can barely be seen.

"When turned slightly to the side, the bone behind her ear was a little conspicuous. When turned around to the back, her shoulder blades were hidden by fat when her arms hung loosely down. Thus, the delineation of her two shoulder blades was discernible.

"The reason is an abnormally deep spine passes down Yurako's back. Therefore, the young woman's back resembles two cylinders stuck together. The groove at the boundary between the cylinders is the spine.

"A dark shadow will form in the depression of the groove. Unless hit directly from the front by strong light, the shadow does not disappear completely.

"When she stood up straight, the end of her spine, the hip joint area, and the bulge of her buttocks deepened the shadow.

"When she twisted her body to the left, two thick rolls formed on the twisted side. The flesh between the rolls rose into one round mound. At the same time, only the lowest curve under the ribs faintly appeared on her right side."

While thinking he was a horrible man, when I heard this, the shape of your beautiful back vividly floated into my heart. Perhaps when you read this, will you be uneasily standing naked in front of a mirror? While trying to see the depth of your spine, two rolls form on your side and your ribs are exposed. Can you imagine this man closely watching your films? Does this spook you as it did me?

Without thinking, I had to say, "Yes, yes. What you say is true. How about parts other than the back?"

The man said, "Do you have a pencil?"

He opened the menu paper on the table.

"It's too clumsy to say it in words. I'll draw a picture as I explain."

Then he began to draw your arms like this, hands like this, thighs like this, your lower legs like this in order. I thought he lacked technique in drawing lines. (Would I later find out my guess that he couldn't draw was right?)

As he spoke, "This place is like this," he slowly drew sloppy lines. From time to time, he shut his eyes, turned his face up, and seemed to fill his mind with visions. His mysterious, faltering pencil traces gradually produced a crude sketch. In the childish drawing, the strange details he couldn't draw as an amateur, through malice, and vulgarity, took a form resembling obsession.

One feature captured skillfully was a recognizable caricature of a face, which is not a difficult act. But what he drew was not a face. Your arms, your fingers, and your thighs were drawn disconnected. They conveyed the feelings to my eyes of no one else but you.

He knew about your body, everything, your dimples, your creases. Although this can't be called art, his power of memory was surprising. He gathered the places he remembered without losing one and meticulously expressed them on paper.

Later when I passed by Arita Drug Store, I often recalled the sketches drawn by this man. The sickening feeling of waxy hands, neck, and oily chest ... the feeling of human skin anywhere ... this man's drawing portrayed all of that.

He represented the bulge of flesh with fine lines and shadows and precisely depicted the slippery, fleshy places. This man intimated your feet by only drawing the connection from your round heels to the arches. He didn't overlook your second toes being longer than and resting on your big toes.

When he drew the backs of your legs and the pads of your toes, he grasped the special feature of each part.

I could discern details like your toes had no pedicure. I couldn't avoid being embarrassed by this man.

"It was frustrating to discover the form of her breasts and buttocks," the man confessed.

He said almost no part of your body has not been exposed on film, but a thin cloth hid the breast area and a portion of the hips. For a long time, he focused on the two mounds that appeared under the cloth. Luckily for him, in *The Dream Dancer*, you wore chemise, and the cord of the chemise loosened. You picked up a rose that fell to the floor. The moment you picked it up, your body bent forward. From the gap formed when the chemise naturally drooped and the loosened cord, according to his adjectives, your breasts looked "like the breasts of an Indian maiden" and stretched perfectly round from their base "like two huge swellings." Despite being unable to see anything beyond the nipples, the appearance of your breasts he imagined was satisfactory.

If one or two parts of the human body are left out, and the others are known, the unknown values are deduced like solving for unknown values from the known values using algebraic equations.

Through a similar technique, he gathered the unknown

pieces of the body from various scenes. From them, he inferred the unknown parts, the shady and sunny muscles on your buttocks, had to look a certain way.

"What do you think? I can draw a picture without missing a thing in detail like a map at the military staff headquarters of the locations of mountains and rivers. You're her husband, but have you memorized her to this degree?"

How many scraps of paper were scattered on the table? The *map* he drew filled the back of the menu. He searched for and pulled out the Miyako Cinema program from his pocket, wrote on its back, onto a paper napkin, and finally onto the marble. This work seemed to give him extreme excitement and joy. If I didn't say something, he probably would have drawn more pages.

"All right. I get it. I've seen enough. I'm not your enemy."

"From now on, when doing a fight scene or expressing emotional turmoil, stimulate her heavy breathing. By doing that, a tiny bone at the base of the neck will jump from under the fat in this way ..."

"No, enough. Please stop this nonsense."

"Ah, ha, ha. I'm drawing a book of nudes of your beloved woman."

"That's true, but your ability to draw so much is unsettling."

"You say that but photograph your naked wife all year long. Are you eating? This is not worth it to me. It's not easy to draw only this."

"I understand. I get it. I'd like to take this picture and show it to my wife," I said and quickly shoved a paper scrap into my pocket.

Deep inside, did he want to show you to me? Or does he regret the drawing so much, he'll let me do as I wish with it? Of course, I never intended to show you. I immediately ripped it up and threw it in the toilet. If I showed you, your heart would weaken. You can imagine your beautiful body made into a wax figure at Arita Drug Store.

The man said, "If you're going home, I'll leave, too."

We left the cafe around nine. I already spent close to two hours being served sake by this stranger, but for some reason, I wanted to keep company with this man. Perhaps I find him creepy but feel drawn into a strange friendship. Does calling this man creepy mean he bears too much of a resemblance to me?

This man sees every bit of your body through my eyes. But he's never met you in person in this world. Did he fall from heaven or rise from the earth? He unexpectedly appeared before me to make me listen to him describe the beauty of my goddess, my lover no one other than me should know.

I have little reason to be jealous of him as a love rival. What he knows is a vision on film and not you, my wife. Can a man who loves shadows grasp the hand of a man who loves reality so that shadows and reality get along well?

As these thoughts crossed my mind, I matched his walking pace. In Kyogoku, he turned toward Kawaharamachi. He walked north down a dim street. Stars lazily appeared and disappeared behind clouds scattered in the sky in an area shrouded in a fog-like drizzle. At times, his figure emerged from the light of street lamps and looked like an actual shadow.

"Of course, Yurako is yours and no one else's. She surely thinks she's your wife," he said, almost half speaking to himself.

"However, if I say she's my wife at the same time she's your wife, how do you feel?"

"I'm not bothered at all. How is your wife? Does she lavish you with love?" I asked, sounding like I was joking.

"In the end, this means nothing more than a simple film of my wife, Yurako. I don't feel mental anguish or burn with jealousy because you think this way. I have peace of mind."

"If you worried about that, the actress's husband couldn't work one day."

"Of course, that's probably how it is, but think about it a little more. First of all, I want to ask you something. Who do you think is Yurako's husband, you or me? Which husband savors happiness and pleasure more?"

"Hey, this has become a grave problem."

Rather than a joke, I said that because I could say nothing else. That man saw through the dark and peeked at my face with sympathy.

"You must know this is not a joke. I'm serious. If my guess is not wrong, perhaps you think that way. I'm in love with shadows. You're in love with reality. So there should be no problem. But even you recognize that Yurako in films is not a corpse but a living being?"

"I know that. I said so."

"At least, Yurako on film cannot be said to be shadows of Yurako, your wife. She's more than a living being. That's right, she can't forget you, but in a film, she's also an independent real entity.

"My argument is quibbling. If the two things together are true, which was born first in this world? If your wife were not here, the Yurako on film is not born. Maybe, the first exists, and then the second becomes possible. If that's the case, where does the truly beautiful Yurako you love, even worship, exist outside of film?

"The Yurako in your home strikes an alluring pose like those seen in *The Dream Dancer*, *The Woman Who Loves a*

Black Cat, or *The Young Hag*. Each one carries Yurako's life force."

"That makes sense. I've thought that, too, from time to time and call it my *Film Philosophy*."

"Uh-huh, film philosophy?" he said strangely like he was about to pounce on me. "As a result, maybe this can't be said. The Yurako on film is real. Instead, you say your wife is a shadow? What is this philosophy of yours? Although your wife will slowly age, the Yurako on film will forever be young, beautiful, and jump around full of life and charm.

"When ten years pass, you will keenly recall her earlier figure. You will think, Ah, it wasn't like this back then. Those creases were not in those places. When did they appear? And where did the adorable dimples in the joints of her body disappear to? At those times, you'll take out a film one more time and watch it.

"You're sure the dimples disappeared in a flash and discover things attached to her body forever. Your wife may waste away, but even now the round breasts of the dream dancer are concealed under the chemise when she picks up the rose dropped onto the floor.

"The woman who loves a black cat always splashes the water as she enters the bath, probably to play with the cat. At that time, your young, attractive wife escaped into film. You realize that the Yurako beside you now is her cast-off, empty husk.

"You watch those films and don't know how you made them and don't understand how the world shining this light could be created through you and your wife's abilities. Now, it feels so strange. In the end, these are not creations of you and your wife. *The Dream Dancer* and *The Young Hag* were not born from you as the director and your wife as the performer. From the start, both of you lived in those films.

"It was different for your wife. There is the eternal *A Woman Alone*. Your wife is accepted as the goddess of that age; it's only in her looks. I think you're thankful to her for allowing you to make a living."

"Of course, your reasoning is unusual, but as she ages, my wife slowly fades as the woman in the film. Film is not an unchanging medium."

"All right, I have something to say. You may wonder why I see Yurako's film again and again. And why have I committed to memory a detailed understanding of Yurako's geography? Even when I close my eyes like when I tried to draw her earlier, I gaze at her body to my satisfaction.

"If I say, 'Oh, Yurako-san, please stand,' she stands. If I say, 'Please sit' or 'Please lie down,' she does as I say. I get her to take off all her clothes and show me her back, buttocks, any place, and to turn to show the backs of her legs.

"Although you are called the husband, can you treat your wife with so little consideration? Even if she is temporarily free and is walking here now, you can hug her. No matter the time, my Yurako will immediately come if called. No matter how persistent the demand, she'd never look disagreeable.

"Although your wife will age, she—the true Yurako— will live forever in my head despite fading on film. Her body lives in my mind. That's why I say she's a vision on film, and your wife is a vision."

"But as you said earlier, if my wife were not here, the films would not have been born? Without the films, there's nothing in your head, right? Or if you died, what becomes of her eternal essence? Isn't this all a bit nonsensical?"

"That's not it. Before you and I were born into this world, one undying truth was the *figure of Yurako*. That truth appears, is born in your wife, and throws various shadows onto film. For example, I loved Marie Prevost's films in America, and you probably loved that actress, too. No, there's no point in asking again."

My surprise at his words colored my complexion.

"Perhaps when you discovered Yurako, you thought, could she be Japan's Marie Prevost? That said, in one scene, Prevost gets into a bath. She's wearing a sheer gown like Yurako's and puts on slippers at the bathroom door. That may have happened years ago in an old film, but I recall it well even now.

"Back then, Prevost stood facing away, playing the coquette, and slipped on her slippers. It was then we saw the backs of her legs. Is that what you remember The scene was in soft focus. Her entire body looked hazy, but the feelings in her expression and posture were identical to Yurako's?

"Especially when looking at close-ups, the cut of her nostrils when looking up was similar. The dimples in arms and hands were located in the same places. The greatest similarities were seen when naked. Their navels seemed to be innies. Sadly, I'm unfamiliar with Prevost's belly button. I know only Pola Negri's navel I saw in *Sumurun* and Yurako's. It's only Prevost I don't know in that way.

"A few women resembling Yurako still live in this world. You may think it's a lie, but did you buy a woman called F-ko of XX brothel in the Shizuoka red-light district? Of course, she wasn't a beauty like Prevost and Yurako. Some of the style was lost, but she surely had *Yurako's constitution*. The dimples formed all over her body conveyed Yurako's looks. And the greatest similarities were found in the breasts...."

He said this and listed the women with *Yurako's style* only he knew about. Although those women's entire bodies bore a resemblance, they were nothing like you, maybe, just the feel of the skin was the same. But one part closely resembled you. The breasts of F-ko in Shizuoka Prefecture are identical to yours. K-ko, a prostitute in Asakusa in Tokyo has your shoulders. S-ko in OO brothel in Shinshu in Nagano has your buttocks. A certain woman in Hojo, Boshu has your knees. Someone at a hot spring in Beppu, Kyushu has your neck. Your hands and thighs are found all around.

He studies each part of your body not only in the movies but learns from these women. The earlier *map* is a map of you, and at the same time, a map of those women.

He said, "You ... you're in an extremely advantageous position. Yurako's beautiful spine is in this neighborhood. Are you familiar with the Tobita brothel district in Osaka. Go there and ask for the woman A-ko in B brothel to bare her back. Your legs are closer than that in Gobancho in Kyoto. The woman D-ko of C is there. On a Japanese woman, it is rare for the second toe to be longer than the big toe. However, that woman is the spitting image of Yurako...."

He also has a philosophy of *reality* in line with thought-provoking names like Plato or Weininger. I didn't learn his tedious strained logic and didn't have the perseverance to write down each element. In short, Yurako lived in the heart of the universe for eons. As god follows this pattern, he creates specific women in this world and creates men who sense the unique beauty only of these women. He and I are among those men. In our hearts, you are alive. Because this world is already an illusion, the human you is no different from the illusory you on film.

The mythical vision of film will continue forever,

longer than humanity. The visions keep various figures from their youngest and most beautiful times. This is the closest thing to reality on this earth. The process is to restore the illusion called humanity to the heart.

He said, "Isn't that great? When that happens, how different are you and I as Yurako's husbands? Your happiness is one thing I'm not concerned about. Like you, perhaps more than you, I know her body. I call for her in any situation and any place, peel off her kimono, make her lay down and get up, but only that…. But that's not enough. *Yurako* is a perfect being…. Come to my home. To tell you the truth, 'I have one Yurako.'"

Without thinking, I froze and stared at his face.

"Huh? You have a Yurako, too? Is she your wife?"

"Yes, either my wife or your wife is close to the true Yurako. May I show you?"

Needless to say, at this point, my curiosity reached its peak. The more this man said and did, the more surprising were his words and actions.

What he said consistently hit the mark for me. He may not be completely mad. Even if he's a little crazy, I have deep respect for the detailed observations, his uncommon nature, and the keen discernment of his senses. Naturally, I couldn't bear to meet his wife, who he calls Yurako. This man still has not revealed his identity. If I went, finally, I would know.

"Well? Don't you want to meet my wife?" he asked, while not being too pushy, and peeked at my complexion from the side of his eye. "If you're interested, I'll show you."

"I'm not disinterested. I absolutely want to meet her."

"Well, come to my home."

"Yes, I'll visit. When would be a good time?"

"Any time is fine. Tonight is good."

"Tonight?"

"Yes, let's go now."

"But isn't it a little late? Where do you live?"

"Not too far."

"What's not too far?"

"Five or ten minutes away by car."

I realized we were already near Demachi Bridge. It was around ten-thirty. Although this man said, "Let's go now," like it was nothing, did he intend to take me, a man he just met, to his home late at night to meet his wife? Is he that proud of his wife?

"That's odd. You're not trying to trick me."

"Ah, ha, ha, ha. Do I look like that bad of a guy?"

"You say it's okay to visit, but it's already eleven o'clock. What will your wife say?"

"My wife is very flexible. She's never angry, no matter what time I get home. She always greets me smiling and in a good mood. If you call us a compatible couple, I'll show that to you tonight."

"This isn't a joke. You're two lovebirds."

"Yes, it's vital to be prepared for our love."

"Vital?"

"That devotion is frightening."

"Frightening? Maybe a little, it makes me flinch."

"Ah, ha, ha, ha. You show off your wife all year long, but tonight your duty is to see my wife. To escape now is cowardly. Come with me. Let's go."

While speaking, he caught my arm and steadily pulled me to a cab stand at the west end of the bridge.

"No, you can't escape, be brave."

He had me wait in front of the cab stand, boldly walked inside, and whispered the destination. After leaving the cafe, I saw the man's figure for the first time in the light, but the earlier sake seemed to be slowly taking effect.

In no time, his facial features changed into another man's. His brazen, wild eyes gleamed. His mouth no longer stayed shut. His quivering nostrils flared. The old Taiwanese Panama hat deeply covering his eyes slid to the back and pushed back on his head like a kid. The frizzy ends of his shaggy hair fell on his forehead. He looked like an old man-about-town.

Earlier, this old man looked to be in his forties, older than me, but with his hat propped on the back of his head, the skin around his eyes had unexpected fine crow's feet. His dull hair was peppered with gray hairs. Even when looked at with wide eyes, he looked like an old man forty-seven or close to fifty years old. He was drunker than I imagined. His listless movements and gait were illuminated. However, he didn't drink too much.

"Hey, are you ready?"

While a gong rang to summon a driver, the man took a mysterious, unfamiliar case, a container like a thin, flat, silver cigarette case, from his pocket. He frequently drank straight from this flask.

"What's that?" I asked.

"This? This tool conceals American whiskey I secretly carry around. I probably saw it many times in moving pictures."

"Oh, that sort of thing has come to Japan?"

"I bought it over there. It's quite handy. Good for little sips."

"That's wonderful. Do you always carry it around?"

"Only at night. My wife is a strange thing. When the night gets late and I return home drunk, she's very happy."

"Your wife drinks, too?"

"She doesn't drink but enjoys my drunkenness.... I get blind drunk and become a complete fool."

The moment he said this, I had no idea why my body

trembled. He laughed out loud as he spoke fondly of his lusty love. I'm sure my eyes stared with scorn from my pallid face.

He's an eerie, ruddy old man. Is he a madman? ... Although he keeps talking about his wife, does this old guy have a young pretty wife? Is there a mistress locked up in some strange place?

Soon after, the cab we rode rattled along a frighteningly dark road. At that time, I had only been in Kyoto for several days. What did we pass by? Thinking about it now, I didn't see him drink anymore after passing over Demachi Bridge, I couldn't directly see Kamogawa River. I thought the car would turn right and push into the gap between the row houses too narrow for a car to squeeze through, but it turned left this time.

The rain stopped. The sky was so cloudy, the mountains could not be seen. I didn't know which house or door was closed or the situation in town but heard the sounds of the waters of a valley river like the Mizokawa.

From time to time, the man stuck his head out the window and gave directions to the driver.

"Go that way."

"Go this way."

The houses became few and far between. There were rice fields and vast stretches of overgrown weeds. Without a doubt, they had reached the country roads on the outskirts of town.

"I'm surprised how far we've come. Isn't this a long way out?"

"It's all right. You've been quiet since we got in. Leave it to me. Tonight, I'm in charge of your body. Is that okay?"

"But why on earth ... why have we come to this place?"

"It's fine. No matter how drunk I get, do you think I'll miss my own house? ... Would you like a cup?"

Each time the car shook, he lurched toward me. The man took a swig from the shaking flask and then held it out to me. He inched his arm around my neck and slid closer like a woman fooling around. His foul breath and sticky fingers were unpleasant. More sake was no good. The drunkard typically inconveniences other people. Then this repulsive man grabbed me.

"Hey, hey, excuse me but this ... can you let go? It's a little tight."

"Ah, ha, ha, ha. Are you mad?"

"Yes, I am."

"Why don't we kiss one time?"

"You're … you're joking?"

"Ah, ha, ha, ha. How many times do you kiss Yurako in a day? It's all right to say. Three, four times, ... ten times?"

"How many times do you?"

"I can't count how many times. I kiss everywhere. Her face, her hands, her fingers, the backs of her legs ..."

"Uh, hmm ... do you kiss her a little more on the face?"

"It doesn't matter. It doesn't matter. What do you do if Yurako drools? Do you happily lick it up?"

"Is that what you do?"

"Ah, I'll lick it up. Yes, I'll lick it up."

"How stupid."

"The stupidity of being trapped by a woman. The fate of falling in love."

"But licking up drool…. How old is your wife?"

"She's young. How old do you think she is?"

"I have no idea. When I think about your age ..."

"I'm an old man. My wife is much younger. She's excitable like an unbroken horse. How old do you think she is?"

"Is my wife younger or older? Yurako is the same ..."

"She's the same age."

"Your wife is that young? Excuse me for asking but is she your second wife?"

"She's my first and legal wife. She's my unique treasure, more like a goddess."

He laughed out loud as he drooled.

"You're probably impressed. As always, I will take this lonely country road to go home to my wife. I don't take a cab but plod home on foot. There, my wife is listening for my footsteps and dozing inside the curtains of the inner bedroom.

"She waits curled up like a cat like her listless body is bored. She's clean, and a fragrance coats her whole body. As I quietly enter the bedroom and gently part the curtain, I say, 'Yurako, I'm home. I know you missed me.'"

"What?"

"Ah, ha, ha, ha. Did I surprise you?"

"Her name is Yurako, too?"

"Oh, yes. She's Yurako. If not, my heart is not moved."

Finally, the car stopped at the bottom of a hill covered in dense vegetation.

"We're here," he said, jumped out, and climbed the steep stone steps. He took an electric torch from his pocket to light his path. Of course, he returned home late every night. Yellow roses lining both sides of the stairs spread out and were entangled to the foot of the hill. My nose was hit by a strong scent like steamed fresh leaves. Light from the electric torch occasionally shined on fresh greenery.

"Where are we?" I asked, looking up the hill. I saw a white Western-style building lit by a single light at the entryway.

It was dark. I couldn't see much but made out a lone building on the hill. This house had no neighbors. On one side was a grove or a forest. I smelled new leaves and dirt and felt signs of vengeful ghosts. Dense shadows hid the back. Behind the house was a cliff or mountain.

We climbed to the top of the stone stairs. A sunken entrance like a Buddhist altar and a white wall partition stood at the end. I thought the door was a wooden door just three-feet high, but as I got closer, I saw a glass door. The lights were off inside the house, so from a distance, the door looked black.

The point of light peeking from the foot of the stairs entered through the cylindrical jade on the top of the hollow like a Buddhist altar and drew a fuzzy circle on the white wall. Though I called it a Western building, it looked like a square, one-story house, more like a dreary cabin if seen during the day.

The man gasped for air as he pulled a clanking key chain from his pocket and opened the door. I followed him into the dirt-floor room. He locked the door from the inside, removed his muddy shoes, groped for his slippers, and put them on.

There must have been a switch somewhere in the darkness, but he didn't turn on the light. The outside door lamp passed through the glass door and dimly lit the room, but those irregular rays made it impossible for me to make out the room's interior.

From the traces of alcohol in his panting breaths, and the close echoes, I knew this entryway was a narrow space and felt confined in the cramped room. He shined the portable electric torch again.

He pointed the beam at the floor and seemed to be searching for something. In the light skimming past, I could see a Chinese pottery receptacle for walking sticks and a hat rack with a mirror. Four hats hung on the rack: a soft fedora, a dark gray derby hat, a newsboy cap, and an ordinary straw hat.

Several pairs of leather slippers were under the rack, and one pair was inside. A pair of French-style, high-heeled, women's slippers made of gaudy pink silk was mixed in. This was my first surprise. They seemed well worn with oily footprints. He let me glimpse those slippers. I was certain they were yours. They looked exactly like your old pair of slippers in my house. Creases and toe and heel marks formed in the same places, and stains were produced from the same gait.

The moment I saw them, the shapes of your stunning legs vividly rose in my mind. Those slippers were worn by legs identical to yours. I wondered if my wife had come here.

He placed these slippers carefully to the side. Maybe, he deliberately let me see them and then grabbed a pair of leather slippers.

"Put these on, please," he said and tossed them to me. Then his electric torch went out. He stood first and walked straight down the dark hallway ahead of me. The narrow hallway forced us to form a line of two. He staggered as he moved forward bumping into the walls on both sides. Now at home, he may have relaxed. He made me drink too much.

The night was humid like the beginning of the rainy season and felt like a steamy bath. To make matters worse in the house, his sake-soaked breath filled the hallway and blew into my face. It made me raise my collar, and I suddenly felt drunk.

When we came to the end of the hallway, he said, "Please, go in here." I passed into the room on the left. He struck a match, held a quivering light aloft, and took five or six quick steps into the room.

I saw a candlestick on a table. He moved the flame inside his palm to the candlestick. As the tip of the candlestick gradually lengthened, the thick darkness centered on the table inched back. However, I could not discern the size of the room or what was inside.

At this instant, he and I sat facing each other with the candle between us. By accident, my line of sight flowed to his face lit red by the line of firelight before him. I didn't see his face but his shiny bald head, the crown of his head.

He removed his Taiwanese Panama hat and set it on the table. He seemed worn out. He listlessly slid his body closer to the back of the chair, and both arms dangled like a puppet with broken strings. His head was down, and he still gasped for air. Instead of his face, I repeatedly looked right at his bald head.

It took a little time until my drunken eyes perceived a human head. Until now, I couldn't imagine his fine bald head. Of course, unkempt frizzy hair wrapped around reaching his forehead and the back of his head. This was deftly hidden by wearing a hat. I was shocked for a time and stared at the bald part shaped like a serpent's eye. This man was not close to fifty but surely two or three years past fifty.

He abruptly stood and, without a word, rushed to a corner of the room. He seemed to be drinking something. His throat made amazing gulping sounds. I understood. He was drinking water to sober up. He drank voraciously. This was my first thought but looking more closely, five or six bottles of Western liquor were lined up on a shelf in the corner. He stood there drinking alone. After five or six cups, he licked his lips, probably licking away drool. He came back to me and stood there then lifted the candlestick from the table.

"Now, I will introduce you to my wife."

"Oh, where is she?"

"In the room over there. Come with me. She's sleeping peacefully."

"Is she nearby?"

"What? This is my wife's room.

As he spoke, light from the candle in his hand illuminated the entrance to the adjoining room. The room was bizarre. In the candlelight, rather than a room, it looked to have the width of a closet. This so-called room was marked by only a deep pink curtain. When fully opened like a theater curtain, the same color curtains hung on three sides. In the center was a large bed that nearly took up the entire room.

The bed was surrounded on four sides like an old-fashioned Japanese curtained room or a Chinese-style bed. I clearly saw the curtains of this bedroom were made from a material like dark green velvet hanging down in multiple dark layers. It could have been mistaken for the stage of the glamorous woman magician Shokyokusai Tenkatsu.

"My wife is sleeping in here. Which shall I show you first? Her back? Her belly? Her legs?"

He reached out a hand to massage and show what I thought was his wife's body sleeping inside of the curtains. His eyes were oddly bloodshot. An unpleasant smile rose on his mouth.

When I write this, you probably know what is sleeping in the bed. I also believed it was a doll. He intimated this earlier. The growing sense of unease was not only due to the true-to-life copy of you but his having dolls, several *real bodies of Yurako.*

I saw your figure in fifteen or sixteen positions: sleeping, standing, thighs open, torso twisted, every possible obscene position. He told me, "Thirty-one Yurakos live in this house."

I've heard to ease boredom when out to sea, sailors have female dolls fabricated from rubber casing. I never knew whether it was true. Although I doubted its veracity, this man's dolls were real.

He neatly folded and wrapped each of his thirty *wives* in a wrapping cloth and set them on shelves. Like a typical apparatus used by Tenkatsu, the shelves in the shadows of the curtains hanging on three sides of the bed were built in several levels. A cryptic character was affixed to each level.

Like the head clerk in a kimono fabric shop taking out fabric, he cheerfully said, "Now, I'll show you my wife squatting."

I imagined the places where these life-size figures, fifteen or sixteen of you, stood in the room on a calm night, and watched. And if I said he had a technique to blow up the flat, folded objects, he had a lot of practice. He twisted on the tap water and lit the gas stove. The device immediately sent out hot water. He pulled a tube from there and attached it to a hole in the doll. While I watched, he inflated the doll.

He gradually prepared one human figure. As the curves vividly appeared, from the arms, the shoulders, the back, and the legs, it was unmistakably you. He paid an absurd level of attention to the fabrication method and the position of the hole for pouring in water. It was not a clumsy device like the cap of a rubber hot-water bottle.

I thought each doll had its uses but felt it would be blasphemy to you to explain the details and will speak no more on this.

Perhaps, he only pleasured himself by pouring in the water. Then he said, "I am doing the same work as God, the Creator. The ancient God blew in breath from somewhere when he created Adam and Eve and, amusingly, he could not stop."

If I told you those things looked like you, you'd probably expect little from rubber casing and find this absurd. He was able to sew the elaborate casings with surprising intricacy. Even if he hadn't described the staggering hardships, it was a reasonable belief. I could never copy it if I tried. From buying the materials to adding the finishing touches, he did everything by hand. If you entered his studio, you'd see I'm not lying.

There you'd discover the reference materials obtained in the struggle for your flesh and gathered through extraordinary persistence and meticulous care. If a person is locked in a room with mirrors stuck to all the surfaces, he'll eventually go insane. You'd surely share the same feelings.

"Come see this room," he said and took me to his studio on the other side of the hall. My eyes were struck by pieces of your hands and feet on display indiscriminately throughout the entire space of the floor, ceiling, and walls.

Particularly weird were the striking enlarged photographs of your body parts—secret places and details to muscle sinews—pasted all over. Of course, if he gazed at these photographs every day, there's no mystery about the rough sketch influenced by the ingenious Arita Drug Store style. But how did he get his hands on these pictures? How did he photograph you if he's never met you?

To answer this question, he showed me scraps cut from various old films. The shortest ones were one or two frames. The longest ones were about ten to twenty frames. He collected all the critical scenes from all of your films.

The scenes from *The Dream Dancer* included the dancer picking up the rose that fell to the floor, dancing on the stage with feet dripping blood, close-ups of the bloody toe prints, the scene depicting the area at the pit of your stomach under the breasts in *The Young Hag*, and the innie navel in *Love on Summer Nights*. Surprisingly, numerous scenes were represented in his detailed sketches.

He knew the shapes of your ears and the alignment of the teeth in your mouth. These could have been obtained from one clear frame of film. He followed a single film from cinema to cinema. He said one time he went to Okayama and another time to Utsunomiya.

"While there I discovered there are many whimsical fellows like me in this world. How? One of Yurako's films premiered in Tokyo and Kyoto. As the film was slowly distributed to the smaller cities in the provinces, the number of frames mysteriously decreased. Of course, regional censors made some cuts. However, they didn't recklessly cut the film based on a general standard for the prefectures.

"The scene in the first twenty frames becomes fifteen and then ten frames in the trip from one town to the next. In the worst case, the film disappears. Isn't that odd? These cuts are made along the way. They wait for Yurako to come and like a wolf hungry yanks off and leaves with her hands and legs.

"By questioning the film technicians at movie theaters in country towns, I have proof of the existence of many men like this. They understand. If money is paid, the desired scene becomes one or two frames. The film is secretly cut and handed over to become part of a secret stash."

The job of an archaeologist closely resembled his work. Archaeologists scatter throughout Japan to dig up remains deep in the earth from several centuries ago and group them based on the shapes of the animals that lived thousands of years ago. Eventually, he built a perfect *you*.

The enlarged photographs affixed to the walls were from the films he obtained. He enlarged each part with constant proportion and created a clay model from them. He stitched together the rubber doll using this model as the insert. The procedure is identical to how a shoemaker sews together the leather pushed onto a wooden mold. We did not discuss the difficulty of this work that day.

First, he worked hard to obtain rubber having realistic coloring and flexibility for your skin. When I touched your hand, its texture closely resembled a waterproof cloth pulled from rubber to thin silk that is used for women's raincoats but, more importantly, was close to human skin.

He sent orders to various stores in Osaka, Kobe, and Tokyo and finally obtained the products of interest at the fifth store. Not only did he use the model constructed from clay for sewing, but he also inserted the places not well known in the live models.

He especially carried the fully sewn rubber casing all the way to Shizuoka and combined the breasts of F-ko of XX brothel, the buttocks of S-ko of OO brothel carried to Shinshu in Nagano, the shoulders of K-ko in Asakusa in Tokyo, the back of A-ko in Goban-cho in Kyoto, the knees of a woman from Hojo in Boshu, and the neck of a woman at a hot spring in Beppu.

I wondered how did he create lips with that fire and arrange rows of teeth like pearls behind those lips? How was he able to successfully grow satiny hair and eyelashes and insert vibrant eyes? How did he make her tongue, fingernails, and toenails? More than being inexplicable, I couldn't imagine how he found these materials.

"That's a secret," he said and smirked. His faint smile did not tell me anything and possibly implied something frightening. A chill ran through me as I wondered, Aren't the materials, in some way, indecent, ghastly, and immoral?

The stories of rubber dolls as playthings for sailors out to sea may be true, but they were never this elaborate. If a casing sewn together had some degree of resemblance to a human, there may be no impossible parts. These rubber casings had nostrils and mucous in them. It had the same body temperature as a human, body odor, an oily feel, drool dripping from the shoulders, and sweat coming from the armpits. When I asked, "Why had he prepared thirty bodies like this?" he answered, "Because various poses are needed." For example, there's a pose when sitting on a lap, a pose when kissing while standing...

I was stunned.

As he said, "It's like this," right in front of me, he demonstrated his peculiar pleasures with these dolls. (He always drank sake to pep up.) Then he asked, "What does this snot taste like?" After he was entwined for some time, he let me watch him licking it up.

"Oh, so you said it's stupid to lick my wife's drool. Look, I do it like this ... I lick it up like this. Not from here ..."

All of a sudden, he lay face up on the floor. A doll with thighs open squatted above his face. From below, he raised both hands and pressed hard on the doll's stomach and listened to the sounds of gas leaking from the doll's anus. The discharge started to flow and stick to the face and bald head of this freakish old man. I didn't need to see anymore and flew outside through a window. I fled at full speed to the dark country road.

YURAKO, I only wanted to tell you the truth. I pray from my heart that this story makes you smile. I pray the spell cast makes you happy. But this incident happened to me. I lost all interest in making your films and was engulfed by fear.

I created a beautiful star out of you. I can't help feeling that the result of repeatedly putting your figure on film was to rob you.

Without your knowledge, you were stripped naked by that old man. He played with your hands, your legs, every part of your body. That alone might have been fine, but my beloved, adorable Yurako is unique in this world and, I believed, mine alone. But since that evening, that belief faded.

Your body is scattered throughout Japan and piled on the shelves in a closet in that old man's bedroom. You are one of his many Yurakos, nothing more than a shadow.

When these feelings surge in me, even if I have you in a strong embrace, I don't feel like this is the only, true you. In the end, I think you are like a shadow and I've become a shadow. The unbreakable true love between us is so hollow, a lie, and nothing more than a scene in a single frame of film.

Even as I mourn now, it's irreparable. It would have been better not to have met that old man that night. How many times has that night darkened my dreams?

I prayed that man and that eerie house on that hill were phantoms that would go away without leaving a trace. However, when I passed through later to look at that hill in daylight, the house was there. I've since learned the name of that old man and what kind of man he is, but that's not all.

I've met them all, A-ko of brothel B in Goban-cho who he said has your back muscles, F-ko in Shizuoka who has your breasts, and the women with your shoulders, buttocks, and neck. I saw for myself that his words were not lies. Although those women do not know his real name, they all said he was an unusual sexual pervert, sometimes brought photographic equipment and a rubber casing and made unreasonable demands, and called these women, Yurako.

But Yurako is mine! The real Yurako! I don't want you to know the name or identity of this man. You shouldn't want to know either. I will look at the current situation and hide from you. I firmly believe I will meet you in the next world. I will leave a step ahead of you to the phantom world....

CREDITS

Japanese Stories and Novellas:

Tanizaki, Jun'ichiro. *Along the Way* (途上) (in Japanese). Input by sogo. Revised by Matsumoko.

https://www.aozora.gr.jp/cards/001383/card56849.html Accessed September 9, 2016.

Tanizaki, Jun'ichiro. *The Secret* (祕密), *The Yanagiyu Incident* (柳湯の事件), *The Passing of a Young Man* (或る少年の怯れ), *Gold & Silver* (金と銀), *The Tumor With a Human Face* (人面疽), *The Story of Mr. Aotsuka* (青塚氏の話) in *The Complete Collection of Japanese Detective Novels (Tanizaki Jun'ichiro Edition)*, (日本探偵小説全集 第5篇 (谷崎潤一郎集)). Vol. 5, Tokyo: Kaizou-sha, 1929 (in Japanese).

https://dl.ndl.go.jp/info:ndljp/pid/1194276 Accessed March 11, 2022.

Cover image:

Shinjuku: Lithographs by Oda Kazuma (新宿：織田一磨自画石版画集), No. 2, Tokyo: Oda Kazuma, 1930.

https://dl.ndl.go.jp/info:ndljp/pid/2541721 Accessed September 14, 2022.

Photo of Jun'ichiro Tanizaki:

The Complete Collection of Japanese Detective Novels (Tanizaki

Jun'ichiro Edition), (日本探偵小説全集 第5篇 (谷崎潤一郎集)). Vol. 5, Tokyo: Kaizou-sha, 1929.

https://dl.ndl.go.jp/info:ndljp/pid/1194276 Accessed March 11, 2022.

Handwritten Jun'ichiro Tanizaki:

Tanizaki, Jun'ichiro. *Hutari no Chigo* (二人の稚兒), Tanizaki Jun'ichiro, 1918 (in Japanese).

https://dl.ndl.go.jp/info:ndljp/pid/2532509 Accessed June 13, 2022.

ABOUT THE AUTHOR

Jun'ichiro Tanizaki was a Japanese novelist, born July 24, 1886 and died July 30, 1965. His work was acclaimed both in Japan and overseas. In his early years, he was a part of the aestheticism movement although his work contained scandalous elements of excessive gynephilia and masochism, but his style, expression, and subjects changed throughout his life. He employed expressions from Chinese, old Japanese poems, slang, and dialects in his writings. His major works include *Seishi* (*The Tattooer*), *Chijin no Ai* (*Naomi*), *Manji* (*Quicksand*), *Inei Raisan* (*In Praise of Shadows*), and *Sasameyuki* (*The Makioka Sisters*).

(From the Japanese Wikipedia page https://ja.wikipedia.org/wiki/ 谷崎潤一郎 . Accessed September 17, 2022.)

www.ingramcontent.com/pod-product-compliance
Lightning Source LLC
Chambersburg PA
CBHW030814210726
48290CB00002B/577